AN UNCOMMON FAMILY

Family Portrait, Book One

ALSO BY CHRISTA POLKINHORN

NOVELS

Love of a Stonemason
Family Portrait, Book Two

Emilia
Family Portrait, Book Three

The Italian Sister
The Wine Lover's Daughter, Book One

Finding Angelo
The Wine Lover's Daughter, Book Two

Fire in the Vineyard
The Wine Lover's Daughter, Book Three

POETRY
Path of Fire

AN UNCOMMON FAMILY

Family Portrait, Book One

Christa Polkinhorn

Bookworm Press

Bookworm Press
1223 Wilshire Blvd., #1054
Santa Monica, CA 90403

This is a work of fiction. Names, characters, places, and incidents are either the product of the author's imagination or are used fictitiously. Any resemblance to actual events or persons, living or dead, is entirely coincidental.

Cover design and author photo: Diane Busch
Cover images: istock Images

ISBN: 978-0-9600135-3-1

Printed in the United States of America

For Kay Jöelle Spiegel

PART ONE: SEARCHING FOR MOTHER

Chapter 1

Karla licked the crispy cone, trying to catch the sliding droplets before they hit the ground. The raspberry ice cream was a dark purple, her favorite color. She wrinkled her nose as she caught another whiff of exhaust from the busy street along the Limmat River in the city of Zurich. It was August and hot in Switzerland. The six-year-old girl scanned the scenery in front of her with dreamy eyes.

A canoe was sliding by a tourist boat on the river. People with funny-looking sun hats and dark glasses sat on the benches of the boat. Along the river on the other side, the built-together stone houses looked like a row of uneven different-colored teeth, gray, yellow, white, and some with a tint of orange. Behind the houses, on top of the hill, the linden trees at the park shimmered in their pale-green foliage and a curtain of dark-green ivy hid part of the gray granite wall.

Karla took another lick from her ice-cream cone, then turned around and peered through the window of the art shop, where her aunt was picking up two framed pictures. When she looked back at the sidewalk, her breath caught.

"Mama?" she whispered.

She saw the woman only from behind, but the bounce in her step, the long, reddish-blond hair flowing down her back, swaying left and right, the tall, slender figure—it must be her mother. She tossed the rest of the ice cream into the trash can, got up, and ran after the woman.

"Mama!" she called as the woman got ready to cross the street. The light turned from blinking red to solid red, just as

3

the woman reached the other side. Karla rushed after her, barely aware of the honking around her or of the shrill warning bell of the blue-and-white streetcar. She heard someone yell at her but by then she had arrived at the other side. The woman was walking along the river toward the Lake of Zurich.

"Mama, wait!" Karla bumped into someone.

A man stepped aside. "Watch it, kiddo."

"Mama . . ."

The woman finally turned around and looked back, scanning the people behind her, then walked on. Karla stopped dumbfounded. It was the face of a stranger.

A wave of despair washed over her. Not believing that she could have been so wrong, she started to run again. She didn't see the slight indentation in the pavement. As she fell, she barely noticed the searing pain in her knees; the disappointment hurt more. She covered her face with her hands and sobbed. Mama would have helped her. Mama would have picked her up, hugged her, and even sang a little tune to her to make her feel better. But her mother was gone.

"Are you hurt, honey?" a dark voice said. Karla felt a hand on her back. "Come on, let me see."

A pair of strong arms lifted her up. She looked into a face with a gray-white beard and kind, blue eyes below thick tufts of eyebrows. The man was tall and sturdy. He had wildish white hair. He reminded her of Saint Nicholas. But it was summer and Saint Nicholas only appeared in December.

"Are you here alone?" he asked. "Where's your mother?"

The question brought a new flood of tears. "I thought it was Mama," Karla managed to say, her chest heaving with sobs.

"Karla, what happened? Why did you run away?" Aunt Anna came rushing toward her, clutching her purse and a large package. "I thought I'd lost you. Jesus, what happened to your knees?" She bent down, put the package on the concrete, and examined Karla's legs. Brushing a strand of wavy brown hair out of her face, she peered at the man with her gray-blue eyes. "What's going on here?"

"I just happened to walk by when she fell," he explained. "She said something about looking for her mother. Are you her mother?"

Anna shook her head. "No, I'm her aunt. Her mother . . . died half a year ago."

"I'm so sorry." The old man gently touched Karla's cheek. "But she thought she saw her mother."

Anna sighed. "She still hasn't accepted the truth." She turned to Karla. "Tell me what happened, sweetie?"

Karla told her between sobs that a woman had walked by who looked exactly like her mama.

"But you know that's not possible, don't you?" Aunt Anna hugged her. Karla leaned her face against Anna's chest and poured her sorrow into her sweater. It was soft but didn't smell like her mama's. Anna waited for her to calm down. "We have to take care of your knees."

"There's a pharmacy right over there. I'm sure they have something to clean the wound and some bandages. May I?" Saint Nicholas gave Anna an inquiring look.

Anna nodded and the man lifted Karla up. His thick hair tickled her cheek. Karla wrinkled her nose. He gave off a faint whiff of smoke, which reminded her of Anna's woodstove. It felt a little comforting.

At the pharmacy, a friendly lady took care of Karla's knees. She wiped them clean, trying not to hurt Karla, who flinched and gave an occasional sob. "Sorry, honey, but we don't want it to get infected."

While the woman bandaged Karla's legs, Anna unwrapped the package she had been carrying. She handed Karla one of the pictures and held the other one up for her to see. "Don't they look beautiful?"

Karla nodded with a weak smile. They did look nice. She barely recognized them again behind the glass and surrounded by a fine wooden frame. One of them showed a woman, sitting on a chair and holding a little girl in her arm. The woman had long reddish-brown hair and the girl's hair was black. They were sitting in front of a house. The stones in the wall had an irregular shape; they looked a little bit like cobblestones. It had taken Karla a while to make them look right. The other picture showed a tree with large purple and cream-colored blossoms. It was the chestnut tree in front of Karla's old home. She had painted the pictures with her favorite pastel pens.

"They're gorgeous," Saint Nicholas said in his deep voice. "Who painted those?"

"Karla did," Aunt Anna said.

Saint Nicholas stared at her, then at the pictures, then at Karla. "How old is she?"

"Six," Karla said, brushing the last tears off her face. Anna handed her a Kleenex.

"And she painted those by herself, without help?" The man squinted as he scanned the pictures. The wrinkles on his forehead and around his eyes deepened. He truly did look like Saint Nicholas.

"Yes," Aunt Anna said.

"This child is very talented. Does she get any instructtion?"

"I'm actually looking for a teacher for her. She loves to draw and paint. If it was up to her, she'd do it all day long. And it seems to help her with . . . you know, the loss."

6

"Amazing." Saint Nicholas shook his head and continued to scan the pictures. "Well, I happen to be a painter myself. I also teach a few children." He looked at Karla and Anna with a serious face. "I'd love to have her as a student."

"I'll think about it. That would be great," Aunt Anna said.

"Why don't you check me out?" The man pulled his wallet from his back pocket, opened it, and took out a small gray card. "Here is my address and phone number and on the back a few references." He handed Anna the card. "Whatever you decide to do though, you don't want a talent like this go to waste."

Aunt Anna studied the card. "Very interesting, Mr. Bergman."

"Call me Jonas," the man said.

"Anna," Karla's aunt said as the two shook hands.

"You're not Saint Nicholas?" Karla asked, surprised.

Aunt Anna and the man laughed. "No, I'm sorry. You think I look like him?" He brushed through his wavy white hair.

Karla nodded. "But you wouldn't come in summer, would you?" She looked down at her neatly wrapped knees. The talk of drawing and painting had pulled her out of her deep misery. "Are you going to teach me?"

The man smiled at her. "You talk this over with your aunt, all right?" Then he glanced at his watch. "Oops. I guess I missed my appointment."

"I'm so sorry," Anna said. "We caused you all this trouble."

"Don't worry. No problem at all." He bent down and put a hand on Karla's shoulder. "And, Karla, I know how much it hurts. I lost my dear wife a few years ago. We were together for over twenty years. I still miss her. But I can promise you, things will get better with time."

7

Karla took a deep breath and nodded. She had heard the words many times before. "Maja lost her mother, too."

"Maja is a friend of hers, a girl from Croatia," Anna explained. "Her mother died during the war."

At home, in their house in a small town near Zurich, Aunt Anna fixed lunch. She heated up the leftover bean and vegetable soup and made grilled cheese sandwiches with tomatoes. The smell of food awakened Karla's appetite. She was quiet and thoughtful but no longer desperate.

"He was a nice man," she said, folding the colorful paper napkins she had made herself with potato stamps. She put them on the blue-and-white placemats on the oak-wood table in the kitchen.

"Would you like to take drawing and painting lessons from him?" Anna poured the soup into bowls and slid the toasted sandwiches onto the plates.

Karla nodded. "Yeah, that'd be cool." She smiled and traced her finger along the spots on the tabletop. The sunlight, filtered by the leaves of the magnolia tree in front of the kitchen window, had sketched a pattern of light and shadows on the table.

"Cool, huh?" Anna smiled and gave the girl a hug.

Chapter 2

It was quiet now, except for the chirping of crickets and the occasional hoot of the owl in the forest near Anna's home. The air was still warm after the hot summer day. Anna had opened all the windows, hoping for a cooling breeze. It had been an unusually hot summer in a country that wasn't exactly known for its heat waves. The strong pungent scent of basil in between the tomato plants reminded Anna of her gardening chores she kept putting off because of the heat.

After her turbulent day in the city, Karla had finally fallen asleep. Anna sat on the patio, watching the darkness descend upon the trees and meadows and erase the last smirches of crimson and purple on the horizon.

A loud scream, followed by crying, interrupted the peaceful evening. Karla had another one of her nightmares. Anna shot up and rushed into the child's bedroom. Karla sat in bed, shivering in spite of the warmth, her eyes wide open.

"Wake up, sweetie. It's just a dream." Anna sat on the bed next to Karla and hugged her.

"Mama?"

Anna watched as the dream subsided. The expression in the child's eyes changed from confusion and fear to a flicker of hope and then to sadness. Anna pressed the trembling and sobbing body against her chest. "Just a bad dream, honey. I'm here, it's okay."

After Karla had dozed off again, Anna tiptoed out of the room and left the door open. It was the first nightmare in quite a while, perhaps triggered by Karla's experience in the city, when she thought she saw her mother.

Right after the accident, Karla had been plagued by bad dreams almost every night. It was always the same. Screams followed by desperate crying. When Anna woke her up, Karla was distraught. She mentioned fire, flames, red paint, which Anna assumed was blood. In the morning, Karla couldn't remember much of the dream. She didn't remember the actual accident either.

Anna sat in the living room, gazing out the window. By then, the last tinges of color had been swallowed by the night. Tears gathered in her eyes. On days such as these, the pain of loss and the doubts flared up again. She would never forget that fateful day half a year before. She still heard the solemn voice of the police officer telling her that her mother and sister had been killed during a head-on collision with a drunk driver. They told her that a child had been in the backseat in her booster, that the little girl had a shock but was unhurt. They needed Anna to identify the two women. For days and nights afterward, Anna saw the mangled bodies lying on the gurneys and the pale face of her little niece, whose normally vivid large dark eyes now stared at her with an empty look.

From one day to the next, Anna, single and childless, had become the guardian of her niece. She was the only close relative who lived nearby. Laura, her younger sister, had been a single mother. Karla's biological father lived in Peru. With the death of her mother and sister, Anna had lost the last members of her immediate family. Her father as well as her grandparents had passed away years before. There was an uncle, a kind man, who had offered to help Anna financially, should she need it.

It wasn't the money, though, that worried Anna. She was the head of the library in her hometown and owner of the only independent bookstore. The bookstore wasn't a big moneymaking enterprise, but together with her salary and her freelance writing, she would be able to support herself and Karla. Fortunately, the home she had inherited from her mother was paid off.

No, it wasn't the finances; it was the responsibility for her little niece that weighed heavily on her. Her heart ached with the loss of her mother and sister.

"Why? Why did you leave me like this? Don't you realize how much I still need you?" Anna whispered, tears streaming down her face.

Chapter 3

Jonas Bergman put the grocery bags on the floor of the old elevator, which slowly lumbered up to the top of the four-story building. The elevator cabin was open, walled in only by a crisscross of iron bars. He lived in one of the heavy medieval stone houses in the old part of Zurich, called the Niederdorf or Low Village, at the east side of the Limmat River.

Upstairs, the old elevator stopped with a rattling sound and Jonas stepped out. *One day, I'm going to be stuck in here,* he thought, giving the old but so far reliable cabin a suspicious glance. He only used the elevator when he had heavy things to carry. He reached into his pocket, searching for his keys. "Damn it," he muttered as he dropped them. They made a metallic crunching sound on the hardwood floor.

"Let me help you, Mr. Bergman."

Jonas turned around. A stout elderly lady with curly gray hair came out of the apartment next to his. She bent down and picked up the keys.

"Oh, Mrs. Schatz, don't bother. Well, thanks anyway and excuse my language." Jonas watched as the woman slid his apartment key into the keyhole.

"That's okay, I've heard worse." Mrs. Schatz chuckled.

She gave him a critical look, then pointed at the grocery bags. "Looks like you were at the market. Good. Seems like you're eating properly again."

"Yes, Mrs. Schatz, I took your advice to heart," Jonas said. He held one of the bags and tried to pick up the second one.

His neighbor grabbed the second bag and followed him into the apartment.

"Thanks again," Jonas said. "What would I do without you?" He winked at her.

"Come on, Mr. Bergman. What you need is a woman of your own. I've told you many times."

His neighbor had been trying to fix him up with someone for about a year without any success. Mrs. Schatz was married and believed that a single man, particularly a widower of Jonas's age, was doomed.

After she put down the grocery bag on the kitchen counter, she turned to Jonas. "I'll have a few friends over for tea tomorrow afternoon. Why don't you come and join us?"

Jonas grinned. "These friends wouldn't happen to be available women you're trying to hook me up with?"

"What do you mean? I wouldn't do such a thing," the woman said in a huffed tone. "These are very respectable ladies. Many a man would be honored and pleased to be able to enjoy their company."

"Of course, Mrs. Schatz, don't misunderstand me." Jonas tried to calm his neighbor. "I have only met charming women at your tea gatherings. And I'm very grateful for your concern. It's not the women who are the problem. It's me." He gently tapped Mrs. Schatz's arm. "You know, I'm just not ready yet. I know, it's stupid, but I can't help it."

Mrs. Schatz seemed somewhat appeased. "Well, okay, I won't push you. Just remember"—she shook a finger at him—"you're not getting any younger either." She looked him up and down and he instinctively pulled in his slight potbelly. "Well, I've got to go, have some baking to do."

She shuffled across the hallway toward the door. Mentioning the baking was another attempt to lure Jonas. She was an excellent baker and well-known among her neighbors and friends for her cakes and pies. Her heavy hips and the bulges around her waist were a testimony to her love of sweets.

At the door to her apartment, she slightly raised her hand. "If you change your mind, you know where we are."

"Thank you kindly, Mrs. Schatz," Jonas said. "I have quite a lot of work to do, but perhaps next time."

He closed the door and breathed a sigh of relief. In the kitchen, he unpacked the groceries. He put the lettuce, zucchini squash, tomatoes, basil, and a piece of mountain cheese into the refrigerator. Picking up a ripe apricot, he inhaled its sweet smell and bit into it, then went into the living room.

As usual, when he came back from an errand or a trip, he stood a while in front the photo of his wife, Eva. A beautiful face with wavy, shoulder-length blond hair, shiny blue eyes, and the touch of a cute snub-nose smiled at him. He smiled back and sighed. "Hi there," he whispered.

His neighbor wasn't the only person who tried to nudge him toward female companionship. His son in Denmark and his daughter, who spent a year in the United States, brought the topic up occasionally. "Dad, remember what Mom said before she died? You shouldn't pine for her; you should live and have another woman in your life."

He gently touched the frame of the photo. *There is no other woman. Only you.*

He pulled a bottle out of the liquor cabinet and poured himself a shot of whiskey, went into the kitchen and dropped a few ice cubes from the freezer into the glass. He shook the glass and watched the golden liquid swoosh around. Coming back into the living room, he opened a couple of windows and the floor-length glass door, which led to a small patio on the rooftop.

Jonas's penthouse apartment was light and airy and tastefully furnished. Being of Danish background, he loved the uncluttered elegance of the place and the light colors of the sofa, drapes, and the simple wood furniture. A few of his paintings decorated the wall.

To the south, he had a view of a small section of the river and part of the lake. Across the river stood the Fraumünster Cathedral with its five stained-glass windows designed by Marc Chagall. If the weather was good, Jonas could see the mountains in the distance.

It was still warm on this hot summer day. The sun was setting behind the buildings, surrounding them with halos of gold. The strip of the lake Jonas could see from his apartment sparkled in the last light of the evening. Jonas was thinking of the little girl and her aunt. He sighed, remembering the look on the child's face when he lifted her up. How well he could relate to that feeling of sadness and despair.

Jonas loved children and now that his own kids were grown and his grandchildren lived in Denmark, he made do with the children he taught privately. He enjoyed teaching. It made him feel needed and the company of his students helped him push away the loneliness for a few hours.

The thought of working with Karla, however, filled him with excitement for another reason. In the two pictures he had seen of hers, he had detected an unusual talent. Her drawings were still rough and unpolished, of course. But skill and craft could be taught. What was more important was the degree of passion and the level of personal expression, which was rare in a child so young.

What Karla needed now was the willingness to learn and to practice, which Jonas believed she had. He had seen it in her eyes when she asked him if he would teach her. How long her endurance would last, that was another question. Children changed as they grew up; they developed other interests, they got bored. He had seen it happen many times. He remembered his own children, the years of paying for piano and violin lessons and just when they were getting good at it, they became interested in video games and dating.

Jonas picked up his pipe, stuffed it with tobacco, and lit it. He closed his eyes, enjoying the earthy taste. He had stopped smoking cigarettes years before, but he treated himself to an occasional pipe. He stepped outside and stood on the rooftop patio, watching the last golden and orange hues of the setting sun fade into the approaching dark.

He smiled. "Well, Karla, what do you say? I think it's worth a try."

Chapter 4

It was past noon and the sun was high in the sky. Karla and Maja were sitting at the edge of a pond near their home underneath a weeping willow. Its hanging branches formed a bell shape and the leaves skimmed the surface of the water.

The pond was one of Karla's favorite hangouts. She inhaled the earthy smell of algae and clay. Sitting there quietly, she could hear the rustling of leaves in the summer breeze, the quacking of ducks, and an occasional splash from a leaping fish. With her elbows propped on her knees and her head cradled in her hands, she watched as a family of coots slowly emerged from behind a patch of reed. Mother, father, and a flock of chicks floated across the pond. As if on command, the adults dipped their heads into the water and the babies followed. They kept diving and coming up again until the two adult birds swam on and the little ones followed them single file.

Karla watched them disappear behind a bend in the bank where the pond veered off to the left. She felt the familiar sting of homesickness. "A family," she murmured, "a real family." She turned to Maja. "Last night, I dreamt about Mama again. She was standing by my bed. When I woke up, she had disappeared."

Maja nodded and skimmed the water with her hand. "I know how we could see our mamas again," she whispered.

"How?" Karla sat up straight and brushed her shoulder-length black hair out of her face.

Maja was seven, a year older than Karla. She was a thin girl with a skinny, boyish figure, short blond hair, and blue eyes. She scudded closer and gave Karla a conspiratorial smile. "Back home, my grandmother told me once that at night, when there's a full moon, sometimes a gate opens in the sky. You have to be on a mountain or high hill, and then you can see into Heaven." Maja nodded emphatically.

"Have you ever seen it?" Karla asked, wrinkling her forehead.

Maja shook her head. "No, but if you can see into Heaven, you can see the dead, the angels, can't you?"

Karla nodded. "I guess you could."

"Perhaps we could see our mothers," Maja said.

Karla was quiet, thinking things over. She wrapped her arms around her tanned legs and glanced at the pond. Maja's pale calves dangled in the water.

"I'll have to ask Anna," Karla said.

"No. We can't tell the adults."

"Why not?"

"Because Grandma said that adults can't see into Heaven."

"Why not?"

"Because their hearts aren't pure enough. Only young children can see Heaven."

"We can't go alone in the middle of the night without telling the adults," Karla said.

"Of course we can. We just get up after they've gone to bed and sneak out of the house." Maja scratched at a scab on her leg.

"What if Anna or your aunt and uncle check on us?"

"Don't be such a scaredy-cat. Don't you want to see your mama again?"

"Sure, I want to, but . . ."

"Think how much fun that would be. If you are too chicken, I'll go by myself." Maja pulled a snit.

"Okay. I'll come. Do you think they can see us in the dark?" Karla was getting excited as well.

"Of course, silly. And there will be light from the moon." Maja picked up a small flat stone, and skipped it across the water. It bounced off the surface several times.

"We have to find out when the next full moon is," Karla said.

"I have a calendar at home which shows the full and the new moons. I'll bring it to school tomorrow." Maja sat down again.

"But where shall we go? There aren't any high mountains nearby."

"We can climb up to the Egg. That's a high hill. I bet we can see from there." Maja pedaled her legs in the water and splashed a few drops on Karla.

Karla dunked her hand and sprayed Maja, then got up and giggled. "Catch me." They raced across the meadow.

During recess at school the following day, Karla and Maja studied the colorful calendar Maja had brought.

"We're lucky. There's going to be a full moon next Monday." Maja pointed at the round yellow dot next to the date. "That's just when vacation starts. That means we can be out late at night and we don't have to get up early to go to school the next day. Great." Maja playfully punched Karla's arm.

Karla nodded. It sounded like a great adventure. She only wished she could tell Aunt Anna about it. She was sure that

19

Anna had a pure heart and wouldn't spoil it. It was so difficult to keep a secret. But she didn't want to disappoint Maja.

Chapter 5

"Karla is intelligent, but very unfocused," the young man told Anna.

Anna was having a meeting with Karla's main teacher about her progress in school. Mr. Winter was sitting across from her behind his desk, which was stacked with neatly arranged piles of papers and books. The late-afternoon sun shone through the window, bathing the sparse office and the serious face of the handsome young man in a pale light.

"What do you mean?" Anna peered at him.

The teacher sat up straight. "For one thing, her mind wanders and she's often unable to concentrate. She doesn't pay attention. She sits in her chair, either looks at me with a blank expression on her face—you can tell she's not listening—or she gazes out the window. When I call on her with a question, she looks startled, as if she'd just woken up from a dream.

"I tried all kinds of things. I moved her away from the window. I called on her more frequently, so she wouldn't have a chance to fall back into her daydreaming. She tries to listen, but after a while I catch her again staring into space.

"I thought that perhaps the subject I teach doesn't interest her, but the other teachers have the same experience. Karla is very absentminded. Interestingly enough, her written work is better and she excels in her art class. She draws and paints far beyond her age, as the art teacher told me."

Anna nodded. "I know; she loves to draw and paint. It's something that makes her happy. I found a professional art teacher for her."

"Yes, it may encourage and perhaps help her. However, she needs to snap out of her daydreaming during the oral lessons, or she won't be able to graduate to the next class."

"Why wasn't I told of this earlier?" Anna asked in a sharp voice. "I didn't know she was doing poorly. At first, she wasn't happy in school. As you know, her whole life was turned upside down when her mother and grandmother died. She's had so many changes, so I'm not surprised that she's still suffering. But she made a few friends, she did her homework, and she never complained about school."

"I'm sorry. Perhaps I should've let you know earlier, but I also knew about her background and thought that things would improve with time. Lately, however, I realized that she needs help—perhaps counseling—and I was going to call you about it."

Anna sighed. "I took her to a therapist in the beginning, right after she moved in with me. He felt, however, that Karla was dealing with her pain in a normal way and that with lots of love and attention she'd slowly get over it. I think that was an overly optimistic assessment. Perhaps she needs professional help after all."

"I do know of someone I can recommend," Mr. Winter said. "She takes care of some of the children here who have been traumatized. I'm sure we can do something to help Karla."

The teacher shook hands with Anna. It was only now that Anna realized why he looked so familiar to her. His shiny black hair and piercing blue eyes reminded her of Nicolas, her husband.

An Uncommon Family

After meeting with the teacher, Anna went back to her bookstore. It was still quiet there, no customers yet. She watered the few plants, then walked around rearranging some books and putting a few toys, which were lying on the floor in the kids' corner, back into the crates.

Her bookstore was fairly small and it was a constant struggle to find enough room for all the books and videos she kept. Gazing out the window, she squinted her eyes against the glare from the sun. She turned around, and gave the tall birch-wood shelves a last look-over, then turned to a package of new books that had just come in. She unpacked the box, took out each book, opened it, and held it to her nose. She loved the crisp smell of new books, fresh off the press. The ink had a slight synthetic aroma, not unpleasant, but rather exciting. Each book contained a secret, a new insight perhaps, an exciting adventure.

She began to label them and entered their data into the computer. She had a difficult time concentrating on her task, though. After a while, she stopped and sighed. The talk with the teacher worried her. She had had the impression that Karla had been doing okay in school. At least, she didn't seem to have had any major problems.

How could I have missed the signs? she wondered.

One of the books she unpacked was a travel book about the United States. The picture on the cover was of the Statue of Liberty in New York. "America," she murmured as she turned the pages. She scrunched her forehead and took a deep breath.

Why am I surprised? I've missed the signs before.

The resemblance between the teacher and Nicolas, her husband, and the picture on the book reminded her of her life in New York City, where she had lived as a young woman. It had been an intensely happy as well as sad time.

I sure fell for him. I was so much in love. And then —

The doorbell rang and a friend of hers walked in. Anna surreptitiously dabbed her eyes and forced a smile. "Hi there."

Petra peered at her. "Something wrong?"

Anna shook her head, then pointed at the picture of New York. "Just thinking of old times."

Petra came over and looked at the photo. "New York, huh?" She put her hand on Anna's shoulder. "Why does it make you sad? Want to talk about it?"

Petra was a good friend and Anna's hairdresser. They lived in the same village and both loved books. After a slight hesitation, Anna felt she could confide in her. "Why not? Let's have some coffee." She pressed the button on the espresso machine.

"You know that I was married?" Anna said as she put the cups on the small table in the corner.

"Yes, but you never gave me any details. It seems to be a taboo subject."

"Well, yeah, I don't like to dwell on it. But anyway, I met Nicolas, my husband, at a party in New York City. I was studying library science. He was a Mexican citizen and was finishing his degree in architecture."

"I knew you lived in New York for a while. I didn't realize you studied there," Petra said.

"One of the reasons was my father. He was an American citizen. After my parents got divorced, he moved back to the United States. I spent most of my vacations with him in New York City. I loved New York. It was such an exciting place. I applied for the library science program at the Pratt Institute. I got in and decided to stay.

"Anyway, Nico and I started going out and we fell in love. He was very handsome. He had jet-black glossy hair and intense blue eyes." Anna gave a wistful smile. "He was part Gypsy. His mother was a descendent of a tribe of Spanish Romani. His father was English."

"Sounds exotic," Petra said.

"Yes, well, he was everything a young stupid woman like me would fall for. Attractive, charming, mysterious, intelligent . . . and an excellent liar."

"A liar? That doesn't sound so good," Petra said.

"You can say that." Anna sighed.

"So what went wrong? Was he unfaithful?"

"Well, there was more to it."

The door opened and another woman entered. She looked around the bookstore, then came up to the counter and asked Anna about a book she was looking for. Anna went over to the bookshelves. She couldn't find the book, so she did a search on her computer. She turned to Petra. "Sorry, I'll tell you the rest later."

"No problem," Petra said. "I'll have to leave anyway. I have a dental appointment. But I sure want to know more." Petra gave Anna a quick hug and left.

Anna lifted her hand in a good-bye gesture, then continued to search for the book. "It's a children's book," she said to the woman. "I don't have it in stock but I can order it for you."

"That would be great, thanks," the woman said. "It's for my daughter's birthday."

Anna smiled and typed the information into the computer. It was a book of poems for children with cute illustrations. She ordered several copies and decided to give one to Karla.

Chapter 6

The sirens shrieked from far away. Someone banged on the car door. Red paint splashed all over. "Karla, Karla," a muffled voice called.

Karla shot up in bed; her breath came in spurts. Slowly the nightmare dissipated, but the voice and the thudding sounds against the shutter continued. Karla kicked back her comforter, got out of bed, and opened the window. Maja's pale face lit up briefly in the moonlight.

"Let's go," she whispered. "Where have you been? I've been knocking forever."

"Psst. Be quiet. Don't wake Anna. I fell asleep. I'll be right out." Karla was already dressed. She grabbed her jacket and climbed on top of the window sill. Her bedroom was on the first floor and faced the back of the house. There was a light thump as she jumped onto the gravel path in the backyard.

Maja leaned her bicycle against the fence and followed Karla, who walked up the narrow path that led to the main road. They crossed the highway, which was without traffic at this time of the night. Karla turned and looked back. In spite of the moonlight, the house was barely visible underneath the tall birches and pines which shaded it. All of a sudden, the windows in Anna's bedroom lit up. Karla held her breath and stared.

"Come on," Maja whispered.

"Wait," Karla said and continued to watch the window. "I think Anna heard something." She exhaled with relief when the light went out again.

"You're such a chicken," Maja grumbled and began to walk up the hill.

Karla followed her. As long as they were in the open, they easily found their way in the familiar landscape lit by the moon. Once they entered the forest, however, it was too dark to see anything. Maja had brought a small flashlight which gave just enough light so they didn't stumble too often over exposed roots or bump into trees. Every once in a while, they stopped and listened to the noises of the forest: the rustling of some small animal in the leaves on the ground, the crackling of twigs or branches nearby.

At one point, they both let out a muffled scream as a dark shadow leapt up next to them and dashed through the undergrowth.

"A wolf," Maja called and dropped her flashlight.

Karla grabbed her arm. "There're no wolves here, are there?" Her voice quivered.

"Must have been a deer. We probably woke it up," Maja whispered.

"This is spooky. Let's get out of here. We should've asked Anna to come along after all." Karla was still trembling from the shock.

"It's too late for that now. Let's go." Maja sounded less confident than before but she picked up the flashlight and walked on.

After a while, Karla saw a weak band of light ahead of them. They had reached the end of the forest. She sighed with relief as they stepped into a meadow. The moon had risen and bathed the landscape in its milky light. The grass was dewy and soon Karla's sneakers were soaked. She shivered in the cool night.

They found the narrow path which led up to the Egg, a hill behind the village. It was quiet outside the forest; the only sounds were their steps on the gravel path, the occasional crunching of stones, and the increased breathing as they climbed the steep hill. Karla felt warm again and she was beginning to enjoy their nightly adventure.

After about half an hour, they reached the top of the hill. They sat on the wooden bench, from which they were able to see the few lights of the village in the distance. They sat quietly for a while, relaxing from the hike, and waiting for something to happen.

Around them the soft silvery light of the moon spread across the fields. Karla took a deep breath. The air smelled of damp freshly cut grass and sage. She heard the melancholic tune of a night bird nearby.

Would they be able to look into heaven? "What now?" she asked Maja.

"We'll have to watch the moon and wait." Maja's normally confident voice sounded timid.

After a while, Karla's neck began to hurt from the strain of tilting her head back. "Let's lie down; it's easier that way."

Maja stretched out on the bench, supporting her head with her jacket. Karla lay down next to her, wedging her body between her friend's and the backrest of the bench, and put her head on Maja's chest.

The enormous disk of the full moon and the sky with its thousands of stars were enchanting, yet Heaven remained as closed as ever. Karla was only six years old and she longed for her mother with all her heart, but she sensed that there was an insurmountable barrier between the living and the dead. Doubts about the success of their mission lodged in her mind.

"We'll never see our mamas again. They're gone forever." Karla's insight sent a stabbing pain through her chest. A deep sadness overwhelmed her.

"My grandma is crazy. I don't know why I believed her." Maja's voice broke.

Karla felt her friend's heaving chest. She sat up and let a sob escape. "At least, the moon is beautiful. And perhaps our mamas can see us, even if we can't see them," she said, trying unsuccessfully to soften her own as well as Maja's pain.

"I doubt it," Maja said matter-of-factly.

"We should get back." Karla wiped tears from her face with the back of her hand.

They got up and began to walk back without talking. In the forest, Maja turned on her flashlight. They made it through the forest, holding hands, without waking any more animals. After they crossed the highway, Karla's throat tightened. The windows of her house were lit and when they came closer, she saw a car parked in the driveway.

"Oh no. My aunt and uncle," Maja said. "We're going to get such a spanking."

Karla's heart was beating fast. "Anna never spanks me."

"I bet she will this time." Maja's voice quivered.

When they opened the door, three pairs of shocked eyes looked at them. Anna and Maja's aunt came rushing toward them.

"For Heaven's sake, where have you been? What are you doing outside in the middle of the night? You scared the heck out of us. We were just getting ready to look for you," Anna exclaimed. She was dressed in sweatpants, a flannel shirt, and a jacket. She brushed a lock of tangled hair out of her pale face.

"We're sorry," Karla said. "We didn't mean to scare you."

"I woke up and wanted to check on you. You were gone, the window and the shutters were open. I saw Maja's bicycle. So I called her aunt and uncle. What were you thinking, sneaking out like that and running around in the middle of the night?" Anna touched Karla's hand. "And you're all frozen. Take off your shoes and socks." Anna got two large towels out of the bathroom and two pairs of dry socks. Karla and Maja stripped off their muddy shoes and wet socks. It was only now that Karla noticed how cold she was. She began to shiver. Anna helped her dry her feet and put on clean socks.

"You're going to get it." Maja's uncle, a tall, skinny man with a black beard and angry, penetrating eyes, pointed his finger at Maja. "We were just about to call the police. We thought you'd run away."

"We . . . we wanted to see our mamas. Grandma said . . ." Maja burst into tears.

Karla tried to explain. "Her grandma told Maja that during a full moon children can see into Heaven and—"

"What a bunch of crap," the uncle shouted.

"Why don't we listen to what they have to say?" Anna pulled Karla close. "All right, start from the beginning." She brushed a strand of hair out of Karla's face.

After Karla and Maja described their nightly adventure and the disappointment of not seeing their mothers after all, it was quiet in the room. Maja's aunt, a short, stocky woman dressed in black, had tears in her eyes. She hugged Maja and talked to her quietly in a foreign language.

Maja's uncle still paced the floor but seemed less angry. He shook his head. "Your grandmother is a superstitious old bat," he muttered.

"Andro, please." Maja's aunt shook her head and hugged her niece.

"Well, it's true; she shouldn't fill the child's head with such nonsense. It's bad enough having to listen to all the crazy vampire stories she tells her. It only makes things worse. Your mother is dead, Maja. She's with God in Heaven, but we can't see her. Nobody can." He sounded upset again.

Karla remembered Maja's fear of punishment. She turned to Anna. "Are we going to get a spanking now?"

Anna gave Karla a puzzled look, then smiled. "Of course not. Promise me, though. Never do this again. Next time you want to go on a mission like this, you have to tell me. All right?"

Karla nodded and hugged her aunt.

Maja's uncle wasn't appeased as easily. He glared at Maja. "You sure deserve a beating. Scaring us like this."

"They didn't mean any harm and I'm sure they learned their lesson, right?" Anna said.

"Yes," Maja whispered and Karla nodded.

"I think it's time we had a hot cup of tea to calm our frazzled nerves. The girls should go to bed. Why don't you let Maja sleep here? That way she can get warm and have a few hours of sleep. I'll bring her home in the morning. What do you say?" Anna turned to Maja's relatives.

"All right, I guess," her uncle muttered. He narrowed his eyes and pointed his finger at Maja. "You better behave. And don't think this is over with." After a short hesitation, he bent down and gave her a quick hug.

Karla felt relieved. No spanking for Maja this time.

After the girls were tucked away in Karla's bed—Maja wearing one of Karla's warm flannel nightgowns—Anna brought two cups of hot milk with honey. Drinking the soothing liquid, Karla realized how tired she was. She was almost asleep by the time Anna turned off the light.

"Your aunt sure is nice," Maja whispered as they were lying in the dark.

"Yeah, she is," Karla murmured.

Chapter 7

Anna was exhausted after the turbulent night but too keyed up to go back to sleep. She took a hot shower and got dressed, built a fire in the woodstove, and made a pot of coffee. Soon the scent of dark French roast mixed with the fragrance of burning beech logs filled the living room.

She sat by the window, watching the milky light of dawn spreading across the fields. Normally, she loved the early morning hours, the transition from dark to light, the way trees, meadows, and houses emerged from the shadows. A new day meant hope, new chances, fresh possibilities. This morning, however, Anna was preoccupied. She was worried about Karla, about her troubles in school and her inability to accept the death of her mother. Then again, it was natural that Karla still grieved. Perhaps Anna was expecting too much too soon.

Anna loved Karla and couldn't even imagine living without the child anymore. Periodically, however, she was overcome by self-doubt. How could she—a middle-aged woman with no experience of raising children—ever be a good enough guardian or mother for a troubled little girl? When she expressed her misgivings to her uncle or her friends, they reassured her that she was doing a marvelous job. "She'll come around; don't be so impatient."

In her conscious mind, Karla knew her mother was gone and would never come back. Her emotions, however, had not accepted that cruel truth. Anna had told her that her mother would always be with her in spirit, but of course this was an even vaguer concept for a six-year-old than it was for an adult. What did this mean, "in spirit"?

"Can Mama hear me? Can she see me? Where is she now?"

Anna tried to be as honest as possible. She admitted she didn't know but seeing Karla's sad face, she couldn't help but give her some encouragement, even if she knew she was faking.

"We don't know for sure, Karla. But I believe the dead are in Heaven. God takes good care of them and, yes, I believe they can hear and see us. But, honey, they can't come back."

"Why not?"

"That's a secret we human beings don't know. Only God knows why that is."

"I'm mad at God," Karla said with tears in her eyes.

Anna swallowed and took a deep breath. Her first reaction was to tell Karla that was wrong, but she caught herself. How many times since her mother's and sister's deaths had she quarreled with God herself, a god she wasn't even sure she believed in.

"I know, Karla. Sometimes I'm angry at God, too. It's okay. But even if we can't understand him, we have to trust him. And that's very hard sometimes."

Anna took another sip of coffee. By now, the first sun rays had managed to rise above the treetops. The dewdrops on the leaves of the trees and plants glimmered. The sky was cloudless; it would be another sunny day.

I have to learn to trust as well, Anna thought.

33

Chapter 8

Jonas had set up a still life for Karla and explained some basic concepts, such as contour drawing and shading. On a small table, he had placed a couple of apples, a tall vase, and a shawl that he had draped over part of the vase, so Karla could practice drawing the folds. He had moved the table next to the balcony door. The light from outside fell sideways onto the objects, throwing shadows onto the table.

Karla seemed unfocused and distracted this morning. Jonas watched as the child began to sketch without her normal enthusiasm. Her lines were hesitant, she kept erasing them, and finally she put the pencil down and sighed.

"What's the matter, Karla? You're not feeling well?"

Karla shook her head and tears gathered in her eyes. "I dreamt something bad," she said.

"Oh? What was it?"

"It was all red and there were dead people. I think they were dead." Karla's voice quivered.

Jonas was aware of Karla's occasional nightmares about the accident that killed her mother. "Tell you what. Why don't we take a break? I feel like some hot chocolate. What about you?"

Karla nodded. "Okay." She slid down from her chair and followed Jonas into the kitchen.

Jonas heated up some milk and put hot-chocolate powder into two mugs. "Why don't you get the can with the whipped cream out of the refrigerator?" he said. "We'll have a special treat today."

"Whipped cream in a can?" Karla gave him a puzzled look.

"Yes, there it is." Jonas pointed to a can in the compartment of the refrigerator door.

"Is this any good?" Karla scrunched her face as she examined the can. "Anna always makes whipped cream from scratch."

Jonas laughed. "Well, it'll have to do. It's not as good as when you whip it yourself, but it's not bad. I'm a little lazy when it comes to cooking. You know, being by myself. Eva, my wife, always made it from scratch, too."

Jonas poured the milk into the mugs, shook the bottle of whipped cream, and squeezed a dollop out of it. "Try it." He handed a mug to Karla.

Karla took a sip and licked some of the whipped cream off the top. "Good," she said.

They sat on the couch in the living room, sipping hot chocolate. Karla put her mug down on the table and walked over to the wall to look at a photo of Eva. She stood in front of the picture, seemingly absorbed, then turned around. "She's very pretty."

Jonas nodded. "Yes, she was beautiful."

Karla came back to the sofa and picked up her mug again. After she took another sip, she gazed at Jonas with her large dark eyes. "Do you dream about her sometimes?"

"Yes, quite often."

"Do you have scary dreams?"

"Not scary; sometimes they're sad. I dream of her when she was ill and that makes me sad. Sometimes I dream of her when she was still healthy and young. These are beautiful dreams, but when I wake up and realize that she's gone, I get sad."

Karla nodded. She wrinkled her forehead and when she looked at him again, her face was sad. "I don't want to have scary dreams about my mama. I only want happy dreams."

"Do you have happy dreams about her sometimes?"

"Yes, sometimes I dream we're still together and we live in the Ticino and we're with Lena."

"Lena?"

"She's my mama's friend and she watched me when Mama was working."

"What about the scary dreams?"

Karla hesitated. "It's just gobs of red and my mama calls for help . . . and I can't help her because I'm stuck somewhere." Karla's voice broke.

Jonas pulled her close and hugged her. "Karla, Anna told me about the accident. You were strapped in your booster. You couldn't have helped your mother. Both your mother and grandmother died instantly. They didn't have to suffer and they couldn't have called you. You had a shock and that's why you have these dreams."

Jonas hesitated. "Dreams have their own language. It's a language of pictures and sometimes these pictures are confusing for us. Some dreams, such as your nightmare, keep coming back. Perhaps they want to tell us something, but they don't tell us in words. Let's take your dream about your mother calling you for help. Now, we know your mother didn't call you for help, because she was dead. So why do you dream that she's calling you?"

"I don't know," Karla said.

"Perhaps the dream isn't about what really happened. It's about you feeling guilty. The voice you hear in your dream isn't your mother's voice. It is your 'feeling guilty' voice. It's that little being in you that tells you that it's your fault that your mother died." Jonas gently squeezed Karla's arm. "But it's not true. It's not your fault. The voice is lying."

Karla looked at him shocked. "Then what can I do when it calls?"

"You have to tell it to shut up."

Karla gave a hesitant smile. "I can't talk in my dream."

"Well, if you can't say it while dreaming, you can say it after you wake up. You can tell the voice to go away. Your mama is at peace now. She doesn't need your help. She wouldn't be calling you for help now. And you know what else?"

Karla shook her head.

"Your mother wants you to be happy. So, perhaps, we can do something to chase the dreams away."

"What?" Karla asked.

"When you have a bad or scary dream, then the next morning you can draw or paint it. Paint what the dream feels like to you. The painting doesn't have to have real things. Perhaps just colors. Perhaps when you see the dream on paper, then it may not be that scary anymore."

Karla gave a hesitant nod.

"Let's try it. Think about the dream you had last night and make a drawing or a painting. Paint what it feels like." Jonas got up and pulled a large drawing pad out of his desk. He put it in front of Karla and handed her a box of oil pastels.

Karla loved oil pastels. She hesitated at first, then began to draw and paint. After a while, the picture took on the form of a brown-red monster with large fiery eyes and a wide-open mouth. She drew a speech bubble in front of its mouth and wrote in her childlike handwriting "Help Help" on it, and underneath the picture "Go away."

"There," she said and put the crayon down. She took a deep breath and smiled. Her face was flushed from excitement.

"Great, I like it," Jonas said.

The doorbell rang and Jonas pressed the buzzer. It was Anna to pick up Karla from her lesson. When she entered, Jonas looked at her surprised. She looked different—younger, better. He wanted to make her a compliment but couldn't figure out what it was that had changed her. A new outfit? She was wearing black slacks and a black-and-blue patterned blouse, which flattered her facial color and emphasized her blue-gray eyes, but that's not what it was . . . he finally saw it. "Your hair?"

Anna blushed. "Yeah. My hairdresser talked me into adding highlights."

"It looks great," Jonas said.

"Thank you." Anna gave an embarrassed smile, then walked over to Karla and looked at the painting of the monster. "Whoa, that's one scary picture."

Jonas shrugged. "We had a little therapy session."

Anna hugged Karla, then smiled at Jonas. "Thanks."

Chapter 9

Anna had just finished reading stories from Dr. Seuss's *Sleep Book*, one of Karla's favorites. Although Karla was able to read herself, she enjoyed listening to Anna reading before going to sleep. Anna had a soothing voice and it made Karla feel good. She was even better at reading and telling stories than her mama had been. She remembered the times Aunt Anna had come to visit her when she still lived at home. Her mother had always let Anna read stories to Karla. She would sit next to Karla and they would both listen.

Perhaps her mama was listening now as well.

Anna put the book aside and smiled. "More tomorrow, okay? Time to sleep." She kissed Karla good night and blew out the candle on the small shrine in the corner of her bedroom. Anna and Karla had built the shrine as a memory to Karla's mother. On a small chestnut-wood table, Karla had set up a few things from her mother: photos, an amber necklace, and a few colored stones Karla and her mother had collected during a vacation in the mountains. A vase with fresh flowers stood next to a candle, which Anna lit in the evening during story time and when Karla said her prayers.

Karla yawned and fell asleep, thinking about the drowsy creatures in Dr. Seuss's book. In the middle of the night, she woke from a dream. She had been walking around the graveyard together with her mother. They stood in front of her mother's plot, which was piled high with flowers and wreaths: white, yellow, and pink lilies; dark-blue irises; bright-red tulips; and more. Her mother was standing next to her. She was alive. They looked at her grave, at the decorations, but they weren't sad. They smiled.

It was a beautiful dream and Karla wanted to go back to it. Lying in the dark, she remembered a story she had heard in Sunday school. It was the story of Lazarus, one of the miracles Jesus had performed. Lazarus had died and Jesus had brought him back from the dead. The story had made a deep impression on Karla. During church on Sunday, the priest had talked about prayers. He had said that God heard our prayers.

Karla shot up in bed. Her heart was beating fast. It all made sense now. If Jesus made Lazarus alive again, perhaps he could do the same for Karla's mother. And if Karla prayed really hard, God or Jesus would hear her. Karla turned on the light. She wrapped her arms around her knees and stared at the shrine. Anna had said that the dead didn't come back, ever. But in the Bible it said that miracles could happen, so perhaps Anna was wrong. Perhaps a miracle would happen for Karla, too.

Karla slipped out of bed. She picked up the box with the matches, then hesitated for a moment. Anna had warned her not to light the candle by herself, that it was too dangerous. But everything looked more beautiful with candlelight and Karla was sure God would like it. It would be all right. He would protect her. Karla carefully struck the match and lit the candle. She smiled as she watched the flame flicker in the light breeze from the half-open window. She turned off the light and kneeled down on the pillow next to the shrine. The flame tossed a pattern of light and shadows on the wall. The scented candle gave off a whiff of lavender. But it was still dark in the room and Karla remembered the many candles in church people lit for dead members of their family or friends.

Karla needed more candles. She wanted to do this right; it had to be festive if she wanted to get God's attention.

She opened and closed the door carefully and tiptoed through the hallway. In front of Anna's bedroom, she stopped for a moment. Perhaps she should tell Anna, but Anna was probably asleep. She didn't want to wake her. She knew where Anna kept the candles in the kitchen. She opened the bottom drawer of the kitchen cabinet. The drawer was stuck and squeaked when she pulled at it. It always did that in the hot summer months. Karla held her breath and listened, but nothing stirred in the house. She grabbed a bunch of candles and tiptoed back to the bedroom.

When she opened the door, the draft from the hallway and from the open window blew the curtain back and forth. It brushed against the candle flame, extinguishing it, but the old dry cloth had caught on fire. At first, it was just smoldering, but another draft fanned the flames and made them shoot high up, consuming the curtain and licking at the ceiling.

Karla dropped the candles and stared at the fire, paralyzed. Images of a burning car, of two bodies leaning over the dashboard flashed before her eyes. The sickening smell of burning cloth finally ripped her out of her apathy. She began to scream loud and long. Someone called her and then everything went dark.

When she woke up, she was lying on the sofa in the living room. Anna, her hair tousled, looked at her with fearful eyes. She gently stroked her forehead. A man whom Karla recognized as her doctor stood next to her. A few men in uniform were walking back and forth talking loudly. *Firefighters*, Karla thought.

"How are you feeling?" the doctor asked.

"Okay," Karla whispered.

The doctor put one of those funny-looking instruments on Karla's chest. If felt cool on her skin. Then the doctor asked her to sit up. "Are you feeling sick?"

Karla shook her head. "What happened?" Then she remembered and started to cry. "I wanted to light a candle and pray."

Anna hugged her. "It's all right. I was able to extinguish it in time. The curtain burned and the wall needs to be painted, but it could've been worse. And the neighbors saw the flames and called the fire department."

"She'll be okay. She must have fainted from the shock more than from the smoke," the doctor said. "You caught her in time. Just make sure she doesn't sleep in her bedroom tonight. There may still be fumes. If she starts feeling ill, let me know right away, but I think she'll be fine."

"Oh, no, she'll sleep in my room," Anna said. She sounded relieved but she was still pale.

The doctor touched Karla's cheek. "Sleep tight and no more matches and candles tonight, okay?"

Karla nodded. She was still confused. Everything had happened so fast. One of the firefighters with a hard hat stepped out of her bedroom. "Okay, we're done. No major damage. You were very lucky."

Then he turned to Karla, and said in a serious and somewhat commanding voice: "Now listen, little girl. You know this could've gone bad. You have to be very careful with matches. Next time, tell your mother to be with you and let her light the candle, okay?"

Karla's eyes filled with tears. "I wanted to pray for my mama and it all went wrong." She began to sob again.

The firefighter looked at Anna startled. "I'm sorry, I didn't realize . . ."

"It's okay," Anna said. "Her mother died. I'm her aunt."

"So sorry." His face softened. He gently patted Karla's head. "Just be careful, honey, okay?"

Karla nodded and lowered her eyes.

Anna accompanied the firefighters to the door. After they had left, Karla got up and walked to her bedroom. The wall above the window and part of the ceiling was black. The curtain, all black, was lying on the floor. Otherwise nothing was burnt. It smelled icky, though, and Karla began to feel nauseated. She stepped back out of the room.

Anna put her hand on her shoulder. "I'll call the painter tomorrow. We'll buy a new curtain. It'll be okay. But tell me, what happened? Why did you light the candle again? I told you not to play with matches when you're alone."

Karla told her how she tried to make the room look pretty, that she had wanted to pray and ask God to bring her mama back, just like he had done with Lazarus.

"Lazarus?" Anna looked at her puzzled.

"The priest at Sunday school told us that Jesus brought Lazarus back from the dead. He called him in his grave and Lazarus stood up and walked around."

Anna sighed and shook her head. "I'll try to explain that thing with Lazarus tomorrow, okay? Now let's just go to bed and get some sleep."

Karla was lying next to Anna, listening to her steady breathing. Branches of the tall pine tree next to the window squeaked once in a while in the breeze. The trunk of the tree, lit by a lantern behind it, cast a long shadow across the bed through the half-open window. It was peaceful after the turmoil of the fire, but Karla couldn't settle down. Tears kept gathering in her eyes and a feeling of deep disappointment hurt her chest.

It wasn't fair. She had wanted to do everything right. She had prayed and God hadn't answered her. He hadn't protect-ted her. He had let the curtain burn and the ceiling get all black and ugly. And her mama, who they all said was watching over her, hadn't helped her, either. Slowly, her sadness turned to anger.

For the first time, she began to doubt the stories she was told, the stories of a kind and just God who loved his children. "God is mean," Karla murmured. She wondered if she would now be punished, but nothing happened. It was dark and quiet in the room, no stern voice sounded from Heaven. Karla disentangled herself from Anna's embrace. She sat up. "God is mean." Her voice was defiant.

"Hush." Anna pulled her down next to her. "Calm down and let's get some sleep."

"I hate God. He doesn't even listen," Karla said, her voice breaking.

Anna sighed. "I guess we might as well forget about sleep. Okay, let's get up. I'll make us some tea and milk."

Chapter 10

While the Earl Gray tea was steeping, Anna watched through the kitchen window as dawn began to spread. It was going to be another hot day. In the distance, a rooster crowed on one of the last remaining farms in town, which had seen an increase in new homes being built for the growing number of people who moved out of the city to the countryside. The formerly quiet road about a mile away from Anna's house had been widened and now saw a steady stream of cars and trucks driving into Zurich and out of it during rush hour. Freeways began to take the place of formerly two-lane roads. The country was still far away from the urban sprawl she had experienced in the United States, but Anna watched the development and seemingly increased "Americanization" of her hometown with trepidation.

This morning, however, after the shock of the fire, she was concerned about other things. She heated some milk and checked on Karla, who had finally succumbed to sleep. Anna picked up the down comforter, which had slipped onto the floor as a result of the child's tossing and turning, and covered her gently. She tiptoed out of the room and closed the door.

She poured herself a cup of tea and went into the living room. Standing by the window, she inhaled the tart bergamot-oil fragrance before taking the first sip. The scent dispersed the still-lingering smell of the fire somewhat. She sighed, trying to think of a way to explain the meaning behind the tales in the Bible, the story of Lazarus and of the miracles that Jesus supposedly had performed.

Anna's own attitude toward miracles was quite jaded. She had had her share of so-called miracles in her life. While she had lived in the United States, she had been a member of one of the many New Age meditation centers. It was after a disastrous love affair, when she was looking for a higher kind of love, unsoiled from the earthly human betrayals and mistakes. She realized soon enough, however, that the members of spiritual communities were—well—human and had all the flaws the rest of humanity grappled with. And most of the miracles turned out to be mere illusions in the end.

On the one hand, Anna was glad that Karla found some solace in the stories of the Bible and she had done her part to make her believe that God was watching over Karla and her mother. On the other hand, Anna's own beliefs were on shaky ground. Was there a god?

Anna took a deep breath and watched as the sun rose behind the trees, bathing the tops in a halo of brilliant light. There were moments when she felt that there truly was a benevolent force. At other times, the world and humanity seemed to her rudderless, tainted, convoluted at best, and vicious at worst. And love? Well, she hadn't had much luck with love, at least not with love for a man. The one she had loved the most had caused her so much heartache that she had begun to doubt that such a thing even existed.

That was until Karla came along. Her niece had given her back some of the trust in love. The little girl had been able to soften and warm that hard, cold place in her chest. Anna would do anything to help her. But how?

Outside, it was getting light. Anna gazed at the thin strips of crimson and orange on the horizon. The maple tree and the birches in front of the house were ablaze in the first sun rays and the dewdrops on the fleshy leaves of the rhododendron shrubs sparkled in the light. The beautiful scenery soothed her worries. She nodded and gave a smile. All she could do at the moment was to answer the child's questions as honestly as possible. And it meant saying she didn't know rather than trying to pretend she believed in something she didn't. Children knew when you were faking.

"That story about Lazarus," Anna began as she and Karla sat at the breakfast table. "I'll try to explain it to you as well as I can. A lot of the stories in the Bible are mysterious. They were written a long, long time ago in a language very different from our own. A lot of very intelligent people have been trying to interpret them and they often disagree.

"So what I tell you is my own opinion and other people may not agree with me. Your priest for instance. But you are a smart girl and, when you are a little older, you will have your own ideas about what the stories mean."

Karla, holding a piece of bread smeared with butter and jam in her hand, stopped chewing and gazed at Anna with intensity.

Anna smiled. "Why don't we finish breakfast first and then I'll tell you. Okay?"

Karla nodded and kept on eating.

After breakfast, they cleared away the dishes and Anna poured another cup of tea for herself and milk for Karla. They sat on the sofa next to the window. The sun stood tall above the pine trees of the forest. A thin layer of white haze floated around the tree tops.

Anna cleared her throat. "Have you ever heard of 'near death' experiences?" she asked Karla.

Karla shrugged, then shook her head.

47

"Sometimes, when a person is very ill or had a severe accident, he or she almost dies. They even stop breathing for some time, but they're still alive. Sometimes, someone can be in a coma. That's a very deep sleep."

"Like the woman in the hospital?" Karla asked.

"Yes, like that woman." Anna and Karla had visited a sick friend of Anna's and in a bed next to her had been a woman who had been in a coma for several years. Karla had been fascinated and somewhat uneasy about the experience and had asked many questions.

"Nowadays," Anna continued, "doctors can tell if a person is dead or only seemingly dead. But in the past, thousands of years ago, when Jesus was alive, doctors didn't have that kind of knowledge. So, perhaps, Lazarus was only near death and his family put him into a tomb. That's not like our graves but rather like a small stone house for the dead. Anyway, when Jesus called him, Lazarus may have just woken up from his coma. And the people thought it was a miracle. Do you understand?"

Karla nodded. She looked disappointed. "Then Jesus didn't do any miracles?"

"I didn't say that. He may have performed miracles. But you know, people have different ideas of what a miracle is. For instance, sometimes a person is very ill and recovers and that's like a miracle, isn't it?"

Karla didn't look convinced. Obviously for her a miracle was something much more magical, something exotic, like Jesus walking on water.

"You were angry at God yesterday because you felt he didn't help you," Anna continued. "But think about it. That fire could've been a lot worse. The whole house could've burned down and you could've been hurt badly. But that didn't happen, did it? I woke up in time because I felt in my sleep that something was wrong." *Anna, try to stay true to the facts here. You heard her scream.*

"You think God made you wake up?" Karla's face brightened.

Anna smiled at Karla. "What do you think?"

Karla nodded. "Cool."

Anna laughed. "I guess you could call it that."

There was a sudden lightness in the air. "So, God may have also taught us a lesson. No more lighting candles without me being present, okay?"

Karla nodded. "Can I paint now?"

"Of course you can."

Karla got up, ran to her room, and dug out her drawing pad from underneath the pile of art utensils.

Did we achieve anything? Anna wondered. At least Karla seemed happier again.

As Anna expected, Karla made a drawing of her experience at night. She drew the inside of her bedroom. A little girl was standing next to the window, looking at flames consuming the curtain. In the next room, a woman was lying in bed. A long arm, clothed in white, reached down from above through the roof, and a large hand touched the woman's shoulder.

Anna nodded and smiled as Karla showed her the picture. *She needs to believe.*

Chapter 11

"Mama, today we went to the Albis. It's a mountain near Zurich. There's a restaurant there called Gingerbread House. A witch came out of the house. Of course, it's not a real witch, Anna said. Just the owner dressed up as a witch. At first, I was a little scared, but she was a kind witch. She gave the children candy. She was a little mean to the adults, though. She grabbed a lady's purse and snatched a hat off an old man's head. But she gave the things back. It was funny.

"Mama, I wish you could've seen her. She was wearing a long black coat and a black hood and she had a long red nose. She had a broom and swept people's feet away. I asked Anna if you were able to see her from Heaven. Anna said she didn't know for sure but she believed you could. I wish you could let me know if you can see me.

"I miss you, Mama." Karla swallowed and took a deep breath. She was sitting in bed before going to sleep, cuddling her patchwork doll. The flame of the candle on her mother's shrine flickered lightly. Anna had bought her a new glass candleholder, which enclosed the candle and was safer than the old open candle. They had moved the shrine away from the window. After the fire, Anna had decided they might as well paint the whole room, not just the one wall. Karla had been allowed to pick out the color. It was a very light green, which matched the color of the rug and Karla's green-and-yellow bedspread.

It was Sunday evening. Anna and Karla had been on an outing and before going to sleep, Karla told her mother about

50

her day. The occasional flickering of the candlelight made Karla feel that her mother was listening.

"Next to the Gingerbread House, there's a farm with lots of animals: cows, sheep, goats, donkeys and chickens and rabbits. After lunch, Anna took me there and I got to watch the farmer milk the cows and I got to pet the sheep and the baby cows.

"Maja came with us. She misses her mama, too. Sometimes, we tell each other stories about you and her mama. Sometimes we get sad and cry, but the stories are fun.

"I don't think it's right that God takes people away and won't let them come back. Maja said that God needs people to help him in Heaven. But he should take people who don't have little children. Anna says that sometimes we don't understand God, but we have to trust him. I don't understand God. But I don't want him to be mad at me. I pray every night and sometimes that makes me feel better.

"Anna says she thinks you can hear me, although I can't hear you. Sometimes, I can feel you. It makes me feel better, better than praying to God even. I hope God isn't mad now. Anna says not to worry. He's very generous and kind. All right, good night, Mama. Sleep well. I'll talk to you again tomorrow."

Chapter 12

Anna smiled as she kissed Karla's flushed cheek. She blew out the candle on the shrine and opened the window. It was still warm after a scorching day. She left the door to the living room open, so the nightly breeze would cool the room enough for Karla to be able to sleep. Tonight, however, she might sleep soundly after the fun and excitement during the day's outing.

Anna had listened as Karla told her mother about her day. The evening "talk" had become a ritual just like the story time, the shrine, and her evening prayer. They seemed to help her. She had become a little happier overall during the past few weeks, ever since she started her art lessons with Jonas. She had bonded with her teacher right away. Anna hoped it would last. It would be good for Karla to have a male role model in her life. And Jonas seemed a very caring person and good with children.

There were still times when Karla was desperate. A few nights before, she had woken up and screamed. When Anna came rushing into her bedroom, thinking that the child had another one of her nightmares, she found Karla wide-awake in bed. She seemed all confused.

"I can't remember what Mama looked like," she cried.

Anna hugged her and pointed at the photo of her mother on the chest of drawers. "You just need to look at the picture of her, then you'll remember," she told her.

Karla eventually calmed down. Anna put her mother's photo on the nightstand right next to her bed. Karla looked at the picture for a while, then her eyelids fluttered and she fell asleep again.

Such incidents showed Anna that the hurt was still there. The open wounds may heal with time but the scars would remain. The traumatic event of the car accident and her mother's and grandmother's deaths had robbed her of that feeling of security that was so important in a young child's life.

Anna remembered the pain of loss when she was little and her father and mother split up for some time. It was much less traumatic than what happened to Karla, but even decades later, Anna could still feel the terror, when the so-far secure world at home became undone.

Anna's parents were a strangely matched couple. Father, the American artist, the freedom-loving creative dreamer and Mother, the strong woman, too demanding of herself and of others. They quarreled about everything.

One day after school, Anna noticed her father's car in front of the house. He normally wasn't home that early. She opened the door, dropped her schoolbag next to the wardrobe, and rushed to meet him. A few steps into the hallway, she stopped, hearing loud voices in the kitchen. Then the door opened and her father stepped outside, his face flushed. Anna saw her mother sitting at the table. She was supporting her head with her hands. Her blond hair, which was usually tied in a neat bun, had become loose and was hanging into her face. Her shoulders were heaving. A head of lettuce, carrots, and a colander with green beans were spread out on the kitchen table, waiting to be transformed into dinner.

Anna was familiar with her parents' fights, but somehow, this time, she felt that things were more serious. "Why is Mama crying?"

Her father bent down and hugged her. "Anna," he said. He spoke with a slight American accent. "Mother and I are having problems. I'm going to move out for a while until things get better again."

Anna's heart stopped. She held on to her father, digging her fingers into his arms. She searched his eyes for any kind of sign that this all wasn't true.

"Don't worry, we'll still be together. You can visit me and I'll visit you all the time."

It was only then that Anna saw the suitcase next to the wardrobe. "Don't leave, Daddy, please. Don't leave." Anna's head was spinning and she felt she was suffocating.

"Anna, you have to be brave. Be kind to your mother. She needs you now. I'll call you tonight, all right?" He picked up the suitcase and opened the door.

"No," Anna screamed at the top of her lungs. "Don't go." She fell to her knees and began to cry loudly. The world as she had known it shattered and a cold wave of fear washed over her.

"Anna, come here." Her mother stood at the kitchen door. Her face was swollen from crying. She held out her arms. "Come, honey. It'll be okay. I promise."

Eventually, things were okay again, at least on the surface. After a few weeks, her father moved back in. The feeling of abandonment Anna had felt that day, the fear of everything safe and secure being snatched away from her, never quite left her, though. Sometimes, when she came home from school and saw her father's car outside, she was overcome by dread. Would he leave again?

Chapter 13

It was another hot summer day. The horizon above the lake to the south was tinged with a smoky yellowish haze. Jonas kept the balcony door and the windows open, but there was hardly a breeze. He stepped out on the balcony. In the north, heaps of black-gray thunderclouds began to form.

Inside in his studio, Karla was painting with oil pastels. She wore an apron to protect her clothes. Her hands were smeared and there were streaks of green, blue, and red on her face. Small pearls of sweat had formed on her upper lip and she kept wiping her forehead, adding more color to her face.

Jonas laughed out loud and Karla looked at him surprised.

"Come on, I'll show you something," he said and pointed at the mirror on the closet door. Karla got up and the two stood in front of the glass and grinned at Karla's colorful face.

"Like an Indian on the warpath," Jonas said. "I guess today is almost too hot for working. But let's see what you got."

They looked at Karla's picture. It was a summer scene, a landscape with a pond, skirted by trees and bushes. On a blanket next to the pond was a picnic basket with fruit—apples, bananas, grapes—and a big bottle of what could have been lemonade. A little girl with dark hair stood by the pond, obviously Karla. A woman with long blond hair sat on a blue blanket or towel under a yellow sun umbrella. As in many of Karla's paintings, her mother was present. It was almost an obsession and Jonas knew it was one of the ways Karla tried to keep in touch with her.

Whenever she drew or painted her mother, her painting habits changed. Normally, when Karla drew other objects from imagination, she didn't bother with a realistic outlook of her drawing. She was very inventive and it was that kind of unusual composition that gave her pictures power. However, when Karla drew her mother, she tried very hard to make her look realistic. She kept erasing her drawing, which she didn't do when drawing other objects. It was as if she wanted to re-create an exact likeness. Often the drawings of her mother were less successful and lacked the strength the other objects in her paintings had.

"Your mama?" Jonas asked, pointing at the woman, although he already knew the answer.

"Yeah," Karla said and glanced at him, then looked back down at the picture. "I paint her so I don't forget what she looks like," she said in a low voice.

"Oh, I see," Jonas said. "But you have photos of her, don't you? They'll help you remember."

"Yeah, but it's not the same."

"What do you mean?"

Karla wrinkled her forehead. "It's . . . like cheating."

"Cheating?" Jonas asked.

"Mmm." Karla nodded. "I need to remember without a photo." There was a tinge of panic in her voice.

Jonas sat down and put his hand on her shoulder. He sensed what Karla meant. He remembered the first time he became aware that Eva's face was fading in his memory. It gave him a little jolt and he stood in front of the photo trying to bring her face back. It was a natural progression, time erasing both reality and memories. And for a young child like Karla, it must be frightening.

"I think I know what you mean, but I don't think looking at a photo is cheating. A photo is like any other work of art, like the pictures you draw of your mother. They just help us remember. I look at my wife's photos all the time. See." Jonas got up and opened the door to the living room. "Look at all the pictures of her."

Karla came to the door and nodded, scanning the photos in the living room.

"I don't know, Karla, but sometimes I think the two of us make a mistake."

Karla looked at him surprised. "Why?"

"We live too much in the past. I still grieve for Eva and I know you miss your mama. But we need to move on and live in the present, not always think of those who are gone."

"I don't want to forget my mama," Karla said, her voice determined, almost angry.

"You don't need to forget her. You'll never forget her. But you can let her rest once in a while. And I need to do the same with Eva. Eva and your mama want us to be happy. They don't want us to be sad and always grieve for them."

Karla gave him a thoughtful look. Jonas smiled. "Not convinced, huh? Well, let's try something else for a change." He pointed at Karla's picture. "I like this. I love the colors and I like the fact that the picture fills the whole paper. That's a good composition. Now, put it aside and I'll show you something."

Jonas stepped onto the rooftop patio and waved at Karla to follow him. He pointed north to where the storm clouds were towering over the mountains. "Look at the clouds. Close your eyes halfway and scan them. Take your time; don't focus on them too much. Relax your gaze and try to see the colors in the clouds. When we don't pay attention, storm clouds are just black and gray. But in reality, there are many more colors. Can you see them?"

Karla squinted her eyes and looked toward the north. She nodded her head. "Yes. I can see purple."

"Good," Jonas said. "What else?"

"Yellow and blue and white and orange."

"Excellent. See, there is much more to the world than it looks like on the surface. We just need to learn to see. Drawing and painting are all about learning to see. You understand?"

Karla nodded.

"Now, what about painting the clouds the way you see them?"

Karla's face lit up. "Yeah, that would be cool."

Jonas smiled. "Okay, let's do it. You can use the pastels. But only the sky and the clouds, no people. And if you forget what the sky looks like, you can always come out here and check."

Jonas put a new large piece of paper on Karla's drawing table, then sat at the other end of the room and observed her while she worked. He noticed the change in her right away. A new kind of energy seemed to fill her. Not having to worry about exact forms and figures, she let herself go. Her body and her mind opened up. Her facial color deepened, her arms and hands moved with great agility, and her strokes became bolder.

Karla was a beautiful child. She seemed to have inherited the facial features of her Peruvian father, the large dark eyes, the high cheekbones, and the light-bronze skin. The highlights in her shiny black hair must have come from her Swiss mother's side.

Every once in a while, Karla stepped out on the balcony and looked toward the sky. Then she returned with a smile and continued.

Jonas nodded to himself. There was a lot of passion in the girl and Jonas wanted to find ways for her to express it. Drawing her mother was a basic need for Karla and Jonas didn't want to interfere too much. They just had to find a balance between preserving that link and exploring the rest of the wide and exciting world.

Chapter 14

Fall vacation was almost over and school was about to start again. The October winds had blown many of the colored leaves from the trees. Karla had collected the most beautiful ones and pressed them in a notebook. Once they were dry, she wanted to use them for a collage.

Today, Anna had taken her shopping in the city for a few school supplies. Karla stuffed the notebooks and pens into her backpack but kept her new set of crayons and other painting utensils on the table. She gazed at the window, scrunching her eyes, as if trying to decide what to draw. The sun rays piercing through the windowpane lit up the reddish highlights in her black hair.

"Look, Anna," she said and got up. Her eyes opened wide and she pointed at the window. An almost perfect spider web was stretched between the top of the window and the side frame, its fine threads shimmering in the golden evening light.

"Neat, huh?" Anna said. They both gazed at the perfect work of art.

"I could draw it," Karla said, pointing at the spider web. "I'll add the spider, too, and perhaps the colored leaves." She got excited and hurried back to the table.

Anna sighed. She hated to spoil Karla's enthusiasm, but they needed to talk. They hadn't discussed Karla's last flawed report card yet. The grades hadn't been bad: a high Six, or A-plus, in drawing; a Five, or B, in writing; and a Four, or C, in math. Under "Attitude and Behavior," however, there was a remark about inattentiveness, daydreaming, forgetfulness, and handing in homework late or not at all.

"That sounds like a great idea, Karla, but first we have to talk about school."

"Mmm," Karla said and picked up a pastel pen.

"Put that down and pay attention," Anna said a little more forcefully.

Karla gave her a probing look, then lowered the crayon but kept it in her hand.

"I talked to your teacher and he told me that you did well in your written work but that you don't pay attention during oral lessons. What can we do to improve your performance?"

Karla turned her head and looked out the window. She didn't answer.

"Karla?" Anna put her hand on Karla's shoulder.

Karla turned back and stared at her, her eyes glowering, her full lips pressed into a thin line. There was a new energy about her. So far, Karla had been mostly obedient and quiet, even passive and often sad. Seeing defiance and anger in her face was almost a relief.

Anna kept a straight face, although she felt a smile tickle the corners of her mouth. Perhaps being a little more assertive was a good thing, even if it was for the wrong reason. Her optimism, however, took a dive when she heard Karla's answer.

"Mama said school wasn't important." She angrily pushed the crayon aside.

"When did your mother say that?"

"When I talk to her at night." Karla jutted out her chin.

"I thought she wasn't talking back to you."

"Sometimes, she does."

"Karla, why would your mother say something like that? You know that's not true. Think about it. Remember how your mom would work with you when you still went to kindergarten? You already knew how to read and write before you started school. Do you think your mom would have taught you these things, if she didn't believe school and learning were important?"

Karla shook her head but her face remained hard and tight.

"What did you two do every Wednesday afternoon after kindergarten? Where did you go?"

Karla hesitated, then said, "We went to the library."

"Okay, why did you go there?"

"To check out books for me, of course."

"What kind of books?" Anna prodded.

"All kinds. Books about how to read and write and build things. We once built a whole farm with animals," Karla said, her face brightening a little.

"See, Karla, your mama wanted to prepare you for school. She wanted you to learn things. That's why she took you to the library. Do you really think a mother like this would tell you one day that school wasn't important?"

Karla looked down at the floor and slowly shook her head.

"Do you agree then that it wasn't your mama who told you school wasn't important?"

Karla stared at her. "Then who was it?"

Anna hesitated a moment. "Did you really hear a voice?"

Karla shrugged. "I thought I did."

"Look, Karla, your mama can't talk like a normal person. She's dead, honey. That means her body and her voice are gone. Do you understand?"

Karla nodded hesitantly.

"Karla, next time you think you hear your mother's voice, tell me. Perhaps the two of us can find out what's going on. Promise?"

Karla nodded again, this time with more conviction. "Anna, are there ghosts?"

"I'm not sure, Karla. I've never seen or heard one, but some people claim they exist. If you ever hear or see one, you have to let me know. We have to be together in this, okay?"

"Can I still tell Mama what I'm doing? And tell her secrets?"

"Yes, of course, you can tell her everything. But I hope you tell me as well if something bothers you. Your mama would want that. She would want that I take good care of you. And for that I need to know what's going on with you. I need to know when you have a problem or if you're unhappy about something."

Karla slid down from her chair and hugged Anna. Anna felt tears rise to her eyes. "I love you, Karla. I want you to be happy. But now we have to talk about school and homework and all that."

Anna and Karla came to an agreement. Karla promised to pay more attention in school and to do her homework first thing after school before painting and drawing. Anna would talk to her teacher after a few weeks to find out if Karla needed more help.

"And I want you to take Spanish lessons, too. We'll both take them. I know a little Spanish but I need to improve. And you need to learn," Anna said.

"Why?" Karla looked at her surprised, squinting her eyes, as if Anna was a painting she scanned.

"Because I want you to be able to talk to your father. He wrote to me; he's coming to visit you."

A spark of fear lit up in Karla's eyes. "But I don't know him."

"That's why he's coming to visit, so you can get to know him a little better."

Karla shrugged her shoulder. "But I don't want to go with him. I want to stay with you and Saint Nicholas."

"Of course, you're not going back with him. Not as long as you're little. Don't worry. Perhaps, once you are older, you will want to visit him."

"Maybe." Karla wrapped her arms around Anna again.

Anna gently patted her back. "It will be fun, you'll see. He's only going to stay with us for few weeks."

"Okay," Karla murmured.

"Now then, what about drawing that spider web?" Anna said.

"Yeah, and the spider and the leaves." Karla rushed to the table. She picked up a pastel pen and started to draw.

Chapter 15

"Mama, I've big news. My papa came to visit. I've never met him before. He's real nice and he brought me presents. I got a beautiful doll. She's sitting on top of the dresser. Can you see her? She has long black hair, real hair, Papa said. And look at the beautiful colors in her dress. I also got some clothes for myself: a dress, a skirt, and blouses. They have similar colors: red, blue, green, yellow. They're just like my doll's clothes. Papa said that his wife picked them out. His wife is my stepmother, he said.

"I felt a little strange around Papa. He doesn't speak Italian or German. But he said he understands a lot of Italian. I speak a little Spanish and Anna helps. She translates for us.

"Today was bad weather. April weather, Anna said. It's been very windy and raining and once in a while the sun was shining through the holes in the clouds. I love to look at the sky when it's stormy. There are so many colors and shapes and they change all the time. I love to paint the sky, but it's hard. The clouds move so fast, you have to draw very fast.

"The other day, Papa and me were painting. Papa isn't very good at it, but I helped him. We painted a landscape with animals in it. Papa tried to draw a dog but it looked more like a donkey. I tried not to laugh but I couldn't help it. He didn't mind, though.

"I drew the people in the picture. Papa said that's too difficult for him. So I drew you, Papa, me, and Anna. When I drew you, I got sad. I wanted you to be here and meet Papa. Papa was sad, too. I saw it. His eyes were all wet. The picture turned out pretty nice. Anna put it up on the wall. Can you see it over there?

"I have to think a lot these days. I'm thinking about you and Papa. How come you and Papa don't live together? I mean when you were still here? Papa said I have a step-mother and a sister in Peru and that I'll get to visit them when I'm a little older. But I don't want another mother. I want you. I didn't tell Papa that, but I told Anna. She said that you'll always be my real mother. Rosa can be my second mother. Rosa is Papa's wife. Anna said that a lot of children have a second mother, a stepmother. But I want Anna to be my second mother. So, perhaps, Rosa can be my third mother. It's all so complicated and I get a headache when I think about it. Anna said not to worry about it. That for now she is my second mother, and when I'm older, I can go and visit my Peruvian family.

"I guess it would be fun. And I would get to meet my sister. Papa showed me a photo. She's a little younger than I am and very pretty. Papa told me that in Peru they have llamas. But they're not in the zoo like here in Zurich. They walk around the fields just like our cows.

"And Mama, I have a new kitty. It's a girl. Its fur is black and it has white spots on its forehead and its chest. The paws and its calves are white, so it looks like it's wearing white boots. It's a little naughty. It scratches the sofa to sharpen its claws. Anna said that fortunately we don't have any expensive furniture.

"We have to give it a name. I wanted to name it 'Puss in Boots,' because of its white legs. Anna thinks that's too long of a name. Perhaps, I'll call it 'Dotty,' because it has white dots. Right now, it's lying on my bed, all curled up and purring. I wish it could sleep with me but Anna wants it to sleep in the kitchen for a while, so it gets used to the litter box.

"Yesterday, Papa flew back to Peru. I was sad for a while. But tomorrow we're going to see Saint Nicholas again. I almost didn't think about him when Papa was here. But I'm looking forward to my class. When Anna and Saint Nicholas and me are together, it almost feels like a family.

"I'm tired now, Mama. Bye-bye until tomorrow. Do people sleep in Heaven? I'll have to ask Anna."

PART TWO: JONAS'S STORY

Chapter 16

Anna glanced out the window as the train passed by a large dug-up field being prepared for a group of new homes. She wondered once again how the originally small farm villages had grown into towns and agglomerations. The rolling hills and woods in the distance, the occasional homesteads and small pastures were the last remnants of the predominantly agricultural area Anna had grown up in.

Anna and Karla were on the way to Zurich to Karla's drawing and painting lesson. It was a twenty-minute ride from their town to the center of the city. When the train arrived in the large modern train station, they got out and let themselves be transported to the main hall on the escalators. The station had been expanded over the past few years into a vast under-ground shopping mall. It was a tourist's paradise and people from all over the world perused the great variety of stores.

Today, Anna and Karla decided to walk to Jonas's place from the main station. It was a beautiful early fall day in late September. The leaves on the trees along the Bahnhofstrasse were beginning to turn. The shops at the well-known shop-ping street donned their usual displays of clothes, furs, and jewelry.

Anna noticed, though, that some of the former splendor and fame of the street was gone. Many of the old established luxury stores had given way to trendy outlets, to drugstores with colorful displays of makeup articles, chain bookstores, and discount clothing stores. There were still a few of the famous jewelry stores and high-end luxury shops left, but the trend was definitely toward outlets that appealed to the younger generation of shoppers.

Halfway down the Bahnhofstrasse, Anna and Karla turned left and walked across one of the bridges over the Limmat, the main river flowing through Zurich. They headed in the direction of the Bellevue and the Lake of Zurich. Anna saw the sign of the old Grand Café Odeon, where she stopped for coffee once in a while when in town. It, too, harked back to older times. It had been the hangout of famous expatriate writers, musicians, artists, and politicians during the First and Second World Wars. Such diverse celebrities and thinkers as Einstein, Joyce, Kafka, Brecht, Toscanini, Trotsky, and Lenin had gathered there, drinking coffee, discussing art and literature, writing music, and planning revolutions. Later it was taken over by an increasingly unsavory crowd of drug users. It was finally converted into a modern cafeteria. What remained were the photos on the wall, the memories, and the excellent coffee.

Anna and Karla walked up the steep road in the Niederdorf, the old part on the hillside above the river. Karla rang the bell to Jonas's apartment and Anna pushed the door open when she heard the buzzing sound. They walked the four floors to the top, since Anna hated the old, rickety elevator. Jonas had left the door to his apartment open. As Anna and Karla entered, a whiff of paint and lacquer greeted them. Anna liked the simple elegance of the place, the light wooden furniture, and the subtle colors.

Usually, Anna dropped Karla off for her lesson and went bookstore hunting. She visited the owners of a few of the bookstores in the city, with whom she got together occasionally. They exchanged ideas about new authors, new books, and the struggle of maintaining small, independent bookstores. Sometimes, Anna visited a museum or gallery or went shopping.

Today, she had brought a book with her. It was a detective novel she hadn't read yet. She had started it the evening before and couldn't wait to get back to it. Settling into a comfortable chair in the alcove of the living room, she started to read. She took an occasional sip of the freshly brewed coffee Jonas had offered her. Before she knew it, an hour had passed and she heard a child laugh.

"Anna, look." Karla stepped out of Jonas's studio, holding up her newest picture. It was a landscape, very much like the one Anna and Karla could see from their home. It depicted the pond and a blooming canola field next to it. The yellow and gold of the field created a beautiful contrast to the shades of green and blue of the pond and the trees and bushes bordering it.

"These were difficult to paint." Karla pointed at the patch of reeds in the pond. "The stems always came out too thick. Saint Nicholas had to help me."

"That's a very good painting. But Karla, you shouldn't call Mr. Bergman 'Saint Nicholas,'" Anna said. "It's not polite."

"Oh, I don't mind. I actually like my nickname. It's kind of mysterious." Jonas lowered his voice to make it sound like Santa Claus.

"I think Karla is ready for her first exhibition," he added.

"Already?" Anna asked.

Karla was almost eight. She had been taking lessons for close to two years. Her drawing and painting had improved considerably and so had her state of mind. The frequency of her nightmares had decreased and she seemed happier. She had become quite close to Jonas and looked forward to her lessons all week.

"Well, it's a special exhibition for the children. We host it at the art store." Jonas turned to Karla. "Why don't you get the pictures we picked?"

Karla skipped next door. Anna looked after her. "She's doing much better all around, thanks to your help."

"She's doing very well with her painting. I think she'll like the exhibition. We started it a few years ago. It's fun for the children and it boosts their self-esteem. Each child can display several paintings or drawings. They're priced at five francs each. And we make sure that everybody sells at least one picture."

"How do you do this?"

Jonas winked at her. "I have a purchase team. The owner of the art store and the staff take care of it. They buy the paintings." Jonas laughed. "They have a whole collection of children's art at home."

Anna smiled. "You're spoiling them, but I think it's a great idea. It gives them a taste of the art world."

"Most of the children I teach are probably not going to be artists. You know, it's like playing an instrument. Kids are all enthusiastic at first and after a while they get bored or tired of practicing. But at least for a few months or years, they do something meaningful. It beats sitting in front of the TV all day.

"There are always a few exceptions, of course," Jonas continued. "And I think Karla might be one. She's still very young and she might lose interest later on when puberty hits. You never know. But I feel she may pursue it in a serious way. She not only has the talent but the passion for it."

Karla came into the room, carrying a few drawings and paintings. Jonas took them out of her hands and spread them on the table. He pointed to one of them, a picture of a bird—a hawk most likely—flying in the sky. It was a fascinating drawing.

"Other children, even talented ones, might have drawn this bird from the side, either flying or sitting on a branch. Karla picked this very unusual pose. She drew the bird as seen from underneath, as it is flying by. Look at the legs and claws and the beak from below. Quite amazing, and she drew it from imagination." Jonas patted Karla's back.

Anna hugged her. "This is great." She was delighted to see the normally serious child so excited.

"We'll be cleaning up soon," Jonas said. "Would you like another cup of coffee? I could go for some more myself."

"Thanks, that would be nice."

"Let's get some coffee and something for you," Jonas said to Karla, and the two disappeared into the kitchen. Karla came back with a mug of hot chocolate and Jonas carried a tray with two cups of coffee and a plate with *pains de chocolat,* chocolate-filled croissants.

"From my neighbor," he said. "She's afraid I'll starve to death. She obviously hasn't seen me stand on the scale lately." Jonas patted his small pooch.

"Is she still trying to fix you up with someone?" Jonas had made a remark once about Mrs. Schatz's matchmaking attempts.

"Not lately. She must feel I'm hopeless." He laughed and went back into the studio.

Anna put the book aside and took a sip of coffee. She looked around the living room. It struck her once again how many photos of Jonas's wife there were. She looked down from the walls, the bookshelves, and the buffet. *He never got over her.*

Anna took a deep breath and gazed out the window. A thin layer of haze grazed the mountains in the distance. Sirens blared nearby. "The New York City waltz," Anna used to call it back in New York, where the sirens seemed to have been a constant background sound. Her memories of her life in New York were tightly knit with memories of Nicolas.

Did I ever get over him? Anna wondered, thinking of her former husband.

Chapter 17

It was during the seventies, over fifteen years before, when Nico and Anna got married in New York City. They had been dating for two years. Anna was working as an assistant librarian at a public library on Fifth Avenue and 42nd Street. Nico had finished his degree in architecture and received a job offer from a company in New York, which had subsidiaries in Mexico.

The wedding ceremony at New York City Hall was anything but romantic. Couples were standing in line in the gloomy hallway of an old government building, waiting their turn to tie the knot. Some of the young men and women were smiling nervously, others were joking around. One young African American couple was ahead of Anna and Nico. The skinny young man in his dark suit pretended to sneak away. The bride, a beautiful tall woman, kept grabbing him and pulling him back.

Finally, it was Anna and Nico's turn. Anna was wearing a simple green silk dress and Nico a suit and tie. Anna was proud of her fiancé. He looked stunning in his black suit and aqua-blue shirt, which matched his shiny black hair and emphasized the color of his eyes. His lips curled into his charming, slightly lopsided smile.

Their close friends, Susan and George, were the witnesses. Anna's hand trembled as she signed her new name, "Anna Foster-Frei." Nico signed with a flourish. Then the civil servant, an overweight, bored-looking man, read the vows in a monotone voice. One of the buttons on his jacket was missing and his gut was sticking out. Anna forgave him his shabby appearance, thinking that he had to read the same lines hundreds of times a day and probably made a lousy salary.

After the somewhat undignified ceremony, Nico and Anna kissed to the applause of George and Susan. Susan and her husband George were in their late twenties. George was a lawyer and Susan worked in a bookstore, which is where Anna had met her one day. They had been friends ever since.

They left the City Clerk's Office in Manhattan and headed to a restaurant for lunch. Anna glanced up and down the street at the rows of cars, which snaked their way slowly through the thicket of traffic. She was so used to the stench of exhaust that she barely noticed it. Tall buildings lined the streets. In the narrower roads, the sun never made it to the ground. New York City was an assault on the senses, the mind, and the emotions, but Anna loved it. She was young and adventurous.

At a traffic light, they crossed one of the wide avenues. "Well, this wasn't the most romantic wedding ceremony," George said.

"You can say that," Nico agreed with a grin. He put his arm around Anna and hugged her. "But we'll have the real celebration in church once my father and Anna's mother get here."

George and Susan invited them to a fancy restaurant nearby. An elderly hostess greeted them with cool and efficient New York politeness and led them to a reserved alcove. The dark wood paneling and the dim light gave the place an elegant but gloomy and almost ghostlike feeling. The booth, however, was nicely decorated and a bottle of champagne was waiting in the ice bucket. The waiter popped the cork and poured them a glass.

"Congratulations," he said, smiling businesslike at Anna.

"To a long and happy life and lots of children," Susan said and raised her glass.

"Let's wait with the children for a while," Nico said. He kissed Anna and she felt she was floating on a cloud of happiness.

Chapter 18

Jonas applied a few stripes of orange to a painting, which consisted of patches and squares of different shades of brown and white. The picture gave the feeling of a quilt and it was one of a series of abstract paintings for an upcoming exhibition. He stepped back and scrunched up his eyes, then dipped the brush into paint thinner and rubbed his hands.

The doorbell rang. The clock on the wall showed two o'clock in the afternoon. He wasn't expecting anybody. He pushed the buzzer, opened the door, and peered over the railing. He saw the top of the head of a woman with light-brown shoulder-length hair who came up the stairs. *Anna?* But it wasn't the day of Karla's painting lessons and the woman was alone. When she turned her head and looked up, he recognized her.

"Anna? What a surprise; I didn't expect you."

"I'm sorry for dropping in unannounced," Anna said as she climbed the last step. She was out of breath, her normally pale cheeks showed a healthy glow. "I was in town to run errands and wanted to drop this off." She held up a shopping bag.

"Well, come on in." Jonas stepped back. "Want some coffee?"

"No, unfortunately I don't have time," Anna said as she walked into the living room. "I have an appointment in about twenty minutes. I just wanted to give you this. It came in yesterday and I know you like his work." Anna pulled a large book out of the bag and handed it to him.

"Wow, this is absolutely gorgeous," Jonas said. He paged through the book. It was the illuminated edition of William Blake's *Songs of Innocence and Experience*. "This is great, but I want to pay you for this. This is expensive."

Anna shook her head. "No, this is a present . . . for all the things you do for Karla."

"Anna, you pay for Karla's lessons."

"So? What you do for her is worth a lot more than money. Besides, you don't pay for a gift." She sounded somewhat abrupt. Had he offended her?

"Thank you very much. I truly appreciate this," he quickly assured her. "And Karla is doing great, by the way. Her painting has really progressed and she seems happier."

"Yes, thank God." Anna gave a weak smile.

"You do a lot for her too, Anna. It must not be easy."

She shrugged. "I try my best. I guess that's all anyone can do." She checked her watch. "But I better hurry or I'll be late."

"Okay, well, thanks again. I'll see you in a couple of days." Jonas followed her to the door.

"See you," she said as she started to walk down the stairs.

"Don't like the elevator either, huh?" he called after her.

She turned around. "No, it just looks a little . . . well—"

"Ancient," Jonas said.

Anna's face stretched into a smile. "I know, it's silly, I'm sure it's perfectly safe. Anyway, I need the exercise."

Jonas went back into his studio, shaking his head. Anna was such a strange bird. One minute she was kind and warm, but at the slightest upset, just like before when he offered to pay for the book, she withdrew into her shell. When she smiled, she looked lovely, almost beautiful.

He picked up the brush and mixed some paint. Just as he was beginning to work, there was a knock at the door. Jonas rolled his eyes, exasperated. "Now what?" *I should paint in my other studio and not here in my apartment where I'm constantly interrupted.* Jonas did his major work in a large studio nearby. He often did touch-up work or smaller paintings as well as his teaching at home.

"Not her again," he muttered under his breath as he saw his neighbor through the peephole. He considered not opening the door, but figured she had already heard his footsteps. He sighed and opened the door. Mrs. Schatz was standing outside, a plate in her hands.

"I made some custard pies, and as usual much too many. I thought you and your lady friend might like some." Mrs. Schatz looked over his shoulders, scanning the apartment.

Jonas suppressed a grin. "What lady friend?"

"Well, you know, the one with the cute little girl."

"She isn't my lady friend. She's the aunt of the little girl, who is my student. She's just a friend."

"Aha. Oh, well, she seems very nice . . . and she's attractive, a little younger than you are and—"

"Yes, Mrs. Matchmaker." Jonas guffawed.

"I'm just concerned for your welfare, Mr. Bergman." Mrs. Schatz lifted her hands.

"Yes, I know. And thanks for the pie. Much appreciated."

Back in his apartment, Jonas shook his head and chuckled. He glanced at Eva's photo. "She's such a busybody, but she has a kind heart."

He put the pie on the kitchen table, cut a piece, and tried it. "Excellent. Her husband is a lucky man, at least where her cooking is concerned." Jonas gave a wistful smile. *Talking to myself again. I guess a solitary life does that to you.*

He went back to his studio and worked for about half an hour, finishing the painting. He stepped back and nodded satisfied. He remembered Anna telling him that his paintings had become more cheerful. It was true; a lot of his older paintings were dark and gloomy. *I must be feeling happier.*

Jonas put down the brush and walked to the window. He looked over the roofs of the buildings toward the lake. The late afternoon sun refracted from the thin layer of mist on the horizon. It was fall and the time of day when the light was diffuse and lacked strength. Normally, that kind of bland atmosphere made him melancholic, but today he felt joyful.

He had to admit he enjoyed the company of Karla and her aunt. They brought a special energy and life to his place. He liked Anna, in spite of the fact that she often struck him as distant. He suspected that underneath the hard shell was a loving heart. He saw it when she was with Karla. Her whole being softened and there was a lively gleam in her eyes.

Something must have happened to her that made her distant and distrustful. He knew Anna had been married but she had never volunteered any details and Jonas didn't want to pry. He had told her a little bit about Eva but in very general terms.

Jonas smiled. There was a concert coming up. He would invite Anna. He knew she loved classical music.

Chapter 19

Karla pulled Anna's sleeve. "I think I just sold one," she whispered. Her face was flushed with excitement and her eyes sparkled.

Anna and Karla watched as Jonas put a red dot next to one of Karla's drawings. He scanned the room and gave Karla the thumbs up. A young man—a younger version of Jonas—was standing next to him. It must be his son, Andrew, who lived in Denmark, Anna thought.

She and Karla had walked to the art store from the train station. It was a cold, sunny day in December but the forecast was for snow. The city was all decked out for Christmas. The windows of the shops were sprayed with artificial snow, and glittering gold and silver decorations gave the streets a festive atmosphere. The smoky scent of roasted chestnuts from the stands up and down the street and of barbecued sausages filled the air. Salvation Army volunteers were ringing their bells and stamping their feet in the cold, hoping for donations for the less fortunate. White mist curled from their mouths as they sang the familiar hymns.

The children's art exhibition was a success. The art and stationary store was located on a busy side street off the Bahnhofstrasse. People walking up and down the street stopped to look at the large colorful posters advertising the event. Some gave the store a cursory glance, smiled, and walked on, but many came inside, out of curiosity and to warm up from the cold.

The pictures were nicely framed and showed all levels of craftsmanship, from simple pencil drawings to more elaborate pastel, water color, and acrylic paintings. Anna noticed with quiet pride that Karla's pictures were among the best.

"They are selling like hotcakes," Jonas said, pointing at the paintings. He introduced his son to Anna and Karla.

"Yes," Andrew said in his deep voice, which reminded Anna of Jonas's. "Someone almost snatched my favorite away from me. But fortunately my father here distracted him, so I was there first."

"Which one did you buy?" Anna asked.

"The one with the upside-down bird," Andrew said.

"That's mine," Karla exclaimed. Her facial color deepened.

Andrew smiled at her. "Great picture. I'll hang it in my office in Copenhagen."

Jonas patted Karla on the head, then walked over to some of the other children.

"This is so nice of your father to do this," Anna said. "The children really enjoy it, too, and it sure does a lot for their self-esteem." She watched as more and more red dots were placed next to the pictures and the smiles on the faces of the girls and boys who had created them brightened.

"I think my father is the one who enjoys the whole thing the most. He's just like a kid." Andrew smiled. "He had more fun playing with our toys than we did when we were little. I think he hated to see us grow up."

"Well, he does a great job teaching children," Anna said. "And I'm sure he loves having you here. Are you going to stay for Christmas?"

Andrew shook his head. "I'm going to spend the holidays with my wife and kids back home. I'm trying to convince Father to join us for Christmas, but he refuses. He doesn't like the gloom and darkness during the winter months when the days are short. It makes him depressed. He prefers to visit in summer. But I worry about him. I know he'll be lonely over the holidays and longing for Mother, although he denies it."

Karla, who had been listening eagerly, patted Anna's arm. "He can stay with us over Christmas, can't he? Oh, please say yes. It would be so much fun having Saint Nicholas for Christmas."

"Saint Nicholas?" Andrew smiled and raised an eyebrow.

"It's a long story." Anna gave Karla a stern look. "You shouldn't call him that."

"He doesn't mind; he said so," Karla said. "Can we ask him?"

"Yes, of course, but let *me* ask him. Okay? I don't want you to nag him about it. He may have other plans or he may prefer to be by himself."

"I'm sure he doesn't have other plans," Andrew said, then stopped talking as Jonas joined them again.

"Well, the opening is winding down. Everybody has sold something. They'll leave the rest of the pictures up for a few more days." Jonas bent down to Karla. "You earned forty francs, my dear."

"That much? What am I going to do with all that money?" Karla wrinkled her forehead.

"Put it in your piggy bank. We'll find something to do with it." Anna laughed.

"I know," Karla said all excited. "I can buy Christmas presents with it."

"There you go. I know exactly what I want." Andrew winked at Karla, who looked at him with a serious face. "Just kidding." He grinned.

"What about a bite to eat?" Jonas slapped Andrew on the back, then turned to Anna. "May I invite you two beautiful ladies for dinner?"

"We would like to invite *you*," Anna said. "For all the work you did."

"Sorry, I beat you to it. This is my turn. Do you like fondue?"

"We love it," Anna said and Karla nodded with a big smile.

"Great. It's Andrew's favorite Swiss dish," Jonas said. "And I know just the place for it. Come on."

Jonas lightly touched Anna's elbow and led her up the street. Andrew and Karla followed.

"You look beautiful today. I like blue on you." Jonas referred to Anna's blue coat and hat. When their eyes met, his gaze made her heart stutter a little. She had almost forgotten what it felt like to be admired by a man.

They walked up the Rennweg through the old part of town and descended toward the Limmat River. As they crossed the river on one of the few bridges, an icy wind began to blow down from the lake. Anna dug her hands deep into the pockets of her coat. Her eyes were watering. She turned around and saw that Karla was wearing Andrew's woolen cap over her own. It was too big for her and covered her face almost to her nose. Karla peeked at Anna from underneath her hat and giggled.

"Aren't you cold?" Anna asked Andrew, shivering at the sight of his bare head. Unlike his father's thick longish mop, his hair was very short.

"Nah, it's nothing. I'm used to the cold." Andrew waved his hand. He removed his woolen scarf and wrapped it around Karla's neck, took her gloved hand and stuck it into his coat pocket. "Have to make sure the little munchkin doesn't catch a cold."

What a kind young man, Anna thought.

They had arrived at the other side of the river and walked up a narrow side street of the Limmatquai, the road along the river. Away from the freezing wind, it felt a little warmer.

"Here we are," Jonas said. He opened the door to a smallish inn. The smell of cheese was almost overpowering. It was a place which specialized in fondue and raclette, another cheese dish. It was a warm and cozy place with rustic furniture. They sat at a table near the large tiled stove.

Waiting for their food, Anna asked Andrew about his plans for the upcoming holidays, waiting for a good opportunity to invite Jonas. She didn't want to make him feel as if they had discussed it with Andrew beforehand. Karla, however, didn't have any such scruples.

"Would you like to spend Christmas with us, Saint . . . Jonas?" She turned to Anna and grabbed her arm. "We want him to, don't we?"

Anna gave Karla a stern look. "Blabbermouth."

Jonas looked puzzled, then chuckled. "I get the impression someone has been a busybody." He turned to Andrew and raised his eyebrows.

"Andrew just told us that you aren't going back to Denmark with him," Anna said. "So Karla and I thought it would be nice if you spent some time with us. We're going to be quite lonely on Christmas Eve. It's just the two of us. Normally some friends celebrate with us. This year, however, everybody has other plans. Anyway, we would be delighted to have you—if you have no other plans, that is."

Jonas laughed. "Well, how could I say no to such a charming invitation? My son put you up to this, didn't he?"

"No, I swear, the invitation was all Anna's idea." Andrew raised his hands in a defensive gesture.

"Aha. Sure. That's all right." Jonas grinned. "I appreciate your concern."

After dinner, Karla and Anna took the train home. Karla was tired from all the excitement, the food, and the late hour, and was halfway asleep. Anna put her arm around her. She smiled as she thought about the pleasant evening. Jonas and his son had been very charming and Anna had enjoyed Jonas's surreptitious admiring glances.

Chapter 20

Jonas put the kettle on the stove. He measured a few teaspoons of black tea into the teapot. As much as he liked cheese fondue, it always made him feel stuffed afterward and tea seemed to help. He hung his jacket, which still smelled of cheese, on the balcony. Andrew had gone out for a few hours with a friend of his.

Jonas stood by the window, waiting for the water to boil. Outside, it had begun to snow. Small flakes danced in front of the window, shimmering in the light of the street lamps. Down below, people were doing their last-minute shopping at the small grocery store across the street. Next to it was a flower shop. A man about Jonas's age came out, carrying a bouquet of roses. He walked up the narrow street, holding the roses carefully with one hand while clutching the collar of his winter coat with the other. Jonas looked after him with a wistful half smile. *Flowers for his wife . . . or girlfriend.*

The teakettle whistled and Jonas poured the hot water into the teapot and let it steep. He sat on the sofa in the living room, propped up his feet on the coffee table, and relaxed. The student exhibition had been a success. Jonas smiled, thinking of the excited faces of the kids. He was glad he had invited Anna and Karla for dinner. They were such good company.

He better think about buying a few presents for Anna and Karla, now that he was invited for Christmas. He had given Andrew some gifts for his wife and children to take along. He had sent a check to Gita, his daughter, who lived in California for a year, studying acting. She had found a boyfriend but they didn't seem in any hurry to tie the knot. Jonas shrugged his shoulders. Gita had inherited Eva's love of the stage as well as her independent spirit.

Jonas went into the kitchen and poured himself a cup of tea. Back in the living room, he pulled a photo album from the bookshelf. The invitation from Anna for Christmas Eve brought back memories of the Christmas celebrations in Denmark, when he and the family visited his parents. Jonas's parents lived in a beautiful old house in a small town near Aarhus, close to the eastern seacoast of Denmark.

After retiring from his job, Jonas's father and mother had decided to move to Denmark, so his father could be closer to his parents, who were getting on in years and needed help occasionally. Jonas's mother, who was Swiss but had always loved Denmark, didn't mind the move.

Back home, Jonas's father devoted himself to his old passion of woodwork and carpentry again. He had made almost all the furniture in the house by himself over the years. The house was featured in one of the home-and-garden magazines as a model of Danish interior decoration.

A friend had once asked Jonas why Danish and Swedish people took such good care of their homes. They were known all over the world for their taste in furniture and interior decoration. Jonas had shrugged and laughed. "It may have to do with the weather," he had said. "The long winters in Sweden and Denmark force people to stay inside a lot, so perhaps they try to make their homes as pleasant as possible."

When the children were little, they had spent a lot of their vacations and holidays in Denmark. Andrew and his younger sister, Gita, had loved Christmas with their grandparents, who had spoiled them with presents and had always made Christmas an especially festive occasion.

Jonas's mother had decorated the tall Nordmann fir which stood in the corner of the living room with delicate ornaments, some of them handmade. The rest of the house was decked out with fragrant pine twigs and cones, hollies, and Christmas cookies in the shapes of angels and reindeers. Those didn't last very long, since the children ate them before Christmas Eve and Jonas's mother and Eva had to bake another batch for Christmas. All through the holidays, it smelled of cooking and baking in the house.

The photos in the album that Jonas looked at were taken ten years before. It was the last Christmas they spent with Eva. She died the following year. In the photos, she was carefully groomed and dressed and still looked beautiful, in spite of the ravages of her illness. The mood was mixed that Christmas. His parents and the rest of the family tried hard to be cheerful, and Eva, although tired a lot, was in good spirits.

Jonas, knowing that Eva's prognosis was poor, tried to hide his anguish. He didn't want to spoil the Christmas spirit. His father, sensing his despair, took him on long walks in the woods nearby, where Jonas had the opportunity to let go of his emotions. They ended their outings with a cup of coffee and a glass of aquavit, a Danish liquor, in the nearby inn. By the time they got home, Jonas had recovered enough that the only signs of his breakdown were his lightly swollen eyelids. He couldn't fool Eva, though.

She hugged him when he came back. "Cheer up, I'm still here," she whispered.

They were in their room, getting ready for dinner. Jonas, still a little dizzy from the aquavit, looked at his wife who was carefully arranging her now somewhat thin blond hair. It was still her own, having grown back after the last series of cancer treatments, but it had lost its shine and sparkle.

As Jonas watched Eva brush her hair, he was once again overcome by deep anguish. He swallowed a sob and stood next to the window. Outside, darkness was beginning to settle on the snow-covered fields and trees. The Christmas lights on the pines in the yard and on the ceramic reindeer twinkled. Jonas thought of the holidays he and Eva had stood at this window, arm in arm, watching the fairy-tale landscape, watching their kids play in the snow, looking forward to the excellent food Jonas's mother prepared. Why? Why did this have to happen? Why did God punish him like this? A sob escaped him. He tried to hide it by clearing his throat.

He felt Eva's hands on his arms. He turned around, hugged her, and buried his face on her shoulder. "How can I ever live without you?" he sobbed and hated himself for his weakness. He was supposed to be strong; he was supposed to cheer up Eva, not the other way round. But Eva had always been the stronger one.

"You will live without me and, in time, you will be happy again," she said, stroking his heaving back.

Yes, Jonas did live without her but it would be a long time before he was able to feel something akin to happiness again.

Chapter 21

The following spring, Eva's health deteriorated fast and she spent most of the time in the hospital. Jonas knew it was the beginning of the end. Watching the world burst into life around him, while the person he loved the most was dying, filled him with anger and despair. *April is the cruelest month . . . The snippet from T. S. Eliot's poem shot through his mind. The new buds on the trees along the Limmatquai, the yellow and blue pansies, and the smell of wet leaves and soil in the parks felt like a slap in the face by a cruel, callous God.

One morning, on the way to the hospital, Jonas stopped by a flower shop. The shop window was full of bouquets of tulips in all colors. Tulips were Eva's favorite flowers. The day before, she had felt a little better. They had been able to sit next to each other in an easy chair by the window in her hospital room and chat. They had had tea and she had even been able to eat a tiny piece of the pastry the nurse had brought without throwing up.

The flower shop was busy and Jonas had to wait for about fifteen minutes until he was served. He left again with a large bouquet of red-and-white tulips. When he arrived at the hospital, he saw that the "occupied" light was on above Eva's room. He waited for a while, thinking the nurses were busy doing the morning toilette. Normally they were through by the time he arrived. He knocked on the door and a nurse opened. Jonas saw right away that something unusual had happened. The doctor and a few nurses were gathered around Eva's bed. She was lying there, pale, eyes closed, without any of the tubes that were usually attached to her. Jonas's heart clenched.

A nurse came to the door. "Mr. Bergman, we tried to call you, but you didn't answer any of your phones." The nurse touched his arm, as if to soften the blow. "Your wife passed away half an hour ago. We're so sorry."

Jonas broke out in a sweat and felt faint. He let the flowers slide to the floor. The nurse helped him to a chair. The doctor came up to him. "I'm very sorry. Perhaps it helps you to know that she died peacefully." Jonas heard the doctor's voice as if through a haze. His mind went into overdrive. Half an hour before, he had been at the flower shop. If he hadn't waited that long for the flowers, he might have been early enough to still see her alive.

"I failed her; she had to die alone. I wasn't here when she needed me the most." Jonas didn't even notice he had said it aloud.

The nurse put a hand on his shoulder. "You didn't fail her, Mr. Bergman. More often than not, people die just when their relatives are not with them. It is as if they needed to be alone to be able to let go."

The nurse meant well, but her words didn't register with Jonas. All he knew was that Eva was dead. He covered his face with his hands and moaned.

"Would you like to have a few minutes alone with her?" the nurse asked.

"Yes, please." His voice sounded hoarse.

After everybody left, he went over to Eva's bed. She was wearing a new nightgown and what remained of her hair was carefully groomed. They must have cleaned and dressed her already. "Why, why couldn't you have waited a little?" he whispered, then broke down and cried, painful sobs racking his body. After a while, he took off his coat and shoes and lay down next to what was left of his wife. He gently stroked her now-cold face, her emaciated body, her thin, silky blond hair. He didn't know how much time had passed when he felt a hand on his shoulder. He turned around and looked into the friendly eyes of the nurse.

Chapter 22

Anna woke up to the sound of slippers tapping over the hardwood floor. The lit face of the alarm clock showed five o'clock in the morning. She grabbed her robe and got up. Yawning and shivering in the morning air, she opened the bedroom door. The house smelled of Christmas; a faint scent of pine and the sweet smell of cookies Anna had baked the evening before lingered in the air.

Karla stood next to the Christmas tree in her pajamas. "I couldn't sleep anymore."

"You're going to be exhausted by tonight. At least get your bathrobe. It's still cold," Anna said.

"Can we light the candles on the tree just to see what they look like?" Karla asked.

"No way. Not yet. But I'll build a fire and make us some hot chocolate." Anna put a fire starter stick into the woodstove, lit it, and arranged a few logs around it. She went into the kitchen, heated some milk, and prepared two cups of hot chocolate.

When she came back into the living room, Karla was sitting on the couch in front of the stove, wrapped in her morning gown, her face flushed with excitement. "When are you going to put the presents under the tree?"

"Tonight, before we light the candles. Otherwise, you'll be shaking the packages all day, trying to figure out what you got." Anna put a mug of hot chocolate in front of Karla. "Careful, it's hot." She sat next to her and the two watched the fire and sipped the sweet hot liquid.

Karla no longer believed in the Christmas Angel who flew down from heaven with all the presents. Anna, however, had kept up the tradition of arranging the presents under the tree and lighting the candles while Karla was banned to her bedroom. Having lived in the United States for many years, she had also kept the American custom of hanging Christmas stockings above the fireplace and stuffing them with small gifts, which Karla got to open on Christmas Day morning.

"Look, it's snowing again," Anna said.

Outside, dawn was spreading, slowly bringing the trees, meadows, and the neighbor's house into focus. Thick snowflakes were falling, covering the landscape with a blanket of white. All at once, the quiet was interrupted by the blinking lights of the snowplow, which drove around the corner and dumped a wall of snow along the sidewalk.

"This is a real white Christmas," Karla said, sitting back down on the sofa. She yawned and leaned her head against the backrest.

"Why don't you take a little nap on the sofa? You're going to be so tired tonight."

"Okay," Karla said and stretched out. "What time is Saint Nicholas coming?"

"Around four o'clock."

Anna had given up encouraging Karla to call Jonas by his proper name, since he seemed to enjoy his nickname. She spread a blanket over Karla, then carried the empty mugs into the kitchen. When she came back, she heard a light snoring sound coming from the sofa. Karla was deep asleep, lying on her back, one arm and a strand of her dark hair hanging over the edge of the sofa. Anna gently slid her arm under the blanket.

It had snowed all morning. Karla was too excited to settle down, so Anna took her on a walk after lunch. When they came back, Anna grabbed a shovel and cleared the snow away from the path and the driveway. Karla, using her small shovel, helped her. "Let's build a snowman," she said, all excited. At that moment, Jonas drove up in his car.

"Saint Nicholas!" Karla tossed the shovel away and rushed to meet him.

Anna watched as Jonas peeled himself out of his Volvo. He was wearing a black winter coat with a hood and a red woolen scarf. *He does look like Santa Claus with his white hair and beard.*

"Hi, sweetheart." Jonas hugged Karla, then turned to Anna. "I should've taken the train. I didn't expect it to snow like that. In the city, there's hardly any snow."

"You may be stuck here if it keeps on like this." Anna shook his hand.

"Oh, yes. Then you'll have to stay overnight," Karla exclaimed. "Can he stay, Anna?"

"Wait a minute. Inviting me for Christmas is one thing, but I don't think I'm ready to move in yet." Jonas laughed. "And I don't have my toothbrush with me."

"Well, that's not a problem. I have a spare toothbrush," Anna said. The idea of him spending the night appealed to her. It would make Christmas much more enjoyable. "I think Karla is right. You should stay. That way you can have a glass of wine and don't have to worry about the roads. I wouldn't want you to drive at night in those conditions. We have a nice guest room, it would be no problem."

"Yes, and tomorrow morning, Anna is going to fix pancakes. They're really good." Karla pulled Jonas's arm. "Pancakes with blueberries and bananas. Please, please stay."

"Pancakes, huh?" Jonas grinned. "How can I resist? All right, I'll stay." He opened the trunk of his car and pulled out a large paper bag full of wrapped presents and a bottle of wine.

"You shouldn't have," Anna said.

"Let me see." Karla tried to peek into the bag. "Presents? For me?"

"Ms. Nosy, why don't you build your snowman?" Anna lifted the bag up high, away from Karla.

"Someone has to help me." Karla gave Jonas an inviting smile.

"All right, Karla, let Jonas relax for a while."

"Well, actually, I could use a little exercise. Besides, I haven't built a snowman in years. We need a carrot, though, and stones for the eyes and a hat."

"Let's go inside first and have a cup of tea or coffee. You can pick out the tools for your work of art." Anna laughed. "If you entertain Karla, I can start preparing dinner."

"Oh, goody." Karla clapped her gloved hands.

It was close to midnight. After all the presents had been unpacked and Karla had finally unwound and succumbed to sleep, Anna and Jonas sat in front of the fireplace, sipping the rest of the wine. An aroma of roasted Christmas goose, fried onions, and burning wood permeated the room.

Jonas got up and poured them both the last drops of wine from the bottle. "We killed that one," he said with a chuckle. "Now I'm glad I'm staying. I might have been caught in a sobriety test."

"Yes, they're really strict these days," Anna said. "Besides, Karla was so excited to have you here. She's gotten quite attached to you. You've become kind of a father figure for her."

"I love her, too. She's a great kid." Jonas cleared his throat. "What about her father? Is he around somewhere?"

"He lives in Peru. My sister was a single mother. She met Arturo on a trip to South America and ended up pregnant. He's a good man. He offered to take Karla with him to Peru after her mother died. But we decided it would be too much of an upheaval for her. He tries to stay in touch, but how can you develop a relationship over such a distance?"

"Yeah, I guess not." Jonas put down his glass. "It's hard enough when your children are adults and move away. I couldn't imagine not having them close when they're little."

"You're still really close, aren't you?" Anna said.

"Yes, we are, thank God." He nodded, then pointed at the window. "It's still snowing a little."

"Isn't the snow pretty at night?" Anna said. "We get sick of it by the end of winter, but it makes everything so peaceful."

Jonas nodded then looked at the fire. It was quiet aside from the hissing of the pine logs and an occasional moaning of the wind. "Eva loved to watch the snow in the dark," he said in a low voice and glanced at Anna. The reflection of the flames from the fire created dancing lights in his eyes. He turned his head and looked toward the fire again. Anna watched his strong profile, the high forehead, covered in part by a strand of thick white hair, the slightly aquiline nose, the neatly trimmed beard.

"I used to wake up in the middle of the night," he continued in a low, dark voice. "The bed next to me was empty. And there she was, in the living room, wrapped in a blanket, gazing outside at the snowflakes."

"How was she? Your wife?" Anna lifted her hand in an impulse to touch his arm but pulled it back instead and let it fall into her lap. "Sorry, I don't want to intrude if it makes you sad."

"That's okay. Eva was wonderful. She was intelligent, beautiful, sexy, and independent." Jonas gave a quick laugh, then his face clouded over. "Losing her independence was the most devastating part of her illness."

"Where did you meet her?" Anna got up and put another log on the fire. The flames flared up and the wood hissed and spit. She moved the fender a little closer to prevent the sparks from shooting out.

"We met in Zurich. She was studying to become an actress," Jonas said.

"Did you already live in Switzerland then? I thought your family was Danish."

Jonas nodded. "My father is Danish; my mother is Swiss. Years ago, my father worked for a Danish company in Zurich, where he met my mother. I was born here and I lived most of my life here. Later, my parents moved to Denmark.

"I studied art and had found a teaching job here in Zurich. And I met Eva, so I ended up staying. We eventually got married."

Jonas gazed out the window, then gave a chuckle. "It almost didn't happen. Eva was a freedom-loving person and I was a jealous young punk. We had quite a few rows while dating."

Eva's work as an actress brought her in touch with many men who flirted with her. She was a free spirit and somewhat of a flirt herself. "It doesn't mean anything," she used to tell Jonas. "It's just a game."

Jonas tried to be open-minded. He knew that Eva's work brought with it invitations by influential men, who promised to further her career and hoped for a few intimate moments or hours in return.

"Don't worry, I know how to keep them at bay," Eva said as she was getting ready to go out with a film producer.

Jonas, racked by feelings of inferiority and fears of losing Eva—after all, he was merely a painting teacher and as yet an unknown artist—began to secretly follow her around. He watched her go into a restaurant with her escort. He waited across the street, hiding in a doorway until they came back out. He followed them as long as possible. Sometimes, they took a taxi and drove away. Jonas, deeply ashamed of his distrust and insecurities, hung his head and went home. Once in a while, the suspicions ate at him so much that he went to Eva's apartment a few streets away from his own and waited there as well, wanting to check if she went into her place alone. One day, Eva caught him spying and it almost cost Jonas the relationship.

It had been one of those gray and gloomy November days. Eva was in a play, which Jonas couldn't attend since he had a class that night. Eva told him she might go out with a few of the actors after the play.

"Come and meet us afterward, we'll probably have a drink at the bar next to the theater," she said.

That evening, Jonas's class at the Kunstgewerbeschule lasted longer than planned. He took the streetcar to the station next to the Kunsthaus, the main art museum of the city. Across the street were the theater and a bar. Jonas recognized a few of the actors but there was no sign of Eva.

"She left about fifteen minutes ago with Ivor," Karl, one of the actors, told him.

Jonas felt his heartbeat speed up. Ivor was a Swedish actor known for his womanizing. Jonas knew that he was after Eva. She had even told him laughingly one night. "He doesn't interest me. He's a good actor but a windbag." So why did she leave with him?

"Have a drink." Karl pointed at the empty chair next to him.

"No thanks, another time." Jonas lifted his hand to wave good-bye. He stepped outside and stopped in front of the theater. There was a poster at the entrance with Eva's picture on it. She had a part in *Mother Courage* by Bertolt Brecht. She played a poor woman, dressed in rags, with dirty limp hair falling into her face, but even so she was beautiful. No wonder she turned every man's head. A wave of anger flooded him, followed by shame. *I don't deserve her.*

Outside, the cold, wet air of a gloomy November evening brushed across his face and a dank smell from wet leaves hung in the air. Jonas shivered and pulled up his coat collar and buried his hands in his pockets. He stopped, not sure what to do. Should he call her? Go by her place? What if she was with Ivor? He couldn't bear it, but not knowing was even worse. He walked across the street to the tram station and boarded one of the blue-and-white streetcars. He sat at the window and looked out into the darkening night. At the Central station, he got off and took a different tram, which brought him up to the University of Zurich. Eva lived in an apartment nearby.

It was one of the old houses, which dated back to the nineteenth century. It had been renovated several times and combined old-fashioned elegance with a few gestures toward modernity. The stone walls of the house had been painted a light yellow, and the green lacquered old-fashioned shutters gave the heavy building a cheerful touch.

Jonas stood in front of the house, looking up to Eva's apartment. There was light in the living room; she must be home. Perhaps he was wrong. She may have just left at the same time as Ivor by accident, thinking Jonas wouldn't come anymore. He saw someone walk by the balcony door. It was Eva. Just as Jonas was getting ready to ring the bell, he saw a second figure. He didn't recognize who it was, since the person stood farther back from the window. Eva turned around and seemed to say something to the person. Then the two disappeared. Jonas waited, his heart beating fast. What should he do? Should he just go inside and confront her? But if it was Ivor, they'd just make up an excuse and Jonas would look like a fool. After all, Eva had the right to invite whomever she wanted into her apartment. Jonas waited for a while, hoping the guy—Jonas assumed it was a man—would step closer to the window, but nothing happened.

Jonas knew what he was about to do was wrong. Eva was somewhat of a flirt but she had never given him any real reason to distrust her. His suspicions clouded his mind, but he couldn't help it. He took a deep breath and went into the small yard at the side of the house. A drainpipe led from the roof along the balcony to the ground. About two feet up from the ground, there was a slight protrusion in the wall, and another larger one somewhat higher up. From there, he could get a good look inside the apartment.

Jonas looked around, feeling like an intruder. He hesitated, then held on to the pipe and pulled himself up, holding the pipe with one hand and reaching for the first jutting stone with the other. He was just about to reach for the second one when he slipped. He held on to the pipe, but one of the clamps connecting the pipe to the wall came off and he slid down the wall, scratching his hand and ripping his pants. There was a loud metallic bang as he pushed against the pipe. He fell to the ground; his hand was bleeding and there was a tear in his pant leg.

The balcony door opened. Eva stepped outside and looked around. Jonas tried to find somewhere to hide but Eva spotted him right away.

"What's going on? What happened to you?" She stared at him stunned.

"Nothing, I . . ."

The visitor stepped out onto the balcony. It was Eva's mother. "Jonas? What a surprise. Why don't you come in?"

Eva narrowed her eyes and her face was flooded with anger.

"Eva, I'm sorry, I can explain," Jonas stuttered.

"Go away." Eva grabbed her mother's arm and tried to drag her inside.

"But Eva?" Her mother looked at her puzzled.

"Never mind, Mom. Come on." Eva turned to Jonas. "Don't try to contact me. Just leave me alone."

"Eva, please . . ." But the balcony door was shut and Eva pulled the drapes.

Jonas slinked away like a beggar. His hand was bleeding, his pants were torn, his heart was crushed, and he felt like a complete fool.

Anna laughed after Jonas finished telling her the story. "You poor guy, that must have been horrible. But you obviously made up again."

Jonas grinned. "Yeah, it took a while. Fortunately, Eva's mother liked me and intervened on my behalf. But she took me aside one day and told me to get my feelings of jealousy under control or I would drive Eva away for good. Eva had been strong-willed and independent even as a child. The minute she felt tied down or trapped, she'd rebel. However, she was also a very loyal person.

"So I had to learn to trust her and it wasn't always easy." Jonas gave a wistful smile. "But it was worth it."

Anna and Jonas were quiet for a while, gazing at the falling snow. Anna got up and extinguished a few of the candles that had burned down on the Christmas tree, then sat down again.

Jonas faced her. "What about you, Anna? You were married once, weren't you?" He could almost feel the woman tense up. Her face hardened and she stared down at her hands. The temperature in the room seemed to drop a few degrees.

"Sorry, I don't mean to pry," Jonas hastened to say. He hesitated, then lightly touched her arm. She seemed to stiffen even more, but then relaxed and exhaled. "It's a long . . . and intense story," she murmured.

"I'm sorry; I shouldn't have brought it up. It's obviously too painful for you."

Anna's shoulders slumped and she looked up at him. "I want to tell you one day, but not tonight. I'd rather wait until we have more time. I'm getting a little tired."

Jonas looked at the clock. "No wonder. It's two o'clock in the morning."

PART THREE: BETRAYED

Chapter 23

Anna sat at her desk in front of the window, gazing at the signs of spring—the yellow and white crocuses, which had shot up spontaneously on the lawn in front of the house. The hazel bushes along the forest were in full bloom. It was a quiet morning. Karla was spending part of her spring break in the south of Switzerland with Lena and her friends. Lena had been a close friend of Karla's mother when she and Karla still lived in the Ticino.

Anna was in the process of making up a list of new books she wanted to order for the library. She also prepared for a couple of events for the bookstore: a storytelling hour for children and their parents and a reading of new books in the evening for the adults.

Maintaining the bookstore was a constant struggle. It was the only one in town and well-liked by the people of the small community. However, the village was only half an hour away from the city of Zurich and many people preferred to shop in the city, where there was a much greater choice of shops and stores. Anna had to constantly think of new ideas to attract customers. Her readings for adults and story hours for the kids were popular, particularly among the older generation and the young children. The adolescents, however, preferred the more glamorous environment of the city with its movie theaters and video stores.

So far, Anna had been able to make a small profit, but for her it was mainly a labor of love. Had it been for the money, she would have sold the store long ago.

It was a gloomy morning outside. In the north, gray-white clouds towered over the mountains. Anna got up to pour herself another cup of coffee when the phone rang. It was Jonas.

"They are playing *Cavalleria Rusticana* at the opera house. Would you be interested?"

Anna faltered for a moment. It was a piece of music she loved but it was associated with both a happy and an intensely sad time in her life.

"Yes, of course," she finally said.

"You're sure?" Jonas must have picked up on her hesitation.

"Yes, the name of the opera just reminded me of something . . . problematic in the past. But I love the piece."

"Great. I'll pick you up."

After Anna hung up the phone, she sat at her desk, looking out the window, daydreaming. She was halfway aware of the gray-white sheets of fog floating by. Toward the south, patches of blue sky were visible.

What a coincidence, she thought. It was during that very opera at the Lincoln Center back in New York City that Nico had kissed her for the first time. And ten years later, after a performance of the same opera, Anna's life had fallen apart. Was it fate that Jonas invited her to the same piece of music? Was it a bad omen?

Jonas was different from Nico. He was a quieter person, not as sparkling as Nico had been. He was kind and gentle with people but intense and passionate about his work. Karla loved him, and Anna once in a while thought he would be a good substitute father for her.

What about my feelings for him? Over the past years, Anna had pushed away any upcoming thoughts or feelings about getting involved with a man. She was content, fulfilled with her work and with Karla. And she wanted to keep it that way, or did she?

Lately, she had caught herself thinking about Jonas more than she wanted to admit. She focused more on her appearance. She chose more colorful outfits, she experimented with makeup. Her hairdresser convinced her to add highlights to give her brown hair more vibrancy.

The changes weren't lost on the people around her. "And who is the lucky guy?" a friend asked her.

"I like that aquamarine blouse, Anna," Karla said. She had just learned the name of the color. Anna noticed Jonas's admiring looks. And every once in a while, she questioned her motive behind all this "beautification" and asked herself what she was trying to do.

And then one night she woke up, feeling sexually aroused, and she knew she had dreamt of Jonas. She got up, brushed her hair from her damp forehead. "Stupid cow," she muttered. She sat next to the window. The first sun rays of the day bathed the top of the pine and birch trees of the woods nearby in a halo of suffused light. Anna felt her eyes fill with tears, blurring the landscape in front of her. *What's happening to me?* She shook her head and brushed her hand across her face.

In the evening, Anna stood in front of her closet and perused her wardrobe. She took out a black dress she usually wore when going to a concert. It was elegant . . . and boring. She put it back and sighed. After some deliberation, she chose a two-piece turquoise silk outfit. She put on some eye makeup and lipstick, stepped back, and looked at herself in the mirror. She shook her head. Her comfortable shoes didn't match the outfit. She chose a pair of high-heeled pumps she hadn't worn in years. They felt tight on her feet but they looked the part. *My feet are going to kill me, why am I doing this to myself?*

She looked at herself in the mirror again. A smile spread across her face and made her look ten years younger. *Oh well, why not? So my feet hurt. We'll be sitting in the theater most of the time.* She shrugged and picked out a matching purse. She looked at her watch. It was six o'clock. Jonas would pick her up in half an hour. They were going to have a bite to eat before the concert.

Anna sat in the living room and kicked off her shoes. She looked down at her feet, which were already starting to hurt, and burst out laughing. She felt ridiculous but strangely happy. She got up and walked barefoot into the kitchen and poured herself a glass of water. Standing next to the window, she took small sips of the cool liquid. Outside, the sky had cleared; the last bit of fog dissolved.

Soon afterward, Jonas drove up in his Volvo. Anna watched him through the window. He was dressed in a dark suit, light-green shirt, and a green-and-turquoise patterned tie. Anna had to admit, he was good-looking. He was of medium height and sturdy. His body was still firm with the exception of the beginning of a little pooch, which wasn't visible under the suit. He had cut his wild white hair somewhat and trimmed his beard.

He smiled at her as she waited for him at the door; his clear, blue eyes, surrounded by a wreath of wrinkles, sparkled. "You look beautiful, as always," he greeted her.

"Thanks," Anna said. "We match," she added with a chuckle and pointed at his tie and her dress.

"Hey, you're right." He gave her a quick hug. Anna smelled the discreet scent of his after shave and thought of the sensuous dream of the other night. She turned around and pretended to fiddle with the lock in the door in order to hide her flushed face.

The drive to the city took about thirty minutes. As they approached the opera house, which was at the Bellevue plaza right at the beginning of the lake, Jonas wondered if they should park the car in a parking garage nearby and walk to the theater, since the few spots next to the theater were usually taken.

Oh, no, my feet, Anna thought. "Hmm . . . as long as it's not too far. I'm . . . not wearing the most comfortable shoes."

Jonas grinned. "How stupid of me. I forgot. Women and their shoes. Why don't I let you off at the restaurant and then go and park the car? Or I could carry you." His blue eyes had a mischievous glint.

Luckily, they did find a spot right next to the restaurant. Jonas parked the car and helped Anna out. "They are nice, though," he said, pointing at Anna's shoes. "Very sexy."

Anna, all flustered, stumbled and held on to Jonas's arm. He put his arm around her. "Careful, careful."

Anna, feeling utterly ridiculous, started to laugh. "I'm sorry. I'm not used to all this."

"Not used to what?" he asked.

"You know, going out, picking out the right clothes, dressing up, and all that."

"I don't know why you worry. You look beautiful," Jonas said with a serious face.

"Thanks," Anna whispered.

"I'm not used to going out much either," Jonas said. "We have to do this more often. You know, practice makes perfect."

Jonas had picked a restaurant next to the opera house with the meaningful name Belcanto. It was a modern but elegant place with huge windows facing the lake, reddish-brown tapestry, and a row of murals with scenes from operas. A young waiter grabbed a handful of large menus and led them to a table next to the window.

They ordered one of the specials, baked European perch with fresh herbs, vegetables, potatoes. While Jonas perused the wine list, Anna glanced at the other guests. People were talking in hushed voices and there was a quiet elegance about the place. Now, Anna was glad she had dressed up. "This is a nice place," she said to Jonas. "Do you come here often?"

Jonas shook his head. "No, very rarely. My normal hang-outs are a little more rustic. But I figured since I was going to the opera with a beautiful woman, I might as well do it in style."

Anna returned his smile, then lowered her eyes. Her face felt warm. She glanced at the lake. The sun had just set and the sky above the hill was ablaze with blotches of purple and red.

At the theater, they sat in one of the loges with a good view of the stage. Anna enjoyed the festive atmosphere and decided to go to the theater more often. She hadn't been out much, except to bookstores and museums. She was sure that Karla would enjoy it as well. They could go to a matinee once in a while.

When the room darkened, there was a hush of voices, an occasional cough, and then it was silent. The music began to play and Anna felt transported into the past. Nico was sitting next to her. His jet-black hair and blue eyes shone in the dim light. They had seen each other a few times and he had invited her to the opera in New York City. She had been nervous that evening, realizing she was falling in love. She smelled his aftershave, felt his touch, and a wave of sadness flooded her.

But no, this was twenty years later. It was Jonas's after shave she smelled, not her husband's. Anna blinked a few times to clear her eyes and brushed a tear away. She felt someone touch her hand.

"Are you all right?" Jonas whispered.

Anna nodded and gave a quick smile. She took a deep breath and pushed the thoughts of the past to the back of her mind. In time, she was able to enjoy the music.

After the concert, Jonas drove Anna home. She invited him in for coffee before his drive back to the city. They discussed the opera. Anna poured the coffee, handed a cup to Jonas, and took a sip.

"You mentioned before that the opera reminded you of something in your past," Jonas said.

"Yes." Anna hesitated, then continued to speak in a low voice. "It reminded me of my husband." Anna glanced at Jonas, then looked down at her hands. "Are you ready for the long story?"

Jonas gave her an encouraging nod.

Anna took a deep breath. "The first seven years of our marriage were wonderful."

Chapter 24

Anna and Nicolas lived in New York City. Nico worked for an engineering firm which had a subsidiary in Guadalajara, Mexico. Aside from her normal librarian work at the public library on Fifth Avenue and 42nd Street, Anna was now in charge of organizing special events such as readings by novelists and poets.

Nico traveled to Mexico on a regular basis, working at the firm in Guadalajara. Once in a while, Anna accompanied him for a couple of days. She spent the days sightseeing, hanging out at museums, or enjoying the many sights and parks of the city.

One summer, when Nico spent several weeks in Mexico working on a joint US and Mexican project, Anna joined him after a few weeks for a two-week stay in Guadalajara. Her library planned to put on a reading and presentation of a few Mexican writers and poets in the fall. Anna was to meet with them and organize the details.

She flew to Guadalajara, where Nico picked her up at the airport. He dropped her off at the pension where he lived during his stays in the city. It was a small two-room suite with a bathroom and a kitchenette. It was located in the old historic center of the city within walking distance of Nico's office and next to one of the many beautiful parks. They had lunch at a small restaurant nearby. Afterward, Nico went back to work and Anna called one of the poets and set up a meeting for the following day.

The next couple of days, Anna met Nico once at work and once for lunch. In the evening, after it had cooled down, they went out to dinner or for a walk. Nico seemed preoccupied. He wasn't his usual bubbly self. When Anna asked him, he waved his hand in front of his face as if warding off a fly.

"It's work," he said. He cleared his throat and sighed. "Business is bad. We don't know if we have the finances to finish this project. They miscalculated the resources, and with the economy in the dumps, this is going to be a real problem. They might have to let a bunch of people go."

Anna peered at him. "Is your job in danger?"

Nico shook his head. "No, it's really the Mexican side of the business that's in trouble. I'm worried about some of my Mexican colleagues. They have families, and if they lose their jobs, it'll almost be impossible to find a new one considering the bad economy." He took a sip of beer.

"Is it certain? That they will lose their jobs?"

Nico lifted his shoulders. "No, we don't know yet. There are talks and meetings going on every day. The next few weeks are really crucial." He glanced at Anna. "I might have to stay longer, until it's all sorted out. You may have to fly back on your own."

"That's all right." Anna reached across and put her hand on his. Nico glanced at his watch. "I need to get going." He gave Anna a quick kiss. "See you tonight."

Anna sighed. At least now she knew why Nico had been in such a strange mood lately. He had been absentminded, often staring into space. She got up and decided to go grocery shopping. She would fix one of Nico's favorite dishes, chicken cacciatore, for dinner.

The following day around lunchtime, Anna decided on the spur of the moment to visit Nico at work. Perhaps they could have lunch together again. When she entered the office on the second floor of one of the few modern buildings in that area of town, the receptionist, a friendly, somewhat over-weight young woman, waved at her.

"You're too late; he already left."

"Hi Gloria. Do you know where he went for lunch?" Anna shook hands with her.

"Let me see." Gloria wrinkled her forehead. "When he goes with his colleagues, they normally go to Lupe's. But today, I saw him leave on his own. He sometimes goes to the park nearby for a walk. You know the one across the street?"

"Yeah, I know which one. I'll give it a try. Maybe I'll find him there."

The Parque Morelos, which ran along Calle Independencia, was a large green area with tall trees, fountains, paths with benches, and picnic areas. It was a favorite spot for families with children and business people taking a break from work. On windy afternoons, kids flew kites.

Anna took a leisurely stroll along one of the paths, looking for Nico. He couldn't have gone too far since he had to be back at the office in less than an hour. She watched as women with small children unpacked their lunches and realized she was hungry. Just as she was about to head to the cafeteria, thinking Nico might be there, she saw him. He was sitting on the lawn underneath a tree near some people, a woman and a little boy. The boy, who was about three or four years old, was playing with a ball. He tossed it in the direction of Nico, who caught it and threw it back. Anna waved, trying to catch his attention. He briefly looked in her direction but didn't see her. He seemed to say something to the little boy or the woman. Anna was too far away to be able to tell whom he was addressing. All of a sudden, he got up, turned around, and started to walk away. Anna called his name. The little boy looked at Anna for a moment, then continued to play. Nico walked in a brisk pace toward the exit of the park. He must not have heard her. She considered trying to catch up with him, but he had already reached the street. He was obviously in a hurry to get back to the office.

It was getting late, and Anna was starved. She walked to the cafeteria, ate a sandwich, and drank a bottle of lemonade. At home, she called another writer and set up a meeting, then took her notebook and went to sit outside on the patio with a cup of tea. She worked on an article for a few hours. In the late afternoon, it was getting hot and Anna went to take a nap.

Nico came home late that evening. After dinner, Anna suggested they take a short walk. It had cooled off and the temperature was balmy. The sun was about to set and colored the sky crimson.

"By the way, I saw you at the park during lunch. I came by the office and Gloria told me you might be there."

"Yeah, she mentioned it. We must have just missed each other." Nico gave her a quick glance.

"I saw you, though. You were sitting next to a beautiful young lady," Anna teased him. "I called you, but you either didn't hear or didn't want to hear."

Nico stared at her. "What are you talking about? Of course I didn't hear you. Why would I have ignored you?" His voice was sharp. "Are you spying on me now?"

Anna was startled at his intense reaction. "I was just kidding. You were sitting next to a woman and were playing ball with a little boy."

"Oh, that?" Nico waved his hand. "I happened to sit next to them and the little boy threw a ball in my direction, so I caught it. I don't know those people."

"It's okay," Anna said. "It just looked like you knew them and then you rushed off—"

"Ah, I get it." Nico picked up his glass of wine and grinned. "You're jealous."

"No, I'm not."

"Yes, you are." He grinned. "I can assure you, I have no idea who those people are." His eyes had a mischievous twinkle. "The woman was pretty, though."

Anna gave him a playful slap. "Stop it."

The following Saturday, Nico had to work. His company had received some encouraging news. The headquarters in the United States had promised them additional funding, so the company decided to push ahead with one of the projects which had been in limbo. Now, they had to make up for lost time.

Anna got up early so Nico and she could have breakfast together. The sun was just rising behind the buildings. It had cooled off a little but it promised to be a sunny day. After Nico had left, Anna sat on the patio, reading for a while, then worked on a book review. Later that morning, she went jogging and walking in the park. The morning before, she had had to struggle closing the zipper on a fairly tight pair of pants. *Too many tortillas*, she thought. She needed to get back to her regular exercise.

She had been walking and running a few rounds when she saw the little boy again who had played with a ball the other day. Two older children, a girl and a boy—teenagers most likely—were playing with him. An older woman, sitting under a tree next to a picnic basket, called to them. It could have been a grandmother or a nanny. The woman Anna had seen the other day wasn't there. The older boy kicked the ball, which rolled toward Anna, and the younger boy ran after it. Anna picked it up and rolled it in his direction.

The boy bent down to pick up the ball and when he stood up again, Anna looked at a pair of striking blue eyes.

"Gracias," he said, then lowered his gaze as she kept staring at him. He ran back to his friends.

Anna's heart skipped a beat. She remembered the photos of Nico as a little boy: the same stark contrast between his jet-black hair and intense blue eyes. The resemblance was eerie. Anna had seen other Mexican and Latin people with fair skin, light-brown hair, and blue eyes, but the combination of blue eyes and black hair—a common feature in Ireland, for instance—was rare in Mexico. Or at least she hadn't seen it except in Nico and the little boy.

Anna watched as the woman and the children gathered their things and began to walk away. On a hunch, Anna decided to follow them. She was careful to leave enough distance so they wouldn't notice her. She had no idea what she would discover but she needed to know. The nanny, or perhaps the grandmother, walked slowly, but the kids ran ahead. When the woman turned the corner on one of the streets behind the park, the children were waiting for her in front of a small, modest house. It was in a rather poor area but the small garden patch in front of the house was well kept with colorful flowers and shrubbery.

Anna stayed back until the woman and children disappeared in the house. She waited a few moments, then carefully advanced until she could read the number on the house. She pulled out her notepad and wrote down the address, then walked back toward the park. She was so preoccupied that she walked past the park and ended up in a shopping street. Feeling very tired, she went to a coffee shop and ordered a cup of cappuccino.

As the coffee and a cool breeze coming from the open space of the park revived her, she tried to make sense of the sequence of strange events over the past couple of days. The longer she thought about them, the more she felt she was being ridiculous. What did she know? She had seen Nico in a park together with a lot of different people. Nico had taken a break from work and happened to sit next to a woman with small children. One of the little boys had blue eyes. So what? There were other children in Mexico with blue eyes.

Anna shook her head. She knew she had a tendency to be obsessive. Once she got an idea in her head, she would pursue it single-mindedly. *Terca como una mula*, stubborn like a mule, Nico sometimes called her. She decided to forget about the whole thing and not bring it up again. She didn't want to give Nico the impression she didn't trust him. If there was any connection between him and those people, he would've told her.

Anna finished her coffee and went grocery shopping on her way home. She would fix cheese-and-green-chili enchiladas for dinner. It was a messy and time-consuming meal, but Nico liked it and Anna felt guilty and ashamed for having acted like a private detective by following the family to their home.

When she returned to the pension, Nico was already there. He had left work early and seemed to be in a better mood than the previous days. He told Anna that the situation at the office had improved and it was now pretty certain that they would get the additional money.

"Don't cook tonight," he said when he came into the kitchen and helped Anna unpack the groceries. "Let's go out for dinner." He pulled her close and kissed her.

A few days later, Nico drove Anna to the airport. After Anna checked in, they sat at a coffee shop, waiting for the boarding announcement.

"I wish we could fly right back to the States from here. I hate having to go back to the office. Things have improved, but there are still some problems," Nico said.

"I'll miss you," Anna said.

"You'll be busy with your work. You won't miss me," Nico mumbled.

"Of course I'll miss you. How can you think otherwise? Won't you miss me?"

"Of course." The answer came fast. "Just wanted to make it easier on us. I mean we'll both be busy and time will fly."

Something in Nico's demeanor startled Anna. He seemed unusually cool and aloof. He gazed into space with a serious face, a sharp furrow between his eyebrows. *He's still worried about work.*

Anna touched his cheek, then gently brushed her hand across his forehead. "Smooth out the worry lines or they'll stick. Relax, it'll be okay."

Nico nodded and smiled, then glanced once again at the clock above him.

"You need to get back to work, don't you?" Anna said. "You don't need to wait. I have a book to read. I'll be fine."

"I'm just a little concerned about traffic back into the city." Nico put his hand on Anna's arm. "You sure you don't mind?"

"No, you should leave. I'll be fine. Really."

"All right. Have a safe flight. Call me as soon as you get in. Okay?" Nico hugged her tight and kissed her. "I'll be home as soon as I can."

Sitting alone, drinking her coffee, Anna felt strangely bereft. She was sorry they weren't able to fly back together.

She shook her head and glanced at her watch. *Time to go.* She picked up her purse and made her way to the gate.

Chapter 25

Late August was still hot and muggy in New York City. Anna took a shuttle from the airport to Grand Central Station and a cab from there to their home in Greenwich Village. She groaned as she entered the hot apartment. She turned on the air conditioner full blast, pulled a pair of shorts and a tank top out of her suitcase. She stripped off her jeans and blouse, which clung to her moist skin, removed her bra and walked into the kitchen. The cold floor felt good on her naked feet. She poured herself a glass of water and sat at the kitchen table. As much as she liked New York City for its excitement and culture, she often wished they could spend the whole summer outside of the city.

Anna checked her watch. It was three o'clock in the afternoon in Guadalajara. She picked up the phone and dialed Nico's office number. He answered right away.

"Hi there, how was your flight?"

"Uneventful." Anna suppressed a yawn. "It's hot and humid here, but that was to be expected."

"It's kind of muggy here, too," Nico said.

"You just say that to make me feel better."

"No, it's true. I was actually sweating when I walked to work today. Everything okay at home? Any mail?"

"I haven't checked yet. Let me see." Anna paged through the mail on the table. "Just the regular stuff," she said. "A couple of bills, your architecture magazine, a letter from . . . England, from your father it looks like. You know, we should visit your father once again. It's been years."

"Yes, I know," Nico said. "We'll do that real soon."

"Sounds good."

"Okay, got to go. I'm glad you made it home safe. Take care of yourself. I'll call you again in a couple of days. I should be home in two or three weeks at the latest. We're winding down here."

"Good. I miss you."

"Miss you, too. *Hasta luego.*"

Anna put down the phone. She took a few sips of water and looked out the window. From their apartment, they had a view of a small park with trees, shrubs, and playground equipment for children. Two Latin-looking women, one with a stroller, were sitting on a bench, watching two kids. A little girl was playing in the sandbox and a boy, probably about four years old, with curly dark hair, was sitting on a swing set. He reminded Anna of the little boy in the park in Guadalajara.

"We should have a baby," she said to herself.

When she and Nico were first married, they had decided to wait a few years. Nico felt they needed to be more settled before having children. At the time, his job hadn't been very secure and he was still waiting for his green card to come through. Now, however, he was more established and had earned a reputation as an industrial architect. It would be a good time to start a family. Anna was twenty-eight and Nico thirty-four, the perfect age. She knew Nico loved children and they loved him. He was always the first to play with the kids when they had visitors with little children. He would make a good father.

The library was quiet during Anna's first day back at work. The normal whispering and humming noises of the patrons were absent. It was vacation time and people who could afford it left the city during the hot and muggy days. The men and women frequenting the library were mostly older, trying to get out of the heat. They sat at the tables, one or several books in front of them. Most of them were nodding. An occasional snore or cough interrupted the silence.

Anna loved the quiet and less busy summer days at the library. It was cool and pleasant. She got to chat with her colleagues, choose and order new books, and work on her own writing. On the third day after returning home, she went out to dinner with Susan, whose husband was out of town. They went to their favorite Italian place in the East Village.

"So, how was Mexico?" Susan asked.

"Great. I got to meet with a few very interesting writers and poets. It was just wonderful to be out of New York City for a while and experience a different environment and culture." Anna took a sip of wine.

"You know," she continued, "I was thinking about having kids, starting a family. And I don't know if New York would be a good place for this. It's a great city in many ways, but I wouldn't want to raise children in this traffic and air pollution."

"Well, a lot of people have families here, too," Susan said. "But you're right, if I had children, I might want to move somewhere a little less crowded myself."

Susan and George lived in the Upper East Side of Manhattan and, according to Susan, they weren't thinking about children yet.

"So, you suddenly got the baby bug?" Susan laughed.

Anna shrugged. "Yeah, I've been thinking about it."

"What does Nico say about this?"

Anna laughed. "The last time we talked was a few years ago and he wasn't too enthusiastic. But that was when we first got married and his career and everything was still up in the air. I think now would be a good time. I've been watching him around children and I think he'd make a good father."

"Yeah, I can see that," Susan said. "He has this Latin warmth and enthusiasm."

Anna looked at her watch. "He's supposed to call me tonight. Do you mind having coffee at my place? I don't want to miss his call."

"Sounds good to me." Susan pushed her empty plate aside. "I just love their spinach ravioli. If only their portions weren't so big. I shouldn't eat the whole thing but I have no self-control."

"Talk about self-control. I have to watch my weight, too. That one pair of pants? I can hardly close the zipper." Anna waved to the waiter.

"Oh, come on. You're so damn skinny. I'm fat compared to you." Susan sighed.

"That's ridiculous and you know it," Anna said.

Susan was a good-looking woman with wavy, naturally blond hair and green eyes. She was a little on the chubby side but it didn't make her any less attractive.

"By the way," Anna said. "I checked a movie out of the library. It's about Italy and an interesting love triangle. Perhaps we can watch it later on, in case you haven't seen it yet."

"That would be fun," Susan said.

At home, Anna turned on the espresso machine and put some cookies on a plate. There was no message on the answering machine, so she tried to call Nico. There was no answer and Anna left a message.

The following day was Saturday. Anna got up early and went to her aerobics class. When she came back home, the sun was shining through the living room window, illuminating the thin layer of dust on top of the bookshelf. Anna sighed. It was time to clean, a chore she didn't enjoy much. She decided to attack Nico's office, which was a mess. Papers and plans were scattered on the desk, table, and floor.

The mess in Nico's office was a bone of contention between them. Nico didn't like Anna to clean his office. He claimed that she misplaced his important papers. Now, however, he wasn't here and Anna was sick and tired of the mess.

She was careful to keep the piles of paper in the order they were in and set them on top of the credenza. While dusting and vacuuming, she remembered the plans of the house Nico had once made for them. They had been talking and dreaming about a future home and Nico had played around with different designs. They were thinking of eventually buying some land outside of the city.

The phone rang. It was Nico. "Hi there," he said. "How are you?"

"Fine. Miss you."

"I miss you, too. I'll be home soon."

"Great. Listen, do you remember the plan you made of our house a few years ago?"

"Yeah? What of it?"

"Where did you put it? I want to have a look at it again."

"It's somewhere either on my credenza or on a bookshelf or in my desk. But why don't you wait until I get back? I'll find it for you. What do you need it for?"

"I've been thinking . . . I've been thinking about having a home outside of the city, having a family, kids, you know?"

It was quiet at the other end.

"Nico? You still there?"

"Yes . . . sure." Nico sounded hesitant. "What brought that on? I thought you liked New York City."

"I do but we have to think about the future, too. We're not getting any younger. It's time to think of a family. Don't you want children?"

"Of course I do. Anna, what's the matter with you? Why are you suddenly thinking about kids?"

"It's not sudden. We've talked about it before and we've been married for seven years. What's wrong with having children?"

"Nothing at all." Nico cleared his throat. "But this is a serious topic, something we need to discuss once I'm back. This isn't the kind of thing you just decide on the phone."

"I know. I'm sorry. Susan was right. I must have the baby bug."

Nico chuckled. "That's okay. Don't worry; we'll have babies, loads of them." He sounded more loving again.

After they hung up, Anna went into the kitchen, fixed a cucumber-and-cheese sandwich, and poured herself a glass of water. She ate the sandwich slowly, thinking about the talk with Nico. He was just being the typical man, a little uneasy about having children, the responsibility, perhaps worried about how it would change their lives. He would come around. She needed to find the design of the house. It might inspire him again. The past couple of years he had spent all his time on commercial buildings. Anna knew that his real ambition was modern one-family homes and interesting public buildings. He was an admirer of architects such as Frank Gehry and Mario Botta.

She searched through the piles of designs on the bookshelves, looking for the plan of the house. She lifted each sketch carefully. There were house plans, floor plans of buildings, large structural designs, but nothing that looked like the design of the cozy home he had shown her. Finally, she opened the drawers of his desk, shuffling through papers and stationary. She found it in the second drawer. The design was different from his other work, more like a regular drawing. He had added a garden with a couple of trees and a flower bed. Anna smiled. She remembered when he first showed it to her.

It had been winter, around Christmas. They had been sitting on the floor in front of the gas fireplace. He had explained the layout to her, the arrangement of the different rooms. She had told him where to put the furniture and he had added the bed, the dining-room table, and chairs. The kitchen was big. They had always wanted a large kitchen with enough room for a breakfast nook or dining area.

Anna folded the design again and put it on the bookshelf. There was something scribbled on the back. She picked up the paper and looked at it more closely. It was a Mexican address, a street name and number in Guadalajara. It looked vaguely familiar but she couldn't remember where she had seen it before. She wrinkled her forehead, then shook her head. Perhaps it was the address of one of Nico's friends or colleagues at work.

The phone rang. It was Susan, reminding her of the concert in the evening. Susan and George had season tickets at the New York Philharmonic, and since George was out of town there was an extra ticket.

Chapter 26

They played the opera *Cavalleria Rusticana* by Pietro Mascagni, a story of love and betrayal with beautiful, passionate singing and music, which brought tears to Anna's eyes. As she was sitting in the dark, listening to the libretto, she remembered that Nico had invited her to a performance of that very opera at the Lincoln Center when they first met. When the lights came on during the intermission, Nico had put his arm around her. He had noticed the tears in her eyes and had kissed her for the first time.

After the opera, Susan dropped Anna off at her apartment. Anna invited her for a drink, but Susan was tired and wanted to go home. Anna, still keyed up after the performance, made herself a cup of herbal tea. Inspired by the music and the story of the opera, she took her journal out of her purse and made a few notes for a poem.

As she paged through the book, she came across the address she had written down in Guadalajara after following the family in the park. She stared at it, stunned. *This can't be possible*, she thought. She got up and picked up the paper with Nico's home design. She turned it around, holding her breath.

Fear gripped her, clenching her stomach and spreading through her body to her chest. The address in the notebook and the one on the back of the plan were the same. Nico knew the woman and the children. He knew where they lived.

Anna stared out the window into the dark. The pictures of the past weeks passed in front of her eyes as in a slide show: Nico sitting next to the woman in the park, playing ball with a little boy with striking blue eyes. Nico's eyes? She still tried to deny it, tried to find another explanation for the resemblance. Who was the woman? Did Nico have an affair? Were they simply relatives? But no, that couldn't be. He would have admitted knowing them. No, there was something else, something so sinister that Anna recoiled from the thought.

Anna wanted to call Nico, wanted to confront him, wanted him to explain, to tell her it was a misunderstanding. But she couldn't, not before she had found out the truth on her own. As if in trance, Anna walked into Nico's office. She sat on his chair, staring at the desk. Slowly, she began to open drawers and searching through his papers. She didn't know what she was looking for. She was afraid of what she might find. The first two drawers didn't contain anything suspicious, just papers from work. She tried to open the bottom drawer, but it seemed stuck. Perhaps it was locked but she couldn't find a key anywhere in the desk.

"Oh, Nico," she whispered. "What's going on?" She couldn't lose her head now. She needed to think clearly.

Anna went into the kitchen and searched through the toolbox for something to open the stuck drawer. She pulled out a screwdriver. Back in the office, she shoved the blade of the screwdriver into the thin slot between the drawer and the frame of the desk. She tried several times until she heard a cracking sound and the drawer finally gave. A thin splinter of wood fell to the floor. She dropped the screwdriver and pulled out the drawer.

It was full of papers and envelopes. Anna grabbed the whole pile and put it on the desk. Her hands were shaking as she lifted each envelope, emptying its contents onto the desk. There was a feeling of relief for each envelope that didn't contain anything suspicious, but it was immediately replaced by fear of what she would find when she opened the next one.

"Nothing," Anna murmured as she reached the bottom of the pile. She grabbed the pile of papers and wanted to put it back into the drawer when she saw something white showing through a thin crack at the bottom of the drawer. She stuck the blade of the screwdriver into the crack and lifted the bottom. Underneath was another envelope. It was sealed.

Anna's heart picked up speed again. She sliced the envelope open. A bunch of papers and pictures fell onto the desk. Anna knew immediately that what she had found would turn her life upside down.

There was only one photo of the woman. She was somewhat younger but it was clearly her, the same long dark hair and intense black eyes. There weren't any photos of the older boy and girl, but there were many of the little boy with the blue eyes. There were pictures of him at different ages. One of them was of Nico holding him. It could have been right after the boy was born.

Anna lifted one of the papers from the pile. It was a document, written in Spanish. Anna's heart stopped. She was barely able to read it, her hands trembled so much. The *acta de matrimonio*, or marriage license, stated that Nicolas Foster and a Carmen Maria Calderón were married in Guadalajara, Mexico, two years before Anna and Nico had met and four years before their own wedding. There were the names of witnesses and a bunch of legalese Anna didn't understand.

This couldn't be true. Anna started to feel sick. She quickly paged through the rest of the documents. She found a birth certificate belonging to the little boy. He was born four years after Nico and Anna had gotten married. The parents were listed as Nicolas and Carmen. There was nothing about the older children.

Anna stared at the floor. Everything was blurry and she noticed only now that she was crying. She dropped the papers and the photos.

"No," she cried out again and again. "No. No. No."

Anna barely had time to rush to the bathroom. She knelt in front of the toilet, retching, but she wasn't able to throw up. After a while, the retching stopped. Anna got up, rinsed her mouth, and went back to Nico's office. She sat at his desk and stared at their wedding photo. Nico was wearing a tux and smiled his lopsided smile. Anna's floor-length dress was made of light-green silk. They looked like the perfect couple.

Overwhelmed by a spurt of fury, Anna screamed and knocked the photo off the desk. It fell to the floor. The sound of shattered glass deflated her anger. She knelt next to the broken picture, her arms crossed in front of her chest, her hands pressed into her armpits. Painful sobs racked her body.

After what seemed to her a long time, her knees began to hurt. She got up from the floor and walked aimlessly around the apartment, not knowing what to do. She picked up the phone and called Susan. Unable to explain, she kept on crying.

Twenty minutes later, she heard knocks on the door. She opened and fell into Susan's arms.

Susan and Anna were sitting on the sofa, sipping tea. Susan stared at the documents and the photos in front of her.

"You're sure there is no divorce certificate?" Susan took Anna's hand.

Anna shook her head. "I can't find one. And even if there was one, Nico never told me he was married. He lied to me the whole time." Her voice broke again. She sobbed quietly.

"And look at the birth certificate of the little boy," she continued. "He was born four years after we were married. Nico must have carried on the relationship the whole time. . . . Married? Susan, we may not even be married." Anna started to cry again.

"That's why we need to talk to George," Susan said. "We need a lawyer. He'll be back tomorrow. When is Nico supposed to come back?"

"In two days. Oh Susan, what am I going to do? He's going to call me tomorrow. What am I going to say? I can't talk to him. I don't even know who he is anymore. I can't stay here. Everything here reminds me of him."

Sunday evening at Susan's home, Anna sat on the bed in the guest room, staring at the half-empty overnight bag in front of her. She had only packed a few clothes and underwear. She pulled out a pair of jeans, then dropped it back into the bag. Finally, Susan helped her unpack and got her settled.

Anna barely touched the light dinner Susan prepared. She drank a glass of wine without tasting it. They watched the news on TV but nothing registered in Anna's mind. Every once in a while, she broke down crying again. Susan kept hugging her.

In spite of the fact that she was exhausted, Anna couldn't fall asleep. She spent most of the night crying. In the morning, her face and eyes were swollen and she was deathly pale.

Susan called the library. Anna wouldn't be in for a few days, she had the flu, she told Anna's boss. She also called Nico. Anna was sitting next to her, her hands clasped tight, her fingers bloodless and white. She listened to Susan tell Nico that Anna was ill and wouldn't be able to pick him up at the airport. She was staying with them. No, it wasn't anything serious, just the flu. Of course, Nico wanted to talk to Anna.

"She's asleep right now. She'll call you later. She says hello. I can pick you up at the airport." Susan rolled her eyes and looked at Anna.

Anna's eyes welled up. She pressed her hand to her mouth, stifling a sob. She wanted to talk to him so badly. She was hoping against all hope that whatever she had discovered over the past couple of days was a big misunderstanding, that it wasn't true. Whenever she thought of Nico and their life together, her heart constricted in pain. She went over the past ten years she had known him in her mind again and again, searching for clues, searching for anything that would have pointed to the fact that her husband—or whatever he was to her—had lived a double life.

"Thank God, he turned down my offer to pick him up," Susan said to Anna after she hung up the phone. "I don't think I could've looked him in the eyes."

Chapter 27

George examined each document and photo carefully, occasionally brushing his hand over his short brown hair. After what seemed to Anna an inordinate amount of time, he looked up and sighed.

"I don't know what to say, Anna. This is incredible. Unfortunately, bigamy is more common than we assume. That doesn't make it any less painful." George put his elbows on the table and leaned his face into his hands. Then he looked up again.

"What can we do?" Susan asked.

George shrugged. "Well, for one thing, bigamy is a class E felony in New York. If convicted, Nico could be fined or he could even go to prison."

"Stop being the lawyer, George," Susan said in an exasperated tone. "Anna is in pain."

"I know. Sorry. Besides, that's not the point now. The question is: Why? Why did he do it? Why didn't he tell you he was married? Why didn't he get a divorce? I mean, we just have to ask him." George wrinkled his forehead. "Of course, that doesn't change the fact that he betrayed you, but perhaps his answer will shed some light—

"Wait a minute." He peered at Anna. "What was his legal status when you first met him?"

"What do you mean?" Anna asked.

"Did he have a green card? A visa?"

"He was here on a student visa. He got his green card after we were married. . . . You don't mean to say he married me, because . . . no, that couldn't be." Anna covered her eyes with her hands. "I don't know what to think anymore."

Susan and George suggested that George would be the one to confront Nico and talk to him first. They were close friends and perhaps a talk between men would shed some light on the situation.

Anna shook her head. "No, I have to talk to him first. He'll know that I know," she said, remembering that she left the desk drawer open and the screwdriver on the floor. "He'll see right away that the envelope with the documents is missing. Unless he comes here first. Besides, I'm his wife; he has to answer to me." Tears welled up in her eyes again. "That's not even true; I may not be his legal wife."

"Well, we really don't know and, in spite of all the evidence, we shouldn't jump to conclusions," George said. "Nico may be divorced and the proof may just not be among the papers you found."

"But he had a child with the woman after we were married. And why didn't he tell me he was married?"

"Well, whatever way you turn it, there's simply no excuse for what Nico did." Susan sounded angry. "Let's face it. He's an adulterer and most likely a bigamist. I'm sorry, Anna, I don't mean to hurt you." Susan put her arm around Anna.

Anna shook her head. "You couldn't hurt me any more than Nico already did. No matter what the real truth is, one thing is for sure. He betrayed me. He's been lying to me for years. How can I ever trust him again?" her voice broke.

Chapter 28

Anna had woken up after a few hours of restless sleep. Like the nights before, the first thought after waking up was of Nico. Unwilling to face the harsh light of reality, she closed her eyes again. The tears soaking into the pillow and the pain in her chest, however, kept sleep at bay. She got up and sat in the easy chair next to the window. The clock on the night table showed two o'clock in the morning. Longing for warmth, she wrapped her robe around her. The leaves on the two birches in the front yard shimmered in the diffuse light of an almost-full moon.

This was the third night after the shocking discovery. Anna had spent hours in front of the window, trying to come to terms with her broken life. How could she have been so blind? It was almost impossible to believe. The man with whom she had had a close and intimate relationship for years had become a complete stranger overnight.

Was there any kind of justification for Nico's actions, anything she could understand and perhaps forgive? Or had he simply used her all these years to be able to stay in the United States? It was just not possible. Not even the best actor in the world could have faked the kind of love and passion she had felt in him. Sure, there had been times when he had been moody or distant. They had had their disagreements, but that happened in every relationship. Nothing she could remember would have pointed to the fact that her husband had lived a secret double life.

And now? What was going to happen now? Anna stared out the window. The trees in the front yard slowly came into focus in the hazy gray of dawn. Soon, patches of crimson, orange, and purple would begin to show behind the buildings, the vibrant colors of a sunrise in a smog-filled city.

Was there any hope left for them? In between fits of rage and despair, there were moments where she longed for Nico with all her heart. She still loved him. If he told her it was her he really loved, if he decided to get a divorce from his first wife, she thought she would be able to forgive him. She would even welcome his children. Anna loved children and she would love Nico's children. They could stay with them during vacation and —

Anna shook her head. The moments of hope were drowned by doubts and misery again. How could she have any expectations? Nico wasn't someone she knew anymore. She was doomed to wait and the waiting was almost unbearable. Completely exhausted, she slipped off her robe and went back to bed, falling asleep almost instantly.

In her dream, she was walking through a forest, feeling Nico's arm around her. She tried to turn around and look at him, but for some reason she wasn't able to move her head sideways. She was forced to walk ahead, assuming it was Nico behind her. There was a terrible noise, as if someone was felling trees. She shot up in bed. The room was bathed in full sunlight. She looked at the clock. It was eleven in the morning.

Someone was knocking at her door. "Yes," she said. She was still half asleep. Her voice sounded hoarse.

"Anna." Susan opened the door. Her face was pale. "Anna. The news . . ."

"What is it?" Anna stared at Susan's terror-stricken face.

143

"Oh, Anna." Susan sat on the bed and put her arm around her.

"What's the matter?" Anna yelled. She jumped out of bed and held on to the headboard, feeling dizzy.

"Are you sure Nico was supposed to come on today's flight?"

"Yes. Why?"

"Anna, I don't want to scare you. Maybe there is more than one flight per day."

Anna was filled with dread. "No, there's only one a day with that particular airline."

"Anna." Susan held her tight. "The plane from Mexico went down. They just announced it on the news. They don't think there were any survivors."

Anna slowly emerged from the darkness. She was lying on the bed. Susan sat next to her, stroking her forehead and her hair. "Anna?"

Anna tried to sit up. Susan held her down. "Just relax. You fainted. George called the doctor."

Anna shook her head. "I don't need a doctor." She sat up and began to tremble violently.

Susan held her. "Yes, you do."

The following few days were a blur of events. Anna lived through them barely conscious. She felt strangely removed from all the action around her. Her tear ducts seemed to have dried out. She couldn't cry, she wasn't able to think clearly. There was a constant pain in her chest and she occasionally wondered if she had one of those silent heart attacks she had read about.

There were visits and phone calls from airline representatives, calls and visits from friends who had heard, a call from Nico's employer, and calls from people from the Guadalajara office. Susan and George answered most of the calls and said that Anna would call back as soon as she was able to.

Anna called her mother in Switzerland. Her mother wanted to fly to New York right away but Anna told her not to. Her mother was a good person but rather bossy and domineering and she would be completely outraged at Nico's double life. Anna needed peace and quiet now and not the additional uproar her well-intentioned mother would certainly create.

The second phone call Anna made was to England to inform Nico's father. She didn't have the heart to call him directly, so she called his sister, Nico's aunt. Anna felt that someone needed to give him the news in person and stay with him.

Anna had met Richard a couple of times before. He had attended their wedding in New York and they had visited him once in England. He was a somewhat withdrawn but kind person and he and Anna had gotten along really well. They had talked on the phone occasionally.

A grief-stricken Richard called Anna right after he had received the news. He, too, offered to help her but she told him that she had all the help she needed. He insisted on flying to New York and Anna couldn't dissuade him. She invited him to stay in their apartment. She was convinced Richard didn't know anything of Nico's marriage to the Mexican woman. She hated the thought of having to tell him. At the same time, it might be a relief to be able to talk about it with someone who had known Nico from childhood. Perhaps he could shed some light on his past.

"What about the funeral?" Richard asked.

Anna sighed. She didn't know what to tell him. *I don't know yet how to bury a husband who might not even be my husband.* "There's going to be a memorial service for the victims in Mexico. That's all I know right now. The body . . ." She couldn't verbalize the fact that there probably would not be a body. "We'll talk about it when you get here," she said.

Anna and Susan were sitting in the living room, trying to compose a list of things that needed to be done. George offered to go to Mexico to take care of as many of the legal and business matters as he could. Anna had given him the power of attorney.

The day before, Gloria, the receptionist at the office in Mexico, had called. During the few times Anna had stayed in Guadalajara, Gloria and she had become friends. She also had been the first one to call right after the plane crash to express her condolences and to offer her help. Now, she called with "a strange piece of news," as she put it.

"I don't know how to tell you this," Gloria said. "We found some papers in Nico's desk. One of them was a life-insurance policy." Gloria hesitated. Anna could hear her sigh. "The name of the beneficiary, however, is a certain Carmen Maria Calderón. This is very odd. We thought that perhaps Nico had been married before and had forgotten to change the name of the beneficiary. We weren't aware of a former marriage and we don't know what the legal ramifications are. Do you know anything about this? I'm sorry to have to bother you with something like this."

"Yes. I know," Anna said in a monotone voice. "I just found out a few days ago. It was such a shock. Obviously, Nico was already married when we got married. I don't know what to tell you and what it all means. But I'm pretty certain that our marriage is void." Anna's voice cracked.

146

"Oh my God, how terrible. I can't believe it."

"Neither can I. But listen, a friend of mine, who is a lawyer and knows a little bit about Mexican law, is flying to Guadalajara in a couple of days. He has my authorization to take care of all the legal stuff. I may have to come down as well. But right now, I don't have the strength." Anna's head ached and she felt all life drain out of her.

"I understand. And if I or the other people in the office can do anything to help, please call us. Nico was a most valuable architect. We're all heartbroken. And now this."

"I know. Well, thanks for everything. I'll talk to you later."

Anna felt as if she had died as well. The doctor had given her tranquilizers but she didn't take them. She was numb without them. She couldn't think straight, she felt empty, and, what was worse, she couldn't truly mourn. She was torn between sorrow and anger.

"I have no closure," Anna said to Susan. "I'll never know the truth. I'll never know why. Why did Nico marry me? I feel as if the past years with him were just a dream . . . or a lie, one big huge lie. How can I mourn a man whom I don't know anymore?"

"You have to trust your feelings, Anna." Susan hugged her. "Nico *must* have loved you. You couldn't have lived with him and not feel it. Perhaps he married you for the wrong reason, but he loved you nevertheless."

"Trust my feelings? How can I, after having been so wrong?"

"Do you think it would help if you went to see his . . . first wife?"

"I thought about it. But what good would it do? What could I say to her? 'Did you know your husband was married twice?' I can't imagine she knew. I couldn't do that to her or to the children. It's not their fault that their father was a liar and a cheat." Anna shook her head. "No, I just have to live with it and try to somehow get over it." A hard sob escaped her, and for the first time in days she cried. The painful sobs, however, brought no relief.

Anna moved back to her apartment. She wanted to prepare for the arrival of Nico's father. Susan came by every day. Other friends dropped by to express their condolences. Anna and Susan decided to have a memorial service at the church in which Nico and Anna had gotten married.

"I don't care what anybody says; to me you were his wife," Susan said. "And in spite of what he did, he was our friend. Perhaps having a small memorial will help all of us."

Anna agreed. "Yes, you're right. Besides, we need to do something for his father."

The memorial service was short. After the ceremony, people came up to Anna to shake hands and express their condolences. Anna tried to put on the best front possible, playing the grieving widow, although she couldn't really mourn. Her sorrow was tinged with a deep sense of lost identity. For over seven years she had lived an unreal life next to a husband who wasn't her husband. And now he was just simply gone, no good-bye, no explanation, no closure.

Chapter 29

Anna glanced at the clock. "Two o'clock, again." She sighed and took a sip of the now-cold coffee. "I told you it was going to be a long story."

Jonas swallowed and touched her arm. "I'm so sorry. This is incredible. I don't even know what to say."

Anna gave a weak smile. "Yeah, sometimes I still can't believe it, even after all this time."

"Did you ever find out anything from Nico's father?" Jonas asked.

Anna shook her head. "He was as shocked as I was. He knew that Nico had had a girlfriend in Mexico but he thought they had broken up before he moved to the United States. He never mentioned the marriage, the children."

"That must have been hard for him, too. To find out that your son is a notorious liar. There must be some explanation?" Jonas gave Anna a cautious look. "You probably don't want to deal with it anymore."

"I had to just go on with my life. But I know that something died in me at that time." Her voice was solemn. "I never quite trusted anybody again . . . men, I mean."

"I can imagine. Did you . . . did you have any relationships after that?" Jonas asked.

Anna shrugged. "Nothing steady or serious. I tried but whenever it got more involved, I pulled back." She paused. "And now, that's okay. I enjoy being with men . . . as friends."

Jonas nodded. "I understand."

Jonas decided to drive home in spite of the late hour. Anna invited him to stay but he knew she had to get up the next morning to pick up Karla from her spring vacation in the Ticino. And Jonas felt he needed to be alone to digest all he had heard over the past few hours. Her story had unsettled him.

At home, he made himself a cup of herbal tea and added a shot of brandy. He stood by the window and gazed into the night without really registering anything.

Now he understood why Anna often appeared withdrawn and distant. But tonight, she had opened up and it had stirred something in him. He couldn't stop thinking about her. The veneer of the strong, aloof, and slightly cold woman had crumbled, exposing her vulnerable inner self.

It had begun earlier in the evening. Her embarrassment about her shoes and outfit and the relaxed conversation at dinner, her tears during the concert had stirred something in him. And when she told him the story of her marriage and the betrayal, he could see in her the young woman in love, full of life and hope, and Jonas was overwhelmed by the desire to hug and kiss her. Just then, however, Anna—as if she had felt the shift in his mood—withdrew into her cautious, remote personality again. And Jonas, too, assumed his former role as compassionate friend.

However, something had changed. For the first time since Eva's death Jonas felt he could fall in love again. Anna was attractive in an unconventional way. She had a good figure, beautiful thick hair, and intense blue-gray eyes. When she smiled—which didn't happen all that often—the slightly harsh features of her face softened. At such moments, Jonas was always startled at how pretty she was. From a conversation they had had, he figured she must be in her late thirties or early forties. Jonas was fifty-three. *I'd be robbing the cradle.* He chuckled, then shook his head.

It was absurd to even think about her that way. There was no chance Anna would return his feelings. She obviously had no interest in a romantic relationship, and who could blame her?

Besides, he told himself, if things didn't work out between them, it might endanger his involvement with Karla. And right now, working with her, helping her a little, and keeping Anna as a friend seemed more important.

Jonas gazed outside, where dawn began to spread. The lake was still dark, a blackish indigo-blue, but in the distance the first glimmers of purple and gold lit up the horizon.

Now, his own bouts of jealousy over Eva seemed even more ridiculous to him. He never had to face the kind of betrayal Anna had experienced. In fact, he was the one who had betrayed Eva. Not with another woman but by withholding a sinister secret from her, a secret in his family's past, which may have affected Eva's Jewish family in a cruel and destructive way. He had been too much of a coward to tell her about the brother of his mother, his uncle Werner, the hater of Jews.

When Jonas was seven years old, he and his parents lived in Zurich. It was two years after the Second World War.

Jonas remembered Uncle Werner as a somewhat crude but funny man. He liked to spend time with him because Uncle Werner brought him presents and played with him. Sometimes, he got to spend a weekend with his uncle who lived in a small village near Zurich.

Uncle Werner let him get away with things his parents wouldn't. He got to stay up later than at home, listen to the radio until late at night, and drink sodas. Uncle Werner even let him suck some foam off his beer mug. And Uncle Werner loved to tell stories, mainly about the war, when Werner was stationed at the border between Germany and Switzerland, defending the "homeland" as he put it.

Uncle Werner was a bachelor, because "who would want such a bigot for a husband?" Jonas heard his mother say once.

"What's a bigot?" Jonas asked.

"Someone who is prejudiced; someone who dislikes people from a different race or religion," his mother said in that curt voice, which meant she wouldn't go into any details.

Jonas knew that Uncle Werner and his mother didn't get along. They argued a lot. He also picked up scraps of conversation between his mother and father.

"I don't understand what happened to Werner that made him so hateful. I remember him as a quiet and somewhat lonely boy, who didn't quite fit in. There were always some problems at home, in school, but nothing that explained his later development," Jonas's mother said.

His father shook his head. "He fell in with a bad lot, a bunch of Nazi sympathizers. And don't forget. It was wartime. People tried to survive and did the best they could. Werner was in charge of part of the border. He had to follow orders."

"You know as well as I do that Werner did more than just follow orders."

"It's easy for us to say in retrospect. How would we have acted, had it been us? We don't know."

"You heard some of his remarks about Jews. It's shameful." Jonas's mother raised her voice, something she rarely did. She got up and left the room, closing the door more forcefully than necessary.

Jonas's father winked at Jonas. "Your mother is a good person. She feels very strongly about what's right or wrong."

An Uncommon Family

Jonas didn't understand his mother's anger, but he knew it had something to do with the war. And Jonas liked the war games Uncle Werner played with him in the forest behind his home. Uncle Werner told him he had to keep their games secret. Jonas felt proud that his uncle trusted him with a secret.

Jonas and Werner were soldiers defending the country. They stood guard at the "border," with large thick sticks, their machine guns. Every once in a while Werner would look around to make sure that nobody saw him, then lifted his stick and shouted, "Stay back, you dirty Jew." He made shotgun noises, "Ta, ta, ta, ta."

And Jonas imitated him. "Dirty Jews, go back. Ta, ta, ta."

"Kill them all," Werner hissed under his breath.

It was only later, when Jonas became friends with Jakob, a Jewish boy in school, that he began to doubt Werner's version of things. He realized that it wasn't the Jews who were the enemy but the Nazis. They had killed the Jews. They had killed part of Jakob's family, who had done nothing wrong.

Why then did Uncle Werner tell him such stories? Why did they play "Killing Jews"?

So the following time, he was alone with Uncle Werner, he asked him. "What did you do during the war, Uncle Werner?" His mother was in the kitchen preparing the meal, and his father had gone to get a bottle of wine from the cellar.

Uncle Werner squinted his small eyes, which made him look mean. "I bet your mother told you all kinds of bad things about me."

Jonas shook his head. "No."

"Oh well. She doesn't understand. She's just too naive." Uncle Werner picked up his mug of beer and took a large swig. Then he put it down on the table with a bang.

"These were rough times, Jonas. All the able-bodied Swiss men were at the border. We were defending our country. Always remember that, Jonas."

Uncle Werner patted Jonas's arm. "Always remember your heritage, Jonas. You are a good Swiss boy." He took another swig from his beer mug. Jonas watched the bulge in his throat as he swallowed and burped. Werner glanced over his shoulder toward the door to the kitchen. Jonas heard his mother and father talking and the clatter of dishes as his mother prepared the meal.

Werner narrowed his eyes and bent his head toward Jonas. A cloud of beer breath hit Jonas's face. "What I tell you now you don't have to repeat to your parents, okay? Your mother and father and I don't see eye to eye on this."

Jonas nodded.

"We defended our country from the Nazis. But we also prevented those dirty Jews from infiltrating our land."

"Why were they dirty?" Jonas stared at Uncle Werner. Jakob wasn't dirty. In fact, he was always well dressed and clean.

Werner waved his hand and spoke in a loud voice. "They stink of money. That's all they ever think about. Making money and hoarding it. A bunch of misers and money-grubbing bastards. Too bad Hitler didn't manage to get rid of all of them."

"Jakob doesn't stink," Jonas said, feeling anger rise in him and his eyes fill with tears. All of a sudden, he realized that something was wrong with the man whom he had admired. The games he had played with him—shooting Jews—now seemed mean. And Jonas was ashamed that he had enjoyed playing them. If Jakob knew—

"Werner!" His mother's voice interrupted Jonas's thoughts. She was at the door, a plate of food in her hands.

She turned around and walked back into the kitchen. When she came back without the plate, her face was red and she was trembling.

"I told you many times not to talk like that. You're polluting Jonas with your sick mind."

Uncle Werner lifted his hands in a defensive gesture. "I'm just telling him the truth."

"No, that's not the truth. These are lies, hateful lies, and I'm ashamed of you being my brother, Werner. I want you to leave, right now."

"Mathilde, calm down." Jonas's father put his hand on her shoulder. But his mother pushed him away.

Jonas saw tears in his mother's eyes. "Please, Werner, just leave. There's no lunch. I'm not hungry anymore." She left the living room and Jonas heard her sob in the kitchen.

Jonas's father shrugged and turned to Werner. "She'll calm down. But I hope you learned your lesson. Don't ever talk to my son like this again."

Werner opened his mouth to say something, then closed it again, shook his head, and got up and left.

Jonas, shocked at his uncle's hateful words and his mother's outburst, went into the kitchen. His mother was standing at the window, looking out. She seemed to have stopped crying.

"Mom?"

His mother turned around and brushed the tears from her face. She held her hands out to Jonas. "Come here, honey."

Jonas went up to her and buried his face in her apron. It smelled of food, a mixture of roasted pork and vegetables. He realized he was hungry. Jonas glanced at his mother's face. "Is there no lunch today?"

His mother gave a quick smile. "Don't worry. We'll eat." Then she put her hand under his chin and looked at him with a serious face. "Don't believe anything Uncle Werner tells you. It's not true." She sighed. "He is my brother, but he is a sick man. I don't know what happened to him."

From that day on, Jonas's family and Uncle Werner barely saw each other anymore. Jonas, feeling guilty for his uncle and his own involvement in the war games, tried to be extra kind to Jakob. Soon, he forgot the incident until many years later when his uncle's words and his role during the war would come to haunt him.

PART FOUR: OF LOVE AND LIES

Chapter 30

Karla and Maja were sitting on a stone bench in the school-yard. It was loud and busy during the first week after summer vacation. Kids exchanged stories about their vacation and teenagers checked out each other's sun tans and new clothes.

Although Karla didn't worry too much about fashion yet, she did change her top three times in the morning. She tried to find the perfect color match for her new pair of khaki pants. She finally picked a green-and-red patterned blouse with a few splashes of the same light brown as her pants. Anna had rolled her eyes as Karla darted out the door. She almost didn't make it in time to her first class.

Karla and Maja had spent three weeks of their vacation with Lena and her new husband, Luigi, in the Vallemaggia in the south of the country. They had helped Luigi, who was a mountain farmer, take care of the sheep and goats up in the Alps. It had been a fun time and Karla had felt like Heidi in the children's novel she had read. She and Maja had learned how to milk goats and had helped a farmer make cheese.

Now, school was in session again. It was late August and Karla tried to get used to the daily routine of getting up early, homework, and new subjects in school.

A few boys were playing soccer nearby. They were a couple of years older than Karla and Maja. Karla was almost ten and Maja was eleven. The boys played rough and were screaming and cursing. One of them tossed the ball at Maja, but only hit the corner of the bench. The ball bounced back and ended up in the ditch.

His friends taunted him as he went to fetch the ball. He bounced it up and down hard, edging closer to the girls. He scanned the schoolyard, checking if a teacher was nearby, then faced Maja. "Hey you, dirty Serb," he yelled at her. He was tall and somewhat overweight, with a fleshy face and mean-looking eyes. He was known for his bullying and ended up in the principal's office quite a lot.

Maja's face darkened. "I'm not a Serb, you idiot. I'm Croatian. Don't you know the difference?"

"All the same to me," he said. "Damn foreigners."

"It's not the same, you dummy," Maja shouted.

Karla put her hand on Maja's shoulder. "Ignore him. He just wants to pick a fight."

The kid scowled at her. "Call me 'dummy' one more time and I'll kill you."

Karla was worried that Maja would make things worse. She was a feisty girl, one who didn't shy away from a fight. She stood up. "Dummy," she repeated in a taunting tone.

Wilhelm scrunched his face, picked up a stone that happened to lie nearby, and tossed it a Maja. She ducked, but the stone hit her on the forehead, leaving a gash. Blood oozed from her wound, sliding in a thin line down her face. She sat down stunned, holding her head. When she saw the blood on her hand, she started to cry. Karla ripped her handkerchief out of her pocket and put it on Maja's forehead, trying to halt the bleeding.

All noise stopped on the schoolyard. The kids stood around and stared at Maja, who wept silently. Wilhelm stood still with his hands deep in his pockets, looking subdued.

When Karla saw Maja's miserable face and the pain in her eyes, something snapped in her. Her fear and pity for her

160

friend turned to rage. She got up and faced Wilhelm. "You're an evil, cruel jerk," she shouted.

Wilhelm shrugged. "She started it."

"That's not true. You insulted her." Karla, not knowing what came over her, charged at him.

He took a step back and his foot caught on a small branch lying on the ground and he stumbled and fell. The next thing Karla knew was that she was on top of him, hammering his chest and face with her fists.

"What is going on here?" Karla heard a teacher's voice. Someone grabbed her by the shoulder and yanked her up. "What do you think you're doing?"

"He threw a stone at Maja," Karla yelled. Realizing she was speaking to a person of authority, she swallowed and stared at the teacher's angry face.

The school nurse took care of Maja's wound. Wilhelm and Karla were sent to the principal's office. Wilhelm was suspended for a few days. He received a warning that next time he was caught bullying, he would be expelled from school. His parents were going to be informed of the incident.

"Now to you." The principal gave Karla a stern look after Wilhelm was dismissed. He was a tall man with a brown crew cut and sharp gray eyes. He reminded Karla of a general in the army and she was always a little afraid of him. She looked down and stared at her shoes.

"I appreciate the fact that you tried to help your friend," the principal said in a gentler tone. "However, beating someone up is not the way to deal with a problem. Next time something like this happens, you tell a teacher about it and let him or her deal with it. Is that clear?"

Karla lifted her head and nodded. She thought she detected a glimmer of humor in the man's eyes. Then his face became serious again.

"And so you won't forget, you're going to write 'Hitting is not the solution' fifty times and hand it in to your teacher tomorrow. Okay?" He squinted his eyes. "Is that scratch on your face from the fight?"

Karla touched her cheek. There was a faint burning sensation. Wilhelm must have scratched her, trying to defend himself. "I guess so," she said.

"Make sure the school nurse or your moth— . . . I mean, your aunt cleanses it so it doesn't get infected, all right?"

"Yes, thanks," Karla whispered.

The principal looked through the window at the courtyard. "I think your friend is waiting for you." He nodded at the door. "You can leave now."

Outside, Maja was sitting on a bench. She had a large Band-Aid on her forehead. "I didn't need stitches," she said as Karla came outside. She got up and gave her a hug. "Thanks. Are you in trouble now?"

Karla glanced back at the principal's office. He was standing at the window, watching them, a touch of a smile on his lips.

"Just a little bit," Karla said and told Maja about the assignment.

Chapter 31

"What happened to your face?" Jonas asked as Karla stepped into the hallway, carrying her art portfolio. Her long dark hair was tied into French braids and there was a whiff of lavender, perhaps from a perfume or body lotion. *She's growing up.* The only small blemish on her beautiful face was a faint scratch all the way across her left cheek.

Karla put her portfolio down and checked herself in the mirror. "I got into a fight with a guy at school," she said.

"You did what?" Jonas raised his eyebrows in astonishment. He couldn't imagine Karla in a fight with anyone, let alone a boy.

Karla grinned and told him of the incident with Maja and Wilhelm a few days before. Jonas burst out laughing and slapped his thigh. "I would've loved to see that. You actually pounded him? I guess that taught him a lesson."

"He's become a little nicer. At least, he keeps away from Maja and me," Karla said.

"Well, I'm proud of you for standing up for your friend. Just be careful. Beating up on a bigger boy may not always go over that well. You may get more than a scratch on your face."

Jonas watched Karla unpack her things. Over the past couple of years he had been working with her, her artwork had matured and he was thinking of new ways to further her talent. "I have an idea," he said. "I received the go-ahead to paint a mural on one of the city walls with a few of my students. Would you be interested? It's a whole different kind of painting but I think you would enjoy it."

Karla gave him a thoughtful look. "I've never painted a mural, but it sounds like fun."

Jonas waved his hand. "It is. Besides, you need to be around other students more. It gets you exposed to different ways of painting and drawing."

Karla shrugged. "Cool. Can we start now? Look what I got." She lifted a new box of oil pastels up in the air and grinned at him. "Anna said she was going to end up in the poorhouse because of me." It was a box of expensive oil pastels Karla had coveted for some time.

"Not bad," Jonas said. "So what made her change her mind and buy them?"

"I helped her with her accounting and I promised to help out in the bookstore once a week after school."

"In other words, you bribed her."

"Yep," Karla said and winked at him.

While Karla was busy painting, Jonas began to work on a draft of a picture of his own. Every once in a while, he glanced at the girl. Today, it became clear to him how much she had changed over the past few years. Not only had her painting improved but she had become a happier, more open and courageous young girl. She was growing up fast. In a couple of years, she would be a teenager.

Her fight with the boy at school reminded him of his own youth. He had to admit that he hadn't been half as courageous when it came to defending a friend who was bullied by others. He was thinking of Jakob, his Jewish friend from school. Jakob came from a fairly Orthodox Jewish family. Some of the other boys had made fun of him because he wore a kippah, the Jewish cap, and went to synagogue on Saturdays.

Jonas and Jakob had been good friends, but Jonas didn't exactly go out of his way to defend Jakob when the other boys teased him. Jonas remembered an incident when someone made an insulting remark and everybody, including himself, had laughed. He stopped as soon as he saw the hurt and disappointment on Jakob's face. He told the others to shut up and leave him alone, but it was too late. He had already betrayed his friend.

Fortunately, Jakob hadn't been the kind of boy who held a grudge. They had continued to be friends. However, Jonas wondered if he had had the courage to defend him against a bunch of bullies the way Karla had done with her friend. Perhaps Karla, who had already experienced the loss of loved ones as a child, was more aware of how precious friends were—something Jonas had only learned later in life. The death of Eva had brought him closer to the people around him that he had up until then taken for granted. They hadn't been able to take away the pain, but they had saved him from the most dangerous plunge into loneliness.

Chapter 32

Jonas and Anna were sitting in front of Anna's home, drinking tea and eating a piece of what was left of Karla's birthday cake. They had celebrated her tenth birthday. Karla and Maja and a few of her other friends were having a sleepover at Anna's. The girls were lying in their sleeping bags in Karla's bedroom and had just quieted down after a lot of talking and giggling.

It was a warm summer night. The light breeze coming from the forest nearby brought the scent of pines and an occasional whiff of honeysuckle. Crickets chirped, and in a nearby tree a mockingbird gave a sample of its plagiarized tunes.

"Ten years old already, I can't believe it." Anna shook her head and poured Jonas another cup of tea.

"Yeah, time flies," Jonas said. "I remember so well when I first met her. She was lying on the ground, in tears, her knees all scraped."

"That was four years ago, almost to the day. It was in August after her sixth birthday," Anna said.

"She's come a long way since then."

Anna turned to Jonas. "You've helped her a lot, you know. I'm really grateful to you."

Jonas waved his hand in a dismissive gesture. "I may have taught her a few things about painting but she more than compensated me for that. She's my favorite student and a great kid." He cleared his throat. "I love her company . . . and yours as well. We make a good team." He hesitated and

Anna felt he wanted to say more. He lifted the teacup, then put it down without drinking.

She glanced at him. His blue eyes gazed at her with great intensity, making her heart pick up speed.

"Anna . . . I've wanted to tell you this, but . . . I guess I'm out of practice. I really enjoy being with you, and . . ." Jonas gave a quick chuckle. "I guess I should stop talking in half sentences." He became serious again. "I love you and . . . I want us to be more than friends."

Anna tried to swallow but her throat squeezed shut. When she found her voice again, it sounded unfamiliar. "Jonas," she finally said. "I enjoy being with you, too. I just don't know . . . I guess I'm afraid."

"I understand," Jonas said. "I don't need an answer today."

Anna noticed her hands were white and she realized she had clamped them together so hard that all the blood had drained out of them. She took a deep breath and relaxed them. *I act worse than a sixteen-year-old.*

Jonas cleared his throat again. "And before you decide, you should know something about me, something I'm not very proud of. I know how you feel about honesty in relationships . . . I did in a way deceive Eva once."

Anna looked at him puzzled. A wave of disappointment surged through her chest. *Not you as well?*

"Not with another woman, not like your husband did. It was more like I withheld something from her that I should have told her. But it was a kind of betrayal, too."

"Yes?" Anna stared at him, relieved that at least he hadn't cheated on his wife, but afraid of what she was going to hear.

"It's kind of a longish story, too. I once told you about an uncle I had, who was a Nazi sympathizer?"

Anna nodded.

Christa Polkinhorn

"Well, there was more to it."

Chapter 33

It was Jonas's third visit to Eva's family. They had just finished lunch and were sitting in the living room. It was a cool fall day and there was a fire burning in the fireplace. A smell of smoke, spareribs, sauerkraut, and German dumplings still lingered in the room. Eva's mother was of German origin and had prepared a typical German meal.

"Excellent but heavy," Eva's stepfather said. "This calls for an after-dinner drink." Kurt got a bottle out of the liquor cabinet and poured them all a brandy.

They sat in the living room, looking out on an apple orchard. Most of the leaves had fallen and formed a yellow carpet on the meadow. The old trees stood naked and sad looking with their gnarled branches exposed. Eva's parents lived in a small town along the Rhine River. They had a view of the river as it snaked around one of its last curves before plunging down the rocks into Europe's largest waterfall.

Somehow, perhaps because of the closeness to the German border, the conversation turned to the Second World War. Jonas knew that Eva's mother was Jewish. Eva had told him that her mother had come to Switzerland during the War and that Eva's stepfather, who had been a young soldier then, had helped her enter the country. Jonas was curious to find out how it all happened. After Sara, Eva's mother, told him the story, however, he wished he had never asked.

"I wasn't alone," Sara said in a low, sad voice. "It was spring 1940. One day, when I came home, the Nazis had taken our parents away. We didn't know where they had taken them to and there was no way we could find out. I was twenty-four and pregnant with our first child. My husband, Joshua, and my sister, Judith, and I decided we needed to leave. The Nazis could come back any minute and take us, too. It was horrible. We were so scared."

Sara's voice broke. Kurt put his hand on Sara's shoulder.

"You don't need to talk about it if it's too painful. I'm sorry; I didn't know . . ." Jonas said.

"No, it's okay," Sara continued, having recovered again. "You should know.

"We packed a few belongings and left. We lived in a small town close to the Austrian and Swiss border and decided to try to get into Switzerland. We knew it would be difficult. The border was closed. In the beginning of the war, lots of refugees made it into Switzerland. It was one of the last neutral countries that hadn't been invaded. But later, most countries, including Switzerland, set up tough restrictions against refugees. We heard of a place near Schaffhausen where people sometimes successfully crossed the border illegally.

"They called it the 'green border,' because it was one of two places where Switzerland extended north of the Rhine. You didn't need to cross the river. The river and Lake Constance were well controlled by the army and border police and the Rhine had a strong current. Some refugees tried to cross the river anyway but not many made it. But crossing the border on land was difficult as well. You had to be familiar with the area in order not to get lost."

Sara took a deep breath. "Well, we didn't have time to find out where to go. We just had a vague idea and we hoped that someone would help us. We knew there were people on both the German and Swiss sides who guided refugees along the erratic course through fields and forests.

"When we got there, we did find a man who showed us a little part of the way, but he turned back, afraid to go on. If you got caught on the Swiss side, you risked being thrown in jail for violating the law, and on the German side . . . well, I don't want to think about it."

Sara became quiet. She lowered her head and looked down at her hands. Jonas thought she didn't want to continue with the story. When Sara looked up again, there was so much pain in her eyes, Jonas felt bad for having brought the topic up in the first place.

"I was the only one who made it across and for years I asked myself, 'Why me?'" Sara's voice broke. "Of course, I knew why. It was because of the baby. God did one good thing during those horrible years." Her tone was bitter. Then she gave a resigned sigh.

"I shouldn't blame God for people's evil ways. Anyway, we were walking through one of the forests. It was late evening. We didn't dare to cross at night for fear of getting lost. At one point, we stopped and Joshua and Judith looked at the map they gave us. I stepped aside because I needed to go into the bushes. I was six months pregnant with Eva and the baby pressed on my bladder." Sara smiled at Eva through tear-filled eyes.

"Oh, Mom. Don't be sad." Eva had tears in her eyes, too, and gave Jonas an imploring look.

"Please, you really don't have to talk about it," he said. "I shouldn't have asked."

"No, no. It's all right," Sara said. "Anyway, I was just about to go back to Joshua and Judith when I heard them. Two kinds of voices calling to my husband and my sister to stop. I was paralyzed with fear. I peeked at them from behind the trees. It was two young men, a soldier and the other one wearing the uniform of the border police. I wanted to rush to help my people but I knew I couldn't do it. If we were sent back, I would not only risk my life but my child's life as well. So I stayed and watched, my knees and my whole body trembling.

"The policeman yelled at Judith and Joshua, asking them for their identification. Joshua handed over his passport. I almost fainted. I didn't realize he had it with him. He shouldn't have taken it along but I guess he forgot. All the Jews had to carry their passport in Germany. I knew right then, they were lost. The passport had the Jewish stamp in it, the *J* that identified them.

"What happened next shocked me so much, I can never forget it," Sara said. "The guy from the border police stared at Joshua and Judith and berated them. 'Go back to where you came from. We have enough of you dirty Jews already,' he yelled at them.

"I was familiar with the anti-Semitism in Germany," Sara continued. "I just didn't expect to find people like that in Switzerland."

Jonas's mouth felt dry. He cleared his throat. "What happened next?"

"The soldier tried to appease the policeman. Then they started to argue. The border policeman pulled a gun and pointed it at Joshua and Judith. He asked them to turn around and forced them to walk back toward the border.

"When I realized that he would lead them back into Germany and hand them over to the German authorities, I almost collapsed," Sara continued. "I was just about to jump up and run after them when I felt a powerful kick in my abdomen." Sara gave a quick sad smile. "My baby stopped me from doing so and saved both our lives."

"Did you . . . what happened to your family?" Jonas managed to say, his voice stuck in his throat.

Sara shook her head. "I never heard from them again." Her voice dropped to a whisper. "After the war, I found out that they both died in the concentration camp in Dachau."

Sara faced Jonas. "Later, I read that the Swiss authorities collaborated with the Germans to mark the Jewish passports with a red *J* so they would be able to tell Jewish people apart from other refugees. I guess it was in part to appease the Germans, so they wouldn't invade the country. But they did this although they knew that people were murdered by the Nazis if they were sent back.

"It took me a long time to forgive Switzerland for this. It was the many Swiss citizens and even some soldiers who helped us anyway and risked being punished." Sara put her hand on Kurt's hand and the two gazed at each other for a moment.

Jonas swallowed and looked at Eva's stepfather. "You mean . . . you were . . . ?"

Kurt smiled and nodded. "Yes, I was that soldier."

"When Judith and Joshua were taken away, I fell to the ground and trembled so hard I was afraid I was going to have a miscarriage," Sara continued. "I pressed my face to the ground and cried, trying not to make any noise. I knew the soldier was still around somewhere.

"Then I heard a voice right next to me. 'Fräulein,' someone whispered. When I looked up, there he was. 'What are you doing here? Don't you know you're not supposed to . . . Are you with them?' he asked, and stared at me shocked.

"By then, I didn't care anymore what would happen to me. I told him everything. He didn't say anything. He bent down and helped me up. He walked me out of the forest. By then, it was almost dark and I had no idea where he took me. I thought I'd end up in some Swiss jail.

173

"As it turned out, Kurt had relatives at a farm nearby. He took me to his aunt and uncle. I stayed with them through the rest of the war. I had my baby there. They were wonderful people. They made me almost forget that ugly man at the border."

Jonas stared at his hands, then lifted his head. He was tortured by a dreadful suspicion. His voice sounded labored. "Do you by any chance know the name of that border policeman?"

Sara looked at Jonas surprised, then nodded. "Yes, actually I do. It was a coincidence. When Kurt tried to silence him when he was insulting us, he called him 'Werner.' I remember because I had an uncle by the same name."

Jonas felt a jolt in his stomach. His heart pounded against his ribs, his ears were ringing. He tried to remember what his uncle had told him. He knew he had been with the border police during the war and that he had been stationed near Schaffhausen, but then again *Werner* was a common name. It could've been someone else. But what if . . . what if it had been Uncle Werner, his own flesh and blood, who had caused the death of Sara's family, of Eva's real father? And even if it hadn't been him at that time, how many other Jewish people had perhaps been murdered because of him?

Someone shook his arm. "Jonas, what's the matter with you? Why are you so pale?" Eva looked at him concerned.

Jonas shook his head and forced a smile. "Nothing," he lied. "It's just such a sad story."

Sara nodded. "The rest of it is happier, though." She touched Kurt's hand again. "While I lived with Kurt's family, Kurt came to visit as often as he was able to. Fortunately, he was stationed at the border nearby. He also kept us informed about the war. I still remember the day he told us that Germany had capitulated and that the war was over. It was one of the happiest days in my life." Sara brushed a strand of hair out of her face. She looked sad again.

"I still hoped that Joshua and Judith were alive some-where. Kurt helped me investigate. Of course, my hopes were crushed. They had become the victims of the Nazis' last desperate purge, the last attempt to rid the world of Jews."

Sara's voice had become hard and bitter again. "I was desperate. I didn't feel like living anymore. I hated the Germans for killing my family; I hated the Swiss for not preventing it."

There was a moment of silence. Jonas stared out the window, but hardly noticed the few remaining yellow autumn leaves on the trees. He felt miserable and guilty, guilty for the fact that a member of his own family may have been responsible for the tragedy.

"But I couldn't go on hating. It wasn't in my nature." Sara's face had softened again. "And so many people here had been so kind and helpful to me and after all, it wasn't their fault. And whenever I saw my little baby's smile, my heart opened up again." Sara looked at Jonas with her clear blue eyes, Eva's eyes.

"I grieved for a long time for my family, but eventually, slowly, I became a little happier again. And then, there was Kurt." Sara smiled.

Kurt cleared his throat. "I was in love with Sara for a long time. But of course I knew she was still grieving for her husband and I didn't have much hope that she would return my feelings. And I was a little scared, too. I was still in the middle of my education and I didn't know if I was ready to take on the responsibility of being a father." He laughed out loud. "But little Eva was so cute; how could I resist?"

They all laughed. Eva smiled at Jonas. His heart warmed and for the first time since Sara had begun to tell her story, Jonas was able to relax a little.

"Anyway," Sara said with a wistful smile. "We fell in love and the sad story had a happy ending after all. And I'm sorry to go on and on with my sad tale and make our guest feel uncomfortable."

"Oh, don't apologize," Jonas said. He hesitated, then turned to Kurt. "I take it you don't know what happened to that guy from the border police? Did you know him at all?"

Kurt shook his head. "No, we just happened to be on duty together that same day. I've no idea what became of him. We weren't exactly friends, if you know what I mean. Why do you ask?"

"No particular reason," Jonas lied. He took a deep breath and pushed the suspicion of his uncle's involvement in this tragedy aside. *It must be a coincidence, nothing more.*

Chapter 34

"Did you ever find out the truth?" Anna peered at Jonas after he had finished telling her the story of his uncle.

Jonas shook his head. "No." He wrinkled his forehead and gave Anna a quick glance, then stared back at the fire. Dusk was settling around them. A breeze rekindled the flames in the outdoor fireplace, flashing an intermittent pattern of light and shadows across his face. "I guess I didn't really want to know."

"Why not? Perhaps, it was a coincidence and your uncle wasn't involved? And even if he was, it wasn't your fault. You were a little kid when this happened."

Jonas shrugged. "I was just afraid and I didn't really want to know the truth. If I knew it had been him, I would've had to tell Eva. As long as it was just a suspicion, I could treat it as such. I was afraid that if I told Eva and her family, something would change between us. They would think less of me and my family. Perhaps . . . perhaps I would even lose Eva."

"So you never told her? You lived your whole life with that uncertainty? That seems to me much worse than knowing the truth, whatever the truth was. If Eva loved you, how could she have blamed you for something you had absolutely no control over, for Christ's sake? I don't get it."

Anna didn't mean to sound so harsh. She tried to squelch the anger that rose in her. She liked Jonas a lot, she had begun to love him, and now he turned out to be a weasel just like her former husband. Why were men such cowards?

"I was a coward, Anna," Jonas echoed her feelings. "There were several occasions I wanted to tell her about my suspicions." He sighed. "But the longer I waited, the more impossible it became. Time has a way of erasing everything. After a while, I hardly thought about it anymore. I had convinced myself that it wasn't my uncle but rather someone else with the same first name.

"I did once try to talk to my uncle. We had lost touch for a long time but I knew that he was quite ill. He lived in a clinic for Alzheimer's patients. My mother visited him on a regular basis. I went there once, but he was too far gone. He couldn't remember anything."

Jonas took a deep breath and said in a low voice, "And to be honest, I was glad. I didn't want to deal with it."

"Do your children know?" Anna asked.

Jonas nodded. "Yeah, I told them. They reacted the same way as you just did. They couldn't believe that I had never told Eva. Andrew said I was stupid to believe that Eva would have blamed me for having an uncle who was a Nazi . . . he also said something, which really hurt me mainly because it was true: 'How could you live with Mother for thirty years and not know her feelings better?'"

"Well, he was right," Anna burst out.

"Yes, I know. I wasn't just a coward. I was a fool." Jonas got up and walked a few steps away, then turned around. "I don't blame you for holding it against me."

"It's not that. I just wish couples could be more honest with each other. Love is based on trust, isn't it? Without trust, you can't truly love someone. How can you live a lie for years? Just like Nico." Anna tried to keep her rising anger under control.

"I don't think that's a fair comparison," Jonas said.

"Okay, maybe not, but still . . ." Anna exhaled deeply.

It was quiet for a while. They both avoided looking at each other.

Jonas cleared his throat. "I just felt you needed to know. I want our relationship to be based on honesty." He looked down at his hands, rubbing his fingers.

Anna finally faced him. "Well, that's neither here nor there, since we're not in an intimate relationship. And what happened between you and Eva has nothing to do with me." She saw the expression of hurt on Jonas's face, and tried to blunt the blow somewhat. "But I'm glad you told me. Friends need to be honest with each other."

"You're right," Jonas said in a curt voice. He glanced at his watch. "It's getting late. I better go."

Anna was upset. She didn't want the evening to end on a bad note. At the same time, she wasn't ready to absolve Jonas. She knew Jonas was a good man and she felt more deeply for him than she had felt for any man since Nico. But his story reminded her too much of her former husband's lack of honesty. It was a breach of trust, not as serious as what her husband had done, but one nevertheless. Anna tried to come to terms with what she had heard. She was confused.

Jonas picked up his jacket and gave her a cautious look. "I'll talk to you later?"

Anna wanted to say something kind. "Thanks, Jonas, for sharing. I'm sorry; I don't mean to be judgmental. I—"

"It's okay, Anna." He tried to smile but his expression looked more like a grimace. He got up and left. Anna was searching for some words of comfort, but he was already gone.

She remained seated for a while, watching as darkness descended fully around her. She gazed at the blackish-blue sky but not even the few blinking stars were able to cheer her up. Flooded by a wave of sadness, she felt her eyes tear up.

The first time she began to open her heart to a man, she was hurt again. She thought about Jonas's confession. Was she too hard on him? He had at least been honest with her. But how many other secrets did he harbor? How well did she really know him? No, she simply couldn't afford to give her heart fully to another man. The last time it had almost killed her. Why go through that again? The solitary life wasn't too bad. She had Karla and her friends. She swallowed her tears, put the tea cups and the pot on the tray, and carried it to the house. Pushing the door open with one arm, she stepped inside and shut the door behind her.

Chapter 35

Jonas caught himself speeding down the hill toward the city of Zurich. It was a thirty-minute drive to the center of the city. He slowed down, checking for possible flashing police lights farther back. Fortunately traffic was light at this hour. *Still, people shouldn't drive when they're upset*, Jonas thought.

The talk with Anna and her reaction disturbed him deeply. He had made himself vulnerable by confiding in her and admitting a mistake he made in his past. He had told her he loved her, and she had practically slapped him in the face. Then again, what did he expect? Anna was extremely sensitive when it came to deceit; no wonder, with her background. But you could hardly compare his admittedly cowardly behavior with the kind of betrayal she had to endure from her husband.

He drove through the nightly city past the main train station, then along the Limmat River toward the Bellevue plaza and the lake and up the narrow road into the old part.

"Damn it," he said through clenched teeth as he stopped his car. Someone had parked in the reserved spot in front of his place. Finding parking in Zurich was almost impossible, so illegal parking was not uncommon. Fortunately, there was a space behind Jonas's reserved one. Just as he opened the car door, a young man came rushing out of the apartment building. It was Mrs. Schatz's nephew.

"Sorry, Mr. Bergman, I thought you were gone. My aunt said you might not be back for the night, so I took the liberty to park in your spot. I'll move the car right away."

"It's okay, don't worry," Jonas said. He glanced up at the building and saw Mrs. Schatz look out the window. She waved.

Jonas gave a slight nod. *That's all I need. And of course the busybody assumed I'd stay the night with my girlfriend—some girlfriend.* He wasn't ready for a talk with his nosy neighbor. After her nephew moved the car and drove off, Jonas parked his car. He decided not to go upstairs yet, but to take a stroll along the Limmatquai, the sidewalk along the river.

The night had settled in for good. A band of whitish haze stretched along the horizon, the last reflections of the sun, which had set hours before. The city lights reflected from the water of the lake. Jonas scanned the sky toward the north, where a heap of billowy dark clouds was building. There was tension in the air as if a thunderstorm was brewing. That might be one of the reasons why Jonas had a headache, the other being his disappointing encounter with Anna.

As Jonas walked along the boardwalk, his irritation and anger slowly gave way to sadness. He couldn't deny it any longer. He was in love with Anna. They had been going out together, and he was a frequent guest at Anna's and Karla's place. Karla was old enough now to take the train alone to Zurich for her art lessons, but Anna would often accompany her, and Jonas and she would engage in lively discussions about all kinds of things. A kind of sexual energy was beginning to develop between them. He also felt that the cocoon Anna had spun around herself was beginning to become unraveled. That's why he had dared to confess his feelings for her.

Now, the walls she had built around herself had become solid again. And all because of his harebrained idea of confiding in her. Why couldn't he have let that old story rest? He had never told Eva, he had even forgotten about it, so why

182

did he have to tell Anna? He was feeling guilty, but why feel guilty toward Anna?

Jonas sometimes felt he had to live up to Anna's high standards of right and wrong. Anna tolerated no falsehood. She would occasionally peer at him with penetrating eyes, as if to dig to the bottom of his soul, uncovering a possible lie or dishonesty. It sometimes made him feel uncomfortable, as if he was hiding something, which wasn't true at all.

Jonas walked fast, not paying attention to the world around him. He was getting angry again. What right did she have? Just because some idiot betrayed her once didn't mean all men were that way. And besides, was she that perfect?

"Self-righteous cow."

A man walking by him gave Jonas a stunned look. Jonas realized he had said it out loud. *Sorry, Anna, I didn't mean that.*

He slowed down and took a deep breath. Standing by the river, he stared at the blackish-blue mass of water flowing steadily away from the lake. He felt homesick for Eva. If only she were here, if only he could talk to her one more time. He would tell her the whole story about his uncle perhaps being responsible for her father's death. She would shake her head, face him, and raise an eyebrow, the way she used to do when she felt he was behaving foolishly.

"Jonas, you're such a dingbat," she would probably say and kiss him. And he longed for a kiss, for an embrace, and more. Jonas brushed his hand across his face and it came away moist.

Chapter 36

"How come Jonas didn't spend the night?" Karla asked, shoveling a large piece of pancake into her mouth. "He said he would."

Karla and Maja were eating breakfast. Anna had made them pancakes with nuts and honey and promised to take them to a nearby pond. It was part of Karla's birthday present.

"He remembered he had something important to do in Zurich," Anna said.

Karla peered at Anna. "He didn't say anything about it yesterday."

"Well, he forgot. It can happen."

"He didn't even say good-bye," Karla said. "Did you two argue?"

"Of course not. But he didn't want to wake you up. He left late. Don't make such a big deal out of it. You'll see him in a few days when you go for your lesson." Anna's face was flushed and she seemed upset.

"Yeah, but . . . it would've been fun. He could've come swimming with us," Karla insisted.

"Maybe another time. Finish your breakfast, so we can leave," Anna said.

"What's all this talk about Jonas?" Maja was wiping the leftover honey off her plate with the last piece of her pancake. "Are you in love with the guy?" She gave Karla a mischievous look.

"Of course not," Karla said matter-of-factly. "He's much too old for me. Besides, he is in love with Anna."

Anna stared at her. "Nonsense," she said rather forcefully.

"Well, he is," Karla said.

"How would you know that?" Anna began to collect the plates.

Karla grinned at her aunt's obvious embarrassment. "I can tell. The way he sometimes looks at you. And he kisses you."

"Those are just kisses between friends. He kisses you, too."

"Yeah, but it's not the same. And he says nice things to you and then you blush." Karla giggled and Maja joined in.

"Okay, that's enough, you two. Help me clean the table and get your stuff. Ready in ten minutes or we won't go."

"I think it would be great if you married him. Then he could stay here all the time and we'd be a real family," Karla said as she picked up her plate.

"That's enough, Karla. I don't want to have this conversation right now."

"Okay, okay." Karla sighed and rolled her eyes at Maja, who kept on snickering.

Karla and Maja sat on a raft in the middle of the pond, relaxing from swimming. Karla waved at Anna, who was sitting on a towel on the lawn, reading. She looked up regularly, lifting her sunglasses and checking on the girls. Karla and Maja were both good swimmers. Karla was proud that she could swim faster than Anna, who didn't know how to do the crawl.

"Did you notice how embarrassed Anna got when I mentioned Jonas?" Karla asked Maja.

"Yep, there must be something there. I wonder if they're doing it."

"Doing what?" Karla asked with an impish smile.

"Oh, you know. Having sex?" She gave her short hair a toss.

"I don't think so," Karla said. "I would've noticed. When Jonas spends the night, he always sleeps in the guest room."

"Well, he could've moved to Anna's room during the night when you were asleep. How would you know?"

Karla shook her head. "No, they don't act that way. I wish they would. I really think it'd be neat if they got together for good. Although . . ." She hesitated. "I just couldn't imagine the two of them having sex. They seem too old."

The girls burst out laughing. Maja stretched out on the raft. "The sun feels good," she moaned.

"Yeah." Karla lay down as well.

They were quiet for a while. Karla enjoyed the sun warming her body. The air smelled fresh, with an occasional whiff of suntan lotion. A few white fluffy clouds floated across an otherwise azure blue sky. She closed her eyes, letting her thoughts drift. The quiet and peace, however, didn't last long. She felt Maja sit up again.

"Was your aunt ever married?" she asked.

Karla sat up as well. "Yes, a long time ago, but her husband died in a plane crash."

"Oh gee, what a bummer," Maja said.

"Yeah," Karla nodded. "She doesn't like to talk about it."

"And Jonas?"

"He was married, too. His wife died of cancer," Karla said.

"Jesus Christ," Maja exclaimed. "Why is everybody dying all the time?"

The two girls gave each other a wistful look. "Don't know," Karla muttered.

"We have to do something to get your aunt and Jonas together," Maja said. "They would be perfect for each other."

"Do what? They've known each other for several years and nothing has really happened. They're just friends."

"I don't know, Karla. The way your aunt reacted this morning when we were teasing her? There is more, I can feel it." Maja gave Karla a knowing smile. There was an excited glint in her eyes.

"You're crazy," Karla said. "We can't get them together."

"Let me think," Maja said. She sat with her arms propped on her knees and her head cradled in her hands. "I bet I can come up with something."

"Oh boy, we're in trouble now." Karla sighed.

Maja loved playing destiny. One time, she wrote a letter in the name of one of her older cousins who she knew was in love with a boy. She imitated her cousin's handwriting and invited him to a family party. She hoped that bringing them together would help ignite the flame in the boy. Of course, she was found out and got a severe spanking from her uncle.

"You can't do anything dumb, I won't let you." Karla was afraid of Maja's love of scheming.

"Don't worry. It doesn't have to be anything serious. They just need a little prodding."

"I'm going swimming again," Karla said, hoping to get Maja's mind off the topic. She stood up and plunged headfirst into the water. Maja followed her, and the two raced each other toward the shore.

Chapter 37

Jonas arranged his paints and filled a cup with turpentine. He opened the window of his studio to get rid of the fumes. Taking a step back, he scanned his work in progress. The large canvas depicted a man, stretched out on the ground, helpless. An oversized monstrous figure, a combination of bird and bat, hovered over him. It was a dark image with dark-red, brown, and black-bluish colors dominating the canvas.

Jonas shook his head and put the brush down. The painting was coming along well but he didn't like the emotions it expressed. It was a reflection of his momentary mood, a mixture of anger and sadness. He sighed and picked up the brush again when the phone rang. There was a familiar voice at the other end.

"Martina! What a surprise. Where are you?"

Martina was another painter who lived in Italy and was on a two-week stay in Zurich, where she had an exhibition in one of the galleries. Jonas and Martina had been friends for many years. She had been the most supportive person during the time he was desperate and grieving for Eva. Eventually, they had eased into a comfortable, uncommitted love relationship.

An unconventional and open-minded woman, Martina had no interest in getting married or even having a close relationship. She had been exactly what Jonas needed at the time, someone he could talk to, who fulfilled his physical needs, and who took away the sharp edge of his loneliness.

And she had made no demands on him. "Don't worry about it," she used to say when Jonas apologized for always talking about his dead wife when they were together. "That's what friends are for."

Later, when Jonas felt a little better again, they would get together off and on whenever Martina was in town. Jonas knew she had other boyfriends; she made no secret of it. The last time she had come for a visit was a year before.

When he heard her cheerful voice, his mood, which had been in the dumps since his last encounter with Anna, improved at once. They decided to have dinner together.

Martina came to his place for an aperitif. When she entered the apartment, it was like a fresh breeze blowing in from the outside. She was a tall woman, a little on the stout side but well-proportioned with wide hips and an ample bosom.

It was a balmy Indian summer evening after a warm day. They sat on the sofa next to the open window, admiring the sunset. The sky blazed with crimson, orange, and yellow shades. They caught up on what had been happening. Martina had an opening at a gallery in town and Jonas showed her his latest paintings.

"You're different, Jonas," Martina said at one point. "You seem preoccupied, kind of absent."

"Really?" Jonas smiled and took another sip of his whiskey. "I'm sorry. I don't mean to be."

"What's going on? Let me think." Martina gave him an impish look. "You're in love."

Jonas grinned. "Well, close."

"What do you mean 'close'? You either are or you're not."

Jonas wrinkled his forehead and sighed. "I'm falling in love with someone who probably won't return my feelings."

"What a drag," Martina said.

"I'm sorry, Martina. Here I haven't seen you in ages and all I can do is burden you once again with my problems about another woman. You deserve better."

Martina gave one of her pearly laughs. "I don't mind being your confidante, even if you want to talk about another woman. And if you told me you found the woman of your dreams, I'd be happy for you."

"I don't know if you could call her the 'woman of my dreams.' Right now, she's rather the 'bane of my existence.'"

"Well, let's go to dinner and you can tell me all about her."

They had dinner at an elegant restaurant along the lake. After sitting down at the window, Jonas remembered that this was the restaurant he had invited Anna to when they went to hear *Cavalleria Rusticana*.

Sitting opposite his cheerful, vivacious friend, who prattled on about all kinds of things, Jonas wondered why he had to fall in love with that cold, distant woman Anna. Why couldn't it be someone like Martina? But he knew, of course, that a relationship with Martina was impossible. She was as unpredictable as the southern wind, blowing in and out of his existence. No, he was too old for that kind of youthful, uncommitted, off-and-on love affair. However, what Martina lacked in severity, Anna had too much of.

"Now, tell me," Martina said after they tasted the wine. She put her hand on Jonas's and gave him an encouraging smile.

So Jonas told her how he had met Anna by chance, that she was the aunt of a student of his, how they had gotten to know each other more closely and how his feelings for her had begun to change. He told her about Anna's fear of betrayal, his unfortunate confession of an incident in his own past, and her rejection of him.

"Well, Jonas," Martina said in an atypically serious tone. "The woman is marked for life; what do you expect?" She took a sip of wine. "She seems paranoid about dishonesty, so your story didn't exactly sit well with her."

"Tell me about it." Jonas sighed.

"Then again, I think you did the right thing telling her. I, of course, wouldn't have told her, no way. But you and I are different. You would've felt guilty not doing it. You're a little more scrupulous than I am." Martina shrugged.

"It seems to me the ball is in her court, now. And, Jonas, if she can't forgive you for that blunder in your past, she isn't worth your affection. You're better off without her. And if you end up heartbroken, then come to Italy for a while, and we'll engage in debauchery and wild sex. That'll cure you." Martina laughed out loud.

"Sounds like a deal," Jonas said with a quick smile.

Later that evening, after making love, Jonas wondered if having sex with Martina was a betrayal of Anna. *To hell with it. She's made it clear she doesn't want me. So what should I do? Live the rest of my life like a monk?* He bent over Martina and kissed her. She gave a sleepy moan, then turned and wrapped her arms and smooth, soft legs around him.

Chapter 38

"There's Jonas," Karla called.

Anna and Karla were in town, shopping. They were walking along the Rennweg, a side street of the Bahnhofstrasse, the main shopping street. Anna looked across the street to where Karla pointed. Jonas stood in front of a store, talking to a woman, his longish white hair tousled by a nippy September breeze. He smiled, gave the woman a kiss on the cheek and a close hug. Anna's heart skipped a beat. *A relative? A girlfriend?*

"Who is she?" Karla asked.

"I don't know," Anna said.

"Don't." She put her hand on Karla's shoulder, trying to prevent her from getting Jonas's attention, but it was too late. Jonas saw Karla wave at him and waved back. Karla ran across the street, which was closed to traffic. Anna sighed and followed at a slow pace.

Jonas gave Anna a quick smile and hugged Karla. "Hello there, I didn't expect you today. Class is only in two days."

"We're shopping for some stuff," Anna explained.

"I see." Jonas seemed a little embarrassed. "Anna, this is Martina, an artist friend of mine." He turned to Martina. "Anna is the aunt of my favorite student." He gave Karla a pat on the back.

Jonas and the woman exchanged a quick glance.

"I'm pleased to meet you," Martina said, and stretched out her hand.

"Pleased to meet you, too." Anna shook hands with her. She surreptitiously checked the woman out. She was younger than Anna, attractive, with shoulder-length mahogany hair. She was wearing boots and was dressed in a somewhat outlandish outfit, a green-and-yellow pantsuit and a longish matching scarf, which fluttered in the wind. *I wonder if she dyes her hair.*

"Martina is in town for a few days. She came to visit me. We haven't seen each other for a long time. She has an exhibition and some paintings in a gallery. We're just on the way there," Jonas went on.

"Oh, how nice." Anna felt awkward. Why did Jonas feel the need to explain all this to her? "Well, I guess we should be on our way. We have some more shopping to do."

"All right," Jonas said with a smile. He seemed relieved. "I guess I'll see you in a couple of days."

"Karla will probably come by herself. I may be too busy," Anna said.

Jonas gave her a quick questioning look, then turned to Karla. "See you soon then?"

Karla nodded. "Bye, Jonas."

Anna was surprised that Karla didn't say good-bye to Jonas's visitor. Since nobody seemed to pay attention, Anna let it go. The woman smiled at both of them. "Bye then . . . Oh, since you're both interested in paintings, I would love to see you at my opening. Here's an invitation. Or if you can't make it, drop by any time after that. The paintings will be up for a few weeks."

She handed Anna a card, who accepted it with a forced smile. "Thank you."

Jonas and his friend walked up the street and Anna and Karla continued in the other direction. Karla turned a few times, looking after them. Anna forced herself not to look back. She glanced at the announcement for the opening, then stuffed it into the pocket of her jacket.

"I wonder who she is," Karla murmured.

"A friend, as Jonas said. I don't know her either." Anna tried not to sound irritated.

"Do you think she's his girlfriend?"

"I don't know, Karla. Probably not. And if she is, why do you care?" *Why do I care?*

"You sound upset." Karla peeked at her, her forehead wrinkled. Then after a pause, "I want you to be his fiancée."

"Karla, stop, please. I'm not in the mood."

"I know why you're upset."

"Karla!"

"All right, all right."

They went to their usual art store to buy some art supplies for Karla. On the way there, Anna secretly tossed the invitation into a trash can. They picked out a few items at the store. However, Karla didn't show her usual enthusiasm at the display of painting paraphernalia. She barely glanced at the hundreds of different crayons, paints, pens, canvasses, and the large selection of drawing pads. Anna wasn't much in the mood either. After they paid for the stuff and left, they decided to skip their usual hangout at the coffee shop and go home early instead.

The trip home was quiet. Karla stared out the window with a morose face. Anna watched the houses flip by and focused on the fields with the ripe corn and golden wheat, on the ponds near their home, trying not to think of the woman.

Chapter 39

Karla sat on her bed, holding the phone and punching Maja's number. It was the evening after her and Anna's shopping spree in the city. "Come on, Maja, answer," Karla murmured, nervously tapping her hand on the bed and staring out the window.

One of the windows in her bedroom faced west and she was able to see the sunset. Normally, she loved to watch the moment when the sun just disappeared behind the hills and the forest and the sky erupted into a lively display of color. As a young child, she had heard a story that it was the sunbeams that painted the sky. During the day, they painted the sky blue, or when storm clouds hovered in the sky, the sunbeams would hide behind the clouds and toss buckets of black and gray paint onto them. In the evening after the sunset, the beams would take their favorite paints and color the evening sky red, orange, and purple and shake the clouds, so they looked like puffy cotton balls. Karla loved the idea that the sunbeams were painters.

This evening, however, such childlike fantasies were far from her mind. "Finally," she said, as she heard her friend's voice at the other end.

"What's the matter?"

"Jonas has another woman," Karla blurted out.

"What are you talking about? How do you know?"

Karla told her how she and Anna met him and this other woman in the city and how he had hugged and kissed her.

"Like a real kiss? On the mouth?" Maja asked, all excited.

"No, on the cheek, but I have a bad feeling. Anna was upset, too. I noticed but of course she won't do anything about it," Karla said, exasperated.

"Is she sexy?" Maja asked.

"I don't know. She's pretty good-looking. She has this long, dark-reddish hair—"

"Red hair?" Maja's voice rose to a high pitch. "That's bad."

"Why?" Karla asked.

"Well, I heard my older cousin once say that women with red hair are hot in bed."

"Really? Oh God. We have to do something."

"Yep. This calls for action. We have to have an emergency meeting. Can you sneak out tonight?"

"No, it's too late. I'd just get into trouble."

"Okay, tomorrow at school then."

"Okay."

"And Karla, don't worry, we'll come up with something."

"'Kay," Karla murmured. "See you tomorrow." She punched the disconnect button and put the phone on the nightstand. Although she was a little worried about Maja's sometimes crazy plans, she was even more worried about Jonas slipping through her and Anna's fingers. Seeing him with that other woman in town had made her aware once again how much she wanted him to be part of her family. She had noticed, too, that for the last couple of years, her aunt had become more cheerful and she knew that Anna enjoyed Jonas's company. She would laugh more when he was around. At least, until that day a few weeks ago, when Jonas had left on her birthday, although he said he would spend the night. And ever since then, Anna had acted strange whenever Karla mentioned Jonas. Something had happened. Adults were so complicated and unpredictable.

Jonas was an important presence in her life. He wasn't just her teacher but he was like a father or an uncle to her. She was still in touch with her real father, Arturo. She had gotten to like him during his visit and she loved the presents he sent her. But he was so far away. Having seen him only once, she didn't really know him. It was Jonas who listened to her and gave her advice when she had a problem. He was like Anna in this respect. Sometimes, she even told him things she kept from Anna.

Like the time she hadn't done her homework for the following day. It was a series of math problems. Karla hated math, so she had put the homework off until the last moment. During her painting lesson on a Sunday, she told Jonas that she was worried she didn't have enough time to do her math homework for the following day and Anna was very strict about homework.

"Well, too bad you don't have the problems with you. You could do them now," Jonas said.

"I have them in my bag," Karla said. "I took them along, so I could do them on the train, but I only got one done."

"Well, take them out."

"But . . . the painting?"

Jonas lifted his hands with the palms facing up and raised an eyebrow, his typical expression meaning *Well? What is it going to be? Make up your mind.*

"All right," Karla said and pulled out her notebook. She sighed as she looked at the scribbles on the page. Truth was, Karla didn't quite understand the new set of math rules they had been taught.

"That's math?" Jonas said as he looked at what Karla had written down. "That looks more like hieroglyphs or modern art."

Karla grinned, then took a deep breath and pointed at one of the problems. "I don't really understand this."

"Okay, let me see."

The following two hours, Jonas helped Karla with her math. Jonas could explain them much better than her teacher. He drew pictures and made them more visual for her. At the end of her lesson, she had done all of the problems and felt she finally understood the concept.

Before she left, Jonas pointed his finger at her. "Next time, bring them to me earlier, not at the last moment. And as a punishment for being tardy, I'll give you painting homework for next time, since we didn't have time today."

"That's not a real punishment," Karla said.

"I know." Jonas chuckled.

Yes, Jonas was her best friend, Karla thought as she got ready for bed. And if Anna was such a stick-in-the-mud and didn't realize that they would all be happy together, then Karla had to make her realize it. Whatever it took.

The following day, Karla and Maja met after school and took a walk along the pond, discussing the situation of "that other woman."

Maja was in her element. She skipped once in a while and waved her hands to underscore a point she made. She scrunched her forehead as she thought of possible solutions to "the problem."

"We have to find ways to get Jonas and Anna together. Didn't you say Jonas had an exhibition coming up?"

"Yes," Karla said, "the opening is in two weeks, I think."

"Hmm. Is Anna going?"

Karla lifted a shoulder. "Don't know. Normally she does, but lately she's been avoiding Jonas."

"Okay, we have to find a way to make her go."

"How?"

"Don't they send out invitations to people? When one of my relatives played in a band, they had a concert, and he sent out flyers."

"Yeah. Jonas has invitations printed out. I saw them at his place."

"Good." Maja nodded. "That's a possibility. Can you get an invitation?"

"I guess so. Jonas would give me one, I'm sure."

"Okay. Get one and bring it home. We'll put a personal message from Jonas on it and send it to Anna. Something like, *Anna, my love, I really want you to come to the opening. Can't live without you.*"

Karla shook her head. "That's stupid. Jonas would never write anything like this. Anna would know right away it wasn't him."

"Okay, we can tone it down a little. Just get an invitation."

"Wait, though," Karla said. "That wouldn't work, because he may send Anna an invitation himself and then she'd get two. She'll get suspicious."

"Hmm." Maja brushed her hand through her short blond hair and squinted her eyes. "I got it," she said after a while. "You go there, you see the invitations, and you ask Jonas if you could take one home with you and give it to Anna. Then he wouldn't send her one. And she'll only get ours." Maja's blue eyes lit up.

Karla saw that it could work, but she felt uneasy about it. "I don't know, Maja. This doesn't feel right."

"What's wrong with it?"

"It's dishonest."

"No, it's not. He would send her an invitation anyway. The only difference is that we make it a little more personal. What's wrong with that?"

Karla shrugged.

"Do you want them to get together or not?" Maja stared at her.

"Yes, but . . . I guess we could try. But . . . the handwriting. Anna would know it wasn't from him."

"Well, has he ever written to her? Does she know his handwriting?"

"I can't remember, but she may have seen notes he has written. And he has sent her tickets for concerts. She must know his signature."

"Okay, so you have to get something with his handwriting when you have your lesson. I know how to imitate handwriting."

"Yeah right, like last time with your cousin. You want another beating from your uncle?"

Maja scrunched her face in disgust. "No, but . . . that won't happen. He won't find out, since it doesn't have to do with my family."

They sat on a bench along the pond. The small lake was covered with water lilies. A small water snake slid across the surface. Insects hovered over the flowers. It smelled of clay and sagebrush. Across the pond, a train rushed by, whistling as it passed.

Karla looked down at her hands, trying to make up her mind. She hated dishonesty probably as much as Anna, but she wanted so much for Anna and Jonas to be together. Besides, the idea with the invitation sounded kind of innocent. She just had to rein in Maja's wild imagination and make the note look friendly but not too gushing. "I guess we could try," she finally said.

Chapter 40

"Hey lady, nice ass. How about it? Want to come home with me?"

Anna turned around, shocked. An older, shabby-looking man, with torn pants and wild, dirty, unkempt hair leered at her. He held a paper bag in his hand with the top of a beer bottle sticking out. He was obviously drunk. His eyes were bloodshot and the white around the pupils had a yellowish tint.

"How dare you?" Anna's voice shook a little. This hadn't ever happened to her in Zurich. *What's this city coming to?* She walked on fast, hearing the man utter an insane laugh. After Anna turned the corner, she noticed she was holding her breath. She exhaled and looked behind her. There was no sign of him anymore.

It's not a big deal, just some poor sucker having a bad day; no reason to take it personally. She hiked up the road in the old part of town, where her friend and hairdresser had her salon. It was a street with many secondhand bookstores. In the middle of the steep hill, she stopped to catch her breath and browsed through the boxes of books that stood in front of the stores. She came across one with the title *Forty and Still Single* and the subtitle *The Problems Middle-Aged Women Face Trying to Find a Suitable Mate.* She gave a weak smile. A few months before, the book wouldn't even have interested her. Now, she picked it up and paged through it, then put it down with a sigh.

Well, I guess there isn't much choice — aside from an old drunk this morning . . . and a man with possibly doubtful moral principles. Anna sighed and walked on. Was she being unfair to Jonas? She had to admit she missed him, their get-togethers, and their talks. She had almost taken the road he lived on — it was a parallel street to the one she was on now — but then had decided against it. Part of her wanted to see him and part was afraid to meet him.

The beauty shop was in a little courtyard among old stone buildings, some of them with carvings above the doors. Linden trees and pots with the first fall flowers — purple asters; white, yellow, and orange sneezeweed; and mums — gave the courtyard a cheerful look. When Anna entered the store, a wave of different kinds of aromas wafted her way: hairsprays, shampoos, and conditioners. It was a pleasant and subtle-enough mixture.

"Hi there. Sit down, I'll be right with you," her friend, a middle-aged woman with a modern short hairstyle and purple lipstick, greeted her. She was alone in the store, cleaning up after a customer who had just left. "How are you?"

"Okay," Anna said. "And you?"

"Great," Petra replied. She motioned Anna to sit in the chair, lowered the backrest, and shampooed Anna's hair.

"So what's been happening since I saw you last?" Petra asked, as she massaged Anna's head.

"Not much that I can think of. Same old story: managing the bookstore, working at the library, taking care of my niece. Sounds kind of boring, doesn't it?" Anna gave a quick chuckle.

"Oh, I don't know, it sounds busy," Petra said. She put Anna's chair in an upright position again and toweled her hair. "What about that man of yours?" she asked with a twinkle in her eyes.

Ever since she had modernized Anna's hairstyle and added highlights, she had been teasing her about trying to seduce a man. Jonas had once passed the beauty shop by accident when she had just finished doing Anna's hair. He had seen them through the window and had come in, complimenting Anna on her looks. The fact that Anna had blushed had given Petra even more ammunition for teasing her.

Anna sighed. "Nothing new," she said in a matter-of-fact tone.

"Nothing?" Petra peered at her in the mirror in front of Anna, then continued styling her hair.

"Well . . . we kind of took a break from each other." *Perhaps for good.*

"Uh-oh. Sounds a little ominous. Want to talk about it?"

Anna debated if she wanted to give Petra more details but she needed someone to talk to. The break with Jonas had troubled her more than she wanted to admit to herself sometimes.

"Well, he told me some things that upset me," Anna began and told Petra of the talk she had had with Jonas about his withholding an important truth from his former wife.

Petra listened and at one point stopped working on Anna's hair. She put her fists on her sides and peered at her friend. "And because of that, you don't want to see him anymore?"

"I have a very hard time with people who aren't honest," Anna said.

"But that whole thing is long past. And obviously the man regretted it, or else he wouldn't have told you. And did he really do something so horrible? What do you want? Perfection?"

"No, just someone I can trust."

"I don't know, Anna. Everybody has flaws. At least he was honest with *you*. People can change, you know."

"I guess so." Anna sighed. "Perhaps, I'm a little too hard on him."

"I'll say." Petra glared at her. "That guy looked like a million bucks to me. Do you know how hard it is to find someone at our age who is unmarried, not gay, and a halfway-decent person and doesn't have a potbelly hanging down to his knees? If I wasn't happily married to Erich, I would take a shot at him."

Anna grinned. "You're funny. I don't know, Petra, I think I'm just hopeless when it comes to relationships. Perhaps I'm just meant to be on my own. Taking care of Karla is more than fulfilling . . . most of the time."

"Well, I'll have to leave it up to you. Anyway, we're done and you look gorgeous once again. I just think it's a pity you want to keep your looks all to yourself." Petra lifted the mirror and turned Anna's chair, so she could take a look at the back of her head.

"Thanks, Petra, I love it." Anna got up, looked in the mirror again, and shook her head a little. She liked what she saw. "All right, thanks, and I'll think about your love advice." She paid and gave Petra a hug.

Petra shook her head and smiled. "Picky, picky."

Chapter 41

There was a knock at the door. "It's open," Jonas called, then regretted it. He was expecting Karla, but it could also be his next-door neighbor. She had been coming around by with treats for him, but he suspected there was another motive for her kindness. She wanted to snoop around to see if his "lady friend" was here. Jonas was tired of coming up with excuses why Anna wasn't a frequent visitor anymore. He was relieved when he saw Karla. He motioned to her to quickly close the door. There was a squeaking sound of someone turning the doorknob in the apartment across from his. He suspected Mrs. Schatz was waiting behind the door, peeking through the peephole.

Jonas put his finger on his lips, signaling Karla to be quiet. Karla grinned and they both stood in the hallway, waiting. Sure enough, they heard the door next door open and then close again.

"*Frau Schnüffler*?" Karla asked. She knew that Mrs. Schatz was a busybody and called her "Mrs. Snoop" once in a while.

Jonas nodded and they both laughed, then went into Jonas's studio. Karla put her portfolio down, walked over to the coffee table, and picked up an invitation for Jonas's next opening.

"Can I have one of these to give to Anna?" she asked.

"Sure, go ahead," Jonas said.

"That way you don't have to send her one."

Jonas peered at her. Her voice sounded a little awkward and her face was flushed. She must feel the slight estrangement between him and Anna. "I'm not sure she'll come, but go ahead and give it to her."

He watched as Karla took the invitation, then dropped it a couple of times before she managed to shove it into her portfolio.

"Anything wrong?" he asked.

She shook her head. "No, why?"

"Just wondering. Anyway, I thought we should do something different today. What about going to the zoo? It's a nice day and we can do some drawings of the animals and the landscape there. It's good practice."

"Yeah, that sounds cool." Karla's face lit up.

"Good, let's go."

Karla gathered her portfolio. "Jonas?"

"Yes?"

"Do you like . . . love Anna?"

So that's what's bothering her. Jonas took a deep breath. "I like Anna very much, yes. Why do you ask?"

"But . . . do you *love* her?" Karla's facial color deepened. She stared down at her hands, then looked up again.

"Karla, what brought that on?" Jonas asked, instead of answering her question. To be honest, Jonas didn't know how to answer her. Yes, he loved Anna; at least he thought he did. Lately, however, Anna's distance didn't exactly engender loving feelings in him.

"Just . . . I feel . . ." Karla struggled with words. "You don't see each other much anymore. Ever since you just up and left on my birthday."

Jonas sighed. Obviously, Karla couldn't be brushed off with a quick, noncommittal answer. "Well, let's just say we had a slight disagreement. I told her something about my past she didn't like. Anna has very high moral standards and it is sometimes difficult to live up to her expectations. Does that make sense?"

"Yeah . . . but what did you tell her?"

"It's a long story, Karla, and I don't want to go into any detail. There was something going on in my family that I should've told my wife. It doesn't matter anymore what it was. What matters is that I didn't tell her. And Anna felt that was cowardly and insincere, and she was right. But people make mistakes in life and sometimes that's difficult for Anna to accept."

"Do you think you'll get back together again?" Karla asked.

"We're not apart, really. I'm sure we'll remain friends. And, Karla, don't worry about what happens between Anna and myself. It has nothing to do with my feelings for you or Anna's feelings for you. We both love you very much. Okay?"

"Yeah, but it was so much better when we did things together . . . and I think you guys should get married," Karla blurted out.

"Whoa. You're moving fast."

"Fast?" Karla peered at him. "You've known each other for years."

Jonas chuckled. "You have a point there. But you know, people can be friends without getting married."

"Yeah . . . but . . ." Karla fiddled with her portfolio. "I think Anna loves you."

"Oh yeah? How do you know? Did she say anything to you?"

"Yes . . . kind of."

"Aha." *She's such a bad liar.* "What exactly? And if you keep pulling on that string, you'll rip it off."

Karla let go of the string of her portfolio. "It's just, I can tell . . . when you say something nice, she blushes." Karla gave him an embarrassed look.

Jonas suppressed a smile. "So, she didn't say anything directly about loving me?"

"Well . . . not directly, but . . ."

"Karla, you can't force these kinds of feelings. You'll understand when you're a little older. Things develop at their own pace. Don't worry about us, okay? And let's go and do something fun."

Karla nodded and picked up her art portfolio. They took the streetcar to the zoo. The white-and-blue tram made its way up the hill above the center of Zurich through the more expensive neighborhoods, the so-called Zürichberg or Zurich Mountain area. It wasn't a real mountain but rather a wide slope from which one had a beautiful view of the city, the lake, the woods behind it, and the mountains in the background. Although the Zürichberg was no longer the exclusive residence of the rich, the old villas still dominated the landscape and gave the area a feeling of subdued elegance. At the last streetcar station, everybody got off and walked the short stretch to the entrance of the zoo.

The Zurich Zoo, one of the best known in Europe, had been extended and modernized over the past years. It had been reconstructed with the health and well-being of the animals in mind. All areas had hiding places so the creatures could have some privacy from the peering eyes of the visitors. It wasn't uncommon to walk through part of the park without seeing many animals.

Karla had told him that her favorite animals were the monkeys. They seemed to love human contact more than some of the other species. They were always present and did their performances and antics to the delight of both children and adults. There was a wide variety of them, from the huge, frightening-looking gorillas to the smaller, faster breeds.

Jonas and Karla watched amused as three baby monkeys jumped from stone to stone, hissing at each other and fighting. The mother got up and walked down the hill. She separated the three, slapping and scolding them with a loud, shrill voice.

In the following area, a whole family of monkeys sat peacefully together: male, female, and a baby on the mother's breast. They sat quietly and looked straight ahead, as if posing for a family photo.

Jonas caught Karla staring at them intently. He put his arm around her. "Want to draw them?"

She looked at him as if she had just woken up from a dream, then nodded. Jonas took out his camera and snapped a picture of the monkey family. "In case they move and get up. That way we can finish the drawing later at home," he explained.

They sat on the bench and began to sketch the trio. Fortunately, the three sat together long enough so they were able to draw a rough outline. After a while, the male stood up and walked away.

"He's bored; he's going for a beer or for a chat with his male friends," Jonas said jokingly.

"No, he's not." Karla gave him a playful push. "Only humans do that."

"Hmm, you may be right," Jonas said.

"They're a nice family, aren't they?" Karla gave Jonas a wistful smile.

"I agree." Jonas took a deep breath. *That's what you need, instead of a father thousands of miles away, a dead mother, and an aunt who may be a little too cold and distant . . . although she is very loving around Karla. I wish it wasn't just around Karla.* He shook his head, as if to disperse the thought.

Chapter 42

Karla's hand trembled as she put the card with the invitation on the coffee table in the living room. "Invitation from Jonas for his exhibition," she said to Anna, who had just come home from the bookstore.

"Thanks," Anna said, paging through the small pile of mail next to the card.

"Aren't you going to look at it?" Karla asked.

"In a minute," Anna mumbled, then picked it up.

Karla's heart beat in her throat. *Is she going to notice?*

Anna read the card, gave a quick smile, and put it down again.

Karla took a deep breath of relief. "Are you going to the opening?"

"Yes, perhaps." Anna picked up another piece of mail.

"It would be fun," Karla continued.

Anna looked up. "Yes. Well, you can go for a little while even if I can't make it. It starts at . . . let me see." She picked up the card again. "Five o'clock. That's still early enough. You can go after school."

"I want you to come, too," Karla said. "I don't like to go by myself."

"Well, I'll see. I might go." Anna looked at the card again and wrinkled her forehead. "That's odd," she mumbled.

Karla's heart skipped a beat. She picked up her school backpack and headed for her room. "Homework," she said.

"Okay." Anna still read the card. She shook her head, and put it down again.

In her room, Karla sat on the bed, listening to Anna moving around the living room. *Did she get suspicious?*

Karla and Maja had taken a long time trying to figure out what to put on the card. They had argued for about an hour. Maja, of course, wanted to put at least one gushing phrase on there. Karla voted against it. They finally agreed on the following:

Dear Anna. I would really love it if you came to my vernisage.
I think of you a lot.
I miss you.
Love always, Jonas.

The door opened. Anna stood in the doorway. "When did Jonas give you this?" she asked.

Karla glanced at her, then averted her gaze as Anna peered at her. "When I had my last class." Her heart pounded.

"Hmm. Did you see him write the message? Was he in a hurry?"

Karla looked at her puzzled. "No . . . I'm not sure. Why?"

"Just wondering." Anna closed the door again.

Karla sighed and tried to calm her heartbeat. She pulled out her books and sat at her desk. She only had to review a chapter in her geography book for the lesson on the following day. She couldn't concentrate, though. After rereading the first paragraph several times without understanding a word, she sighed and pushed the book away.

Now, the whole plan with Jonas's personal invitation sounded stupid to her. Even if Anna believed that Jonas had written the invitation, she might ask him about it or thank him for the personal note. And then what?

Karla picked up the phone in her room and called Maja. She was afraid and upset and needed to talk to someone.

"Yes?" Maja answered with a yawn.

"I think we did something stupid," Karla said.

"Why?" Another yawn.

"Are you asleep?" Karla asked.

"Not yet. I'm reading this boring chapter on history. It puts me to sleep. You know, about the Stone Age. I mean who cares about the Stone Age? But what did we do stupid?"

"The thing with Jonas and Anna."

"Why? Did she read it?"

"Yeah."

"And? Did she notice anything?"

"I hope not. I'm just worried."

"You're such a scaredy-cat. It's going to work; you'll see. Is she going to the opening?"

"She said she might."

"Well, so what are you worried about?"

"What if she says something about the message and Jonas says he didn't write anything?"

"Oh, for God's sake. They won't talk about some stupid message. If she goes, Jonas will be happy, and they'll talk about pictures or whatever."

"Perhaps you're right." Maja's confidence made Karla feel a little better.

"Just relax. And don't worry. Anyway, I have to go back to my dull Stone Age. We have a test tomorrow."

"Okay, bye." Karla pushed the disconnect button and put the receiver on her nightstand. She went back to her geography book, but her ability to concentrate hadn't improved much. She sighed and got up to check what Anna was fixing for dinner. The kitchen was empty; there was a bunch of broccoli, some lettuce on the cutting board, and pieces of chicken in a bowl. It looked like Anna was about to start their evening meal. Anna sat in the den, talking on the phone. She laughed at one point. Was she talking to Jonas perhaps? Karla sat on the sofa in the living room, trying to hear snatches of conversation. At this moment, Anna stopped talking and hung up the phone.

"Who were you talking to?" Karla asked.

"Verena, my friend from the bookstore. Why?"

"Just . . . curious." Karla was both relieved and disappointed; disappointed because she somehow hoped Anna and Jonas had had a pleasant conversation, and relieved because she had been worried that Anna might have brought up the invitation to the opening.

After dinner, Karla helped Anna wash the dishes. Afterward, she tried to read the geography chapter again, and this time she was able to concentrate a little better. Later, she worked on a painting in her artist corner in the den while Anna was taking care of some paperwork. At nine o'clock, Anna leaned back in her chair and stretched.

"I'm getting very sleepy," she said, yawning. "I think I'll turn in early today and read a little in bed. What are you going to do?"

"I'm getting tired, too. I just want to finish the watercolor, so I can let it dry."

"Okay, sweetie, sleep tight. I'll see you in the morning." Anna kissed Karla and yawned again.

Karla added a few more strokes to her painting. It was a still life with a series of colorful fall leaves, an orange, an apple, a cluster of grapes. She glanced once more at her picture and smiled. She hoped Jonas would like it. She closed the paint box, gathered her brushes and the glass of water, and washed everything in the kitchen sink. On the way to her bedroom, she picked up the invitation to the opening again and then she saw it. She gasped. There was a spelling error in the message. Vernisage . . . *that's not right, is it?* Karla dropped the card on the table and went to the bookshelf. She pulled out the dictionary and paged through it. Sure enough, it was *vernissage* with two *s*'s. *Stupid Maja.* And Karla hadn't even noticed it.

She felt fear crawl over her skin, giving her goose bumps. Had Anna seen it? She must have noticed and Karla didn't think Jonas would have made a mistake like this. Was that the reason Anna had asked her if Jonas had written it in a hurry?

Karla grabbed the invitation and took it with her to her bedroom. Perhaps Anna wouldn't look at it again. She knew the date and the time of the exhibition, if she decided to go. Karla undressed, brushed her teeth, and crawled into bed. However, she couldn't fall asleep for a long time. She tossed and turned, worrying about the outcome of this whole charade. "I knew it was a stupid idea," she murmured.

When she finally fell asleep, she dreamed of being in Jonas's apartment. Jonas sat in front of his living room table, sorting through a whole stack of invitations with messages on them. More and more kept flying in through the window and landing on the table.

The following morning, Karla felt like she hadn't slept at all. She sat at the breakfast table bleary-eyed and yawning.

"I hope you're not coming down with something." Anna put her hand on Karla's forehead. "You look pale."

"No, I just didn't sleep well," Karla said, then took another sip of milk.

"Are you nervous about something? Do you have a test today?"

Karla shook her head. "No, just a bad night."

"All right, I hope you feel better. I have to leave a little early today. So don't forget to lock the door when you leave. We'll have spaghetti carbonara tonight. Your favorite."

"Oh, good." Karla forced a smile and waved as Anna darted out the door. She finished her cereal and put the bowl into the kitchen sink, then went to her bedroom to gather her schoolbag. She picked up the invitation on her nightstand, glanced at it again, shook her head, and dropped it into her bag.

Chapter 43

The exhibition took place in a modern two-story gallery with large windows and perfect lighting. Jonas and the owner were still busy setting up the table with the refreshments when the first few guests arrived. It was fifteen minutes before the official opening. A few of Jonas's close friends took the opportunity to chat with him before the place was swamped. Jonas was a well-known artist not just in Switzerland but in Europe and overseas. Some of his work was even represented on postal stamps. In many of his paintings, elements of two of his favorite artists, Picasso and Georges Braque, were visible.

"Great new stuff," one of his friends said, pointing at some of Jonas's large colorful lithographs, prints, and paintings.

"Thanks," Jonas said. He poured them a glass of white wine. They toasted each other. "So what's going on with you?" Jonas asked, getting ready to take a sip. His hand stopped short before reaching his mouth and he didn't hear his friend's answer. He stared at the entrance, where Anna and Karla had just come in.

"Excuse me a moment," he said to his friend. He put down the wineglass and walked to the door, feeling his face stretch into a big smile.

"Hi there, you made it. I'm so glad you came." He greeted Anna with a handshake and lightly touched Karla's shoulder.

"Thanks for the invitation," Anna said. "I haven't seen your work in a while."

"Well, look around." Jonas made a sweeping gesture toward the paintings.

"Very impressive. I love those large ones." Anna gazed at some of Jonas's huge prints with their typical mixture of abstract and dramatic, realistic elements. She sounded genuinely impressed.

One of Jonas's friends came up to him and asked him a question.

"Excuse me," Jonas said to Anna.

"Go ahead." She put her hand on his arm, which made him feel warm inside. An unexpected gesture like this from Anna was a pleasant surprise. "We'll look at the paintings for a while."

"Okay, I'll see you later then," Jonas said.

While Jonas was listening to his friend, he watched Anna and Karla across the room. Anna looked lovely. She was wearing a two-piece mauve outfit, which emphasized her blue-gray eyes and flattered the wavy shoulder-length brown hair with blond highlights. As she gazed at the pictures, her normally tense features softened. She bent her head lightly and said something to Karla, then smiled. *Anna, if you only knew how beautiful you look when you smile.*

Jonas felt a hand on his shoulder. His friend looked at him amused. "Are you dreaming, Jonas?"

"I'm sorry, I was thinking of something."

"Is that *something* perhaps the woman with that cute young girl, by any chance?"

Jonas gave a quick grin. "I guess you found me out."

"Very attractive," his friend said. "Who is she?"

Jonas was spared an answer, since another friend of his came and asked him a question. As the evening wore on and people came and went, Jonas talked to Anna a few more times. To his surprise, he noticed that Karla was unusually quiet. Normally, she admired the paintings and looked at them with interest, but today she seemed to feel uncomfortable and absentminded. Did she have trouble in school or had she had an argument with Anna?

He dodged a small group of people that tried to get his attention and walked over to Anna. "I'm so sorry I don't have more time to talk to you."

"Oh, don't worry. This is your evening; you have to mingle with the art world." Anna laughed. "Karla and I can entertain ourselves, no problem."

"Perhaps . . . I probably have to go out with some of the people for a quick bite to eat. I would love it if you two came along."

"Oh no, not tonight," Anna said. "We have to leave in a few minutes. Karla has school tomorrow. Perhaps some other time."

Jonas bathed in Anna's encouraging smile. "All right, I'll hold you to it." He gave her a quick hug and was pleasantly surprised that she let him do it.

"How are you, Karla? You're so quiet tonight. Something bothering you?"

"I'm fine, just a little tired." A quick smile flashed across her face.

After Anna and Karla had left, Jonas continued to mingle with the guests, trying to sound interested when the journalist asked him the same old questions about his art and to give halfway-intelligent answers. He didn't like the promotional aspect of being an artist. He knew it was necessary but it exhausted him. What he really wanted to do was just paint, have his paintings framed and exhibited, and let someone else take care of public relations. The world, however, wanted the artist in person, the human being behind the work. They wanted to talk to him, to touch him, and, above all, to be noticed by him. So he tried to be attentive but his mind was elsewhere. He thought of Anna and longed to be with her.

Chapter 44

"Great paintings, don't you think so?" Anna asked Karla as they walked toward the train station. She buttoned up her jacket; the evenings in October were getting cool. The few trees along the Bahnhofstrasse donned their yellow-golden fall foliage.

"Yeah. I love them," Karla said. It was the first time she showed any excitement all evening. Anna glanced at her. Jonas was right; she seemed preoccupied and absentminded.

Anna put her arm around Karla. "You sure you're okay? You're so quiet tonight."

"I'm fine, really. I stayed up late last night, studying for that math exam. I'm just tired."

"Well, that's understandable. But you did okay, you said?" Anna brushed a strand of hair from Karla's forehead.

"I think so; I'll find out soon." Karla gave a little snort. "I hate math."

"Don't blame you," Anna said. "It wasn't my favorite subject in school either. Anyway, study hard and do the best you can and don't worry. Okay?"

They walked by the small park at the end of the street. A merchant at the corner was in the process of closing his stand. Anna inhaled the aroma of roasted chestnuts, the scent of fall and approaching winter. She glanced at the statue of Pestalozzi, the Swiss educational reformer, who looked down at them from a tall pedestal, holding a child in his arms. Anna gave Karla a hug and was rewarded with a quick warm smile.

As they sat on the train, leaving the station, Karla leaned her head against the backrest and closed her eyes. Anna observed her for a while. She looked tired; there were dark shadows under her eyes. Something seemed to bother her. Was it school or other problems? Karla was usually forthcoming when something troubled her, but lately she had become more withdrawn. Anna had attributed it to her age. She was at that preteen age with all its changes, when things began to get confusing. Aside from that, she was also becoming more her own person. She had her own circle of friends and probably didn't want to share everything with her aunt. Anna often didn't know how far she should intrude.

"I don't want to bug you, but I hope you tell me if something bothers you," Anna said when Karla opened her eyes again and yawned.

"Yeah, I know. It's nothing really. Just tired."

"Well, the weekend is coming and you can sleep in."

"I know; I can hardly wait. Okay, we're here." Karla got up and Anna followed her to the exit. Their car was parked next to the train station, and it only took them a few minutes to reach home.

Karla went straight to bed and Anna made herself a cup of tea and sat in the living room next to the window, relaxing and thinking about the evening. Now, she was glad she had gone to Jonas's opening. She had hesitated at first. She was still torn about her feelings for him. She hadn't seen much of him and he hadn't made any effort, either, to get in touch. It was of course her fault, because she had pushed him away.

Anna sighed. *Petra is right; I'm too hard on him. I'm too hard on all men.* But was it really worth giving up her independence for an illusory happiness that would just go sour again? Besides, she was happy by herself, wasn't she?

An Uncommon Family

The scarlet-red leaves on the blood maple tree in front of the house fluttered in the evening breeze. Fall was here, and soon another year would come to an end. Anna took a sip of tea and watched as the darkness descended upon the forest and the meadows, leaving a thin layer of orange-yellow on the horizon.

Was she really that happy? She was happy with Karla. She loved her. She had watched her change from a scared, desperate little child to a happier, more self-confident girl. But Karla was growing up. Already now, she showed signs of pulling away, becoming more independent, and spending more time with her friends. In a few years, she would be going to school in the city and after that perhaps study for a few months in a foreign country. Jonas had suggested some art schools in Italy and Germany. And then what? Anna would be by herself again. Her heart clenched at that thought. She didn't even know what it meant to be alone anymore. Was she kidding herself?

Then again, to get involved with a man just to escape loneliness wasn't the right thing either. Besides, Jonas may not be interested in her anymore. There was that other woman she had seen while with Karla in town a few weeks before. They had acted as if they were more than friends. Anna sighed. *I'm second-guessing people again.* But Jonas had been happy to see her tonight. His joy had been unmistakable. And her own heart had beaten fast when she saw him. He had wanted her to come, or else he wouldn't have sent her the personal note.

She got up and searched for Jonas's invitation. She couldn't find it anywhere; she must have misplaced it or perhaps Karla had it. But she remembered the note well. A smile teased her lips. The message had been a little odd, as if he had been uncertain what he wanted to write. And he had made a spelling error, which surprised her, knowing how well educated he was. He must have written the note in a hurry and had probably been nervous. That's what it was; he had worried about her reaction. Would she reject him again?

It was dark now. Anna looked outside and spotted her reflection in the windowpane. She looked at the image startled. Was that really her? Those stern, almost rigid features? What had made her so distant and hard? Or who? Had that man, Nicolas, stolen her life? Was it her fault for letting him do it? "Go away," she said through clenched teeth. The flash of anger turned into sadness.

She went to her room and searched through some papers in her desk. She picked up an envelope, went back to the living room, and opened it. There were two letters in it: one from Richard, Nico's father, to Anna and one from Nico to his father. After Nico's death and after Richard had heard the shocking news of his son's double life, he had sent those letters to Anna "as proof that Nico did love you."

Anna unfolded Nico's letter. He gave his father all kinds of news about his studies and his work in New York. This was followed by a note: *And, Dad, I met a wonderful woman by the name of Anna. I love her very much and we plan to get married soon. Just wanted to give you a heads-up. We want you to come to our wedding.*

For years after the plane crash, Anna had read those four sentences over and over again. They were the only proof that, at some point, Nico had loved her. She hoped that at least he hadn't lied to his father about his feelings for her. Of course, there had been those years of living together, when Anna had felt that Nico loved her, but she still didn't trust her own feelings about that time.

"I love her very much," Anna repeated the words. Her eyes welled up. She sat on the sofa and covered her face with her hands. She cried for a long time. Afterward, she felt better, as if the release of years' worth of pent-up tears had melted a block of ice in her heart.

She picked up the letter again, kissed it, then tossed it into the fireplace and watched the flames flare up and consume it.

"I loved you, Nico, but now you have to let me go. Let me finally live my life and love again." Anna took a deep breath and put another log on the fire.

Chapter 45

"So, how did it go?" Maja peered at Karla from under her rain slicker. They were standing close to the wall underneath the protruding roof of the school building. School was out. It was four o'clock in the afternoon and pouring rain. The schoolyard was strewn with red, brown, and yellow leaves. Karla gazed through the curtain of water at the fields and mountains. Heaps of black oppressive clouds hung in the sky.

She shrugged. "Okay, I guess. We went to the opening and fortunately they didn't mention the invitation."

"Okay, but were they friendly? Anything new?" Maja sounded impatient.

Karla wrapped her rain jacket tight. She shivered lightly in the cool late-October air. "Yeah, they were friendly. Jonas was busy though and they didn't get to talk much. I was glad when it was over with. I was so afraid they'd notice something. I couldn't even enjoy the exhibition."

"Oh, for God's sake, is that all you can think about? I told you they wouldn't talk about some dumb invitation. Are they going to get together again?"

"Anna hasn't said anything. I don't know about Jonas. I'll see him later this week."

"Well, we'll have to plan our next step then." Maja pulled the hood of her raincoat down and shook out her hair.

"Oh no, I can't take this anymore," Karla said. "It's too scary."

"Oh, come on. We can't stop now. They're talking again, they are friendly, so it worked. Why stop now?"

"Maja, please. This is going to end badly."

"No, it's not. Look, didn't you say your aunt was going to have some event at the bookstore next week?"

"Yeah, a reading, so what? Oh no, don't even think about it." Karla picked up her backpack and was getting ready to leave.

"Listen, just one more time. And afterward, they're on their own." Maja pulled up her hood again and followed Karla out into the pouring rain. "We'll send Jonas one of your aunt's invitations and that's it. Perhaps you can even get her to write a note herself, then we don't have to."

"Maybe," Karla mumbled under her hood. She walked fast, trying not to step into the huge puddles on the concrete.

"Well, let's at least talk about it. If you really don't want to, then we'll just drop it."

"Okay," Karla agreed. "I have to stop by Anna's book-store on the way home. Want to come with me? We can do homework at my place. Anna won't be home until later."

"Sounds like a winner. I wish this rain would stop. My feet are soaking wet. Should've worn my boots."

"I hate this weather," Karla grumbled. "I think only my aunt loves rain. She claims that people buy more books during bad weather. Well, here we are." Karla opened the door, which made a bell-like sound.

Anna stood behind the counter and talked to a customer. She looked up briefly and smiled at the girls. "Take off your wet stuff and leave it at the wardrobe."

Maja and Karla stripped off their raincoats and dropped the backpacks at the door. "It's nice and warm in here," Maja said.

"Yeah, I don't want to leave," the woman said, holding a wrapped book in her hand. "Is it still pouring out there? Looks like it."

"Why don't you wait for a while? Sit down over there." Anna pointed at a corner where two tables, chairs, and a sofa stood. "Want a cup of coffee or tea or hot chocolate?"

"Coffee sounds great. That's why I love your bookstore, Anna. You encourage customers to hang out."

"That's the only way I can stay in business," Anna said. "That and the special events and readings. Fortunately, I have some very loyal customers, and one thing they enjoy is sitting here with a cup of java, browsing through books, without feeling pressured to buy something every time." She turned to Karla and Maja. "Want some hot chocolate? I just made a fresh pot. It's in the thermos."

"Great," Maja said. "I may buy a book from my pocket money one of these days." She grinned.

Anna chuckled. "That will be the day. We do have a pretty good young-adult section. You may even find one of your favorite mystery books."

"Cool." Maja sauntered over to the bookshelf, gave it a cursory look, pulled out a book, put it back, and joined Karla at the table with the hot chocolate. "Have to look at it some other time. My mind can't possibly take in any more today. We had a math test this morning and I got totally lost. I mean totally."

"I got a Five on my last one," Karla said.

"Really?" Anna gave Karla a surprised look. "You didn't even tell me. That's good, the second best grade."

"I just got it back yesterday," Karla said and sipped her hot chocolate. She went to the counter and picked up an announcement for the upcoming reading. She looked over at Maja, who winked at her.

"Ahem, are you going to send Jonas one of these?" she asked Anna. "I'm sure he'd love to come."

Anna glanced at the announcement. "Oh yes, why don't you take him one? You'll see him tomorrow."

"Okay . . . want to write something on it?" Karla handed her the card. Her hand was shaking a little.

Anna looked at it, then gave it back to her. "No, that's okay. It has all the information on it. But tell him it would be fun if he could make it."

"Okay." Karla took the announcement and walked over to Maja, who rolled her eyes at her.

"You give up too fast," she whispered.

Karla looked at Anna, but she was busy talking to a new customer who had just come in. "What am I going to say?" she whispered back at Maja.

"Forget it," Maja said. "Let's go to your place."

They put the dirty cups into the small sink at the back of the store, gathered their stuff, and walked to the door. Karla was relieved that the rain had diminished somewhat. It was now more of a drizzle than a downpour.

"Okay, we're going to our place to do homework," Karla said to Anna.

"Good. I'll be home in about an hour or so. Do you want to eat with us, Maja? There's enough."

"Thanks, I'd love to, but my aunt is cooking my favorite tonight. She'd be upset if I didn't come home."

"Okay, sure, some other time then." Anna waved at the two girls.

The weather had improved somewhat. There was even a spot of blue sky in the west. "Look," Karla exclaimed. The sunrays shining through the opening in the clouds painted a stunning rainbow, which arched across the whole sky.

"Cool," Maja said. She shielded her eyes against the glare and nodded.

At home, they unpacked their schoolbags and settled around the dining-room table.

"We'll have to take care of the invitation first, before Anna gets home," Maja said.

Karla nodded. "I wish Anna had written something. She can be such a fuddy-duddy sometimes." Anna's reaction had irritated her.

"That's why we have to take things into our own hands," Maja said. "It's for their own good. Okay, so what are we going to write?"

"Nothing gushing, please. You know, Anna is not the gushing type." Karla rolled her eyes.

"Hmm." Maja put her pen in her mouth, sucking at it. She pulled it out. "What about: 'Dear Jonas, The exhibition was great. Loved it. I hope you can come to my . . .'? What is it?"

"A reading," Karla said.

"Okay. 'I hope . . . with all my heart—'"

"No, no, that's too much. Anna wouldn't write that," Karla said.

"Okay. How about: 'I hope you can come to my reading. Great books. Really, really miss you.'"

"No 'really, really.' Come on."

Maja sighed. "You sure are hard to please. You're almost as bad as your aunt. 'Really miss you.' That's it. No more changes."

"Okay. I guess. But don't make any spelling errors," Karla said.

"Jeez. Just because I made one once—"

"Hurry up, Anna is coming home soon, and we haven't even started our homework yet."

Maja carefully wrote the text and signed it, copying Anna's signature from a piece of paper Karla had given her. "What do you think?"

Karla nodded. "I guess it's okay."

"Just okay? This is a work of art." Maja held the paper away from her and looked at it, squinting her eyes. "Here it is." She handed it to Karla, who slid it in an envelope and put it in her art portfolio.

After a while of fidgeting and fiddling with books and notebooks, Karla and Maja settled down and did their homework. Karla had a composition to finish. She made it through one paragraph when she heard the door. Anna came home, carrying two grocery bags into the kitchen.

"Hi, girls. How is homework?"

They both moaned. "Not done yet."

"Oh? You must have a lot then. Well, it'll take me a while to unpack and fix dinner, so you have some time."

"I better go home. It's getting late. I'll finish at home," Maja said. She stuffed her books into her backpack and gathered her things. She said good-bye to Anna and winked at Karla. "See ya."

"'Kay," Karla murmured, trying to concentrate again on her composition. Her mind, however, kept straying back to the note in her portfolio. It didn't feel right. *This is the very last time I'll do something like this*, she promised herself.

Chapter 46

Jonas put down the newspaper after skimming an article about his exhibition and smiled. He had received some favorable reviews of his new paintings. He got up and checked on the weather. It was cool but no longer raining. The turning leaves on the trees along the river gave the city its last burst of color before it sank into the bland grayish November gloom.

Jonas went into the kitchen and poured a cup of tea. He took a sip, savoring the smoky taste of Lapsang Souchong. The exhibition had been a success. Aside from all the praise he had received, it was above all Anna's visit that made him happy.

"I'm an old fool," he said with a grin, then became serious. Perhaps he once again began to hope for something that may turn out to be an illusion. However, he couldn't help it; the announcement of Anna's reading raised his expectations. Her personal message made it clear that she really wanted him to attend, that she even missed him. That and her coming to the opening showed him that she seemed to have the desire to renew their friendship. He didn't dare to hope for more, not yet.

On the way to his studio, he picked up the invitation again. The message had surprised him at first. It was more personal than anything he had received from her, at least since their falling-out. Something bothered him, though. He couldn't put his finger on it, but the language Anna had used seemed unfamiliar. Jonas shook his head. He put the card down when the phone rang.

"Just the person I was thinking about," Jonas said when he heard Anna's voice.

"Well, I hope good thoughts," Anna said.

"Of course, only the best. You should know that by now," Jonas said jokingly.

"I just wanted to let you know that Karla will be a little late. She missed her regular train. She said she almost forgot that it was the day of her art lesson. Unbelievable, that's the first time ever. She's been very absentminded lately. Anyway, sorry about that."

"No problem," Jonas said. "We changed the schedule, so it's possible." Since Karla was too busy in school during the week, they had decided to have her art lessons on the weekend. "Or perhaps she's in love," he added with a chuckle.

"I don't know, she didn't say anything, but she hasn't exactly been communicative lately."

"Well, Anna, she's growing up. She's getting into the teen years when confiding in her friends is a lot more interesting than talking to her elders. I remember that time very well with my kids."

"Well, let's hope that's what it is."

"Anyway, thanks for the invitation to the reading," Jonas continued, "and for the kind words on the announcement. I'd love to come."

There was a pause. "What words?"

"You know, the personal note."

"Personal note?"

"Didn't you write something on the announcement?"

Another pause. "Not that I remember. No, I'm sure I didn't. In fact, Karla asked me to write something, but I told her that all the information was on there but to let you know that I hoped you could make it . . . Jonas, what are you talking about?"

Jonas swallowed. "Anna, we may have a problem. I don't know how to tell you this, but that's what is on the invitation." Jonas read the short note to her.

There was silence at the other end. "I . . . I don't understand," Anna finally said.

"Well, I'm beginning to understand; at least I think I have some idea." He told Anna about the conversations he had had with Karla, about her hope that they would become really close. He was starting to think that perhaps Karla wanted to help them along a little, so to speak.

"But . . . Karla would never do something like this; at least I don't think so. Oh Jonas, I don't know what to think anymore."

Another pause.

"Wait a minute, that means . . . what about the note on your invitation to the opening?" Anna's voice sounded as if from far away.

"There was a note on that, too?" Jonas asked.

"Yes, wait . . . oh, I don't have it anymore. That's another strange thing. It suddenly disappeared. But it said . . . eh, that you missed me and really wanted me to come to the opening. I was a little surprised, and yes, there was a spelling error. I thought that perhaps you had been in a hurry."

"What spelling error?"

"You wrote *vernissage* with one *s* . . . or whoever wrote it."

In spite of the serious implications, Jonas almost had to laugh. "I certainly would know how to spell that word, I've written it often enough. Didn't you get suspicious?"

"A little, but I thought you might have been preoccupied or in hurry or something. I just never would've thought . . .

Jonas . . ." Anna's voice sounded angry now. "Jonas, if that's true, that's incredible, unacceptable. I mean—"

"Well, let's try to stay calm. If Karla was the culprit, she was totally misguided but she didn't mean any harm. The girl wants a family and—"

"That's no excuse." Anna's voice was shaking.

"I agree and she needs to know that this is wrong, but why don't we wait until we have a chance to talk to her? Listen, Anna, she just got here. I'll try to talk to her and I'll let you know, okay?"

"Okay, but—"

"Anna, I'll talk to you soon." Jonas hung up and took a few deep breaths. He hated having to deal with this. He went to the door and opened it.

The beautiful young girl looked at him with her large dark eyes. "Hi Jonas."

He motioned Karla to come in, but didn't say anything. He picked up the invitation to the reading, held it in front of her eyes, and pointed at the personal note. "Do you know anything about this?"

Karla faltered, her face darkened, and her eyes filled with tears. She swallowed and nodded.

Jonas walked into the living room and slapped the card on the table. He had hoped for a different answer but at least she wasn't lying about it. "What in heaven's name were you thinking? You falsified someone's handwriting and signature? This is criminal behavior."

"I'm sorry, I knew it was wrong all along, but Maja . . ." Karla stopped short, biting her lip. She obviously didn't want to rat on her friend.

"Ah, so it wasn't just you?" *That explains some of it.*

"It's my fault," Karla said. "We thought . . . I thought that perhaps you two would make up and . . . I didn't mean any harm. I'm sorry."

"Karla, I don't know what to say. I told you not to worry about Anna and me. Don't you see? What you did is manipulating people's feelings and that's just wrong. Think about it. I am . . . what if a man was in love with a woman but that woman did not return his feelings? And then someone writes a note like this and gives the man false hope, then when he finds out that it wasn't true, he'd be very hurt. This is cruel."

Karla nodded. "I didn't mean to do that."

"Well, that may be true, but the effect is the same. You cannot manipulate people's feelings like that. It's cheating and lying."

"Don't hate me, please. I'll never do it again."

"Well, I hope so. I don't hate you but I'm disappointed in you, Karla. I really thought you knew better."

A tear slid down Karla's cheek. Jonas hated to see her unhappy but wasn't ready to give in yet. "Stop crying, that doesn't help either." He didn't mean to sound so harsh. He got up and put a box of tissues in front of her. Karla grabbed a few and blew her nose.

"Thanks," she mumbled, trying to get ahold of herself.

"Anyway, no class today," Jonas said. "I need to be alone for a while. You better catch the next train and go home."

"Does Anna know?" Karla asked.

"Yes, that's why the whole thing blew up. She called to tell me you would be late, and I mentioned the note."

"She's upset?"

"Of course she's upset, what do you expect?"

"She'll never forgive me." Karla cried again.

"Well, you should have thought of that before. This is exactly the kind of thing she's extremely sensitive about. Misleading people, lying . . . what's the matter?" Jonas peered at Karla, who had turned ashen and held her stomach.

"I think I'm going to get sick." She rushed to the bathroom. Jonas heard her throw up. *Poor thing. Now you're making me feel guilty.*

When Karla came back out, she was still pale. "I better go home."

"No, sit down for a while. I don't want you to get sick on the way home. Want some tea?"

Karla nodded. "Perhaps."

Jonas went into the kitchen and poured a cup of tea from the thermos. When he came back, Karla was sitting on the sofa, looking miserable. She held her head.

"Are you coming down with something?"

"Don't know. My head is killing me."

He handed her the tea. "Here, it's still warm."

"Thanks," she whispered and took a little sip. She put the cup on the table and folded her arms in front of her. "Are you . . . are you still going to teach me?" Her voice broke again.

"Yes," he said in a curt tone. "Provided you'll never do this again."

"I won't . . . but Jonas, I know what I did was wrong, but I still think Anna loves you."

"Jesus Christ, girl, you still haven't learned your lesson, have you? How would you know that?" Jonas shouted and threw up his hands.

"I just feel it."

"Well, I don't think I'm going to trust your feelings at this point. Karla, you believe this because you want to believe it, because you *want* it to be true, not because it is true. And from now on, I ask you to leave mine and Anna's relationship up to us. You understand? This is my last warning. If you want us to remain friends, you don't interfere anymore."

"I promise." Karla nodded. "I better go home. Anna is going to kill me."

Jonas gave a snort. "I doubt it. She'll forgive you . . . eventually."

Karla held her head again and winced. "God, it hurts."

Jonas wondered if she tried to make him feel sorry for her, but she did look ill and she had thrown up. He touched her forehead. "You're burning up. You must have the flu. You can't go home on the train. Come on, I'll drive you."

"Thanks," Karla whispered. She got up and staggered. Jonas held her. "I feel dizzy, it's probably from the headache." She held on to Jonas. Her face turned white and she would've fallen if Jonas hadn't held her. He lowered her to the sofa. Her face felt hot, but she was shivering. Tears escaped her eyes as she held her head.

"Since when have you been feeling bad?"

"I didn't feel good when I got up, but then it went away."

"I'm going to call Anna. You need to see a doctor. Just wait; don't get up." Jonas remembered he had read somewhere that there were cases of meningitis in the city. *God, I hope it's only the flu.*

He picked up the phone and went into the kitchen. He called Anna, who answered right away. "Well, what did she say?"

"Yes, it was her, but Anna, let's talk about that later. Karla is sick; she threw up and has a terrible headache and is feverish. I'm going to bring her home, but I think you should call the doctor. It's probably just the flu, but just to be safe."

"Well, if it's the flu, the doctor may not come right away. It's the weekend. Unless it's an emergency, he may just put some medicine in his mailbox and check her out on Monday."

"Anna, I don't want to scare you but the severe headache worries me a little. I've heard of a few cases of . . . meningitis, and I just want to make sure—"

"Meningitis?" Anna's voice rose to a high pitch.

Shit, I shouldn't have said anything. "Don't worry, Anna, it's probably false alarm, but I just think we shouldn't take any risks."

"I'll call him right away. How is she now? Can I talk to her?" Panic flooded her voice.

"She is lying down. She had some tea. Don't worry, Anna." Jonas walked into the living room. Karla was sitting up but she was pale and held her jacket close. "Anna wants to talk to you."

Karla's hand shook as she held the receiver. "I'm sorry, Anna," she said and broke down crying. "I didn't mean . . . okay, yes, Jonas is taking me home. Bye." She gave the phone back to Jonas.

"I'm calling the doctor right now," Anna said, her voice trembling.

"Anna, don't panic. I'm an idiot; I shouldn't have mentioned meningitis—"

"Just bring her home, Jonas."

"Okay."

"Meningitis?" Karla stared at him.

"Now, don't go crazy. It's enough that your aunt loses her nerves. I just read somewhere of a few cases. It always happens once in a while. You probably just have the flu." He helped Karla get up.

"But Maja said one of her relatives had it." Karla's dark eyes looked even bigger in her now-pale face.

Jonas suppressed the bout of terror that spread from his stomach to his chest. "No need to worry. Come on, honey, let's get you home." He picked up Karla's portfolio, grabbed his car keys, and took Karla by the arm. He noticed the invitation to Anna's reading and marveled how such a big issue all of a sudden looked insignificant.

Chapter 47

"But it could be meningitis!" Anna almost screamed into the phone. The emergency assistant of the pediatrician told her to hold on. A few seconds later, the doctor answered and asked her about the symptoms. He told her to calm down, it was probably the flu, but he would be by right away.

At first, the words calmed Anna down, but then she got worried again. If the doctor didn't suspect it could be meningitis, he wouldn't come right away, would he? She kept pacing the living room, then forced herself to sit down. *I have to remain calm,* she told herself. She kept looking at the clock. Finally, she heard a car. Thinking it was Jonas, she rushed to the door. It was the doctor.

The young pediatrician smiled at her. "Where is she?"

"She's on the way home. Do you think it could be . . . meningitis?"

The doctor shook his head. "I doubt it, but let's wait."

"You know the relative of a friend of hers had it a few weeks ago."

"Has her friend been in contact with the sick person?"

"I don't . . . think so, but I don't know. Let me call her family." Anna grabbed the phone. At that moment, Jonas's car arrived. Anna watched as Jonas helped Karla out of the car. She was clearly ill; her normally light-bronze skin looked grayish.

Anna dialed the number of Maja's family and waited impatiently. After a few rings, Maja's aunt answered. To Anna's relief, she told her that Maja had not been in contact

241

with the sick relative, and it turned out that it hadn't been meningitis after all. "Thank God," Anna said.

"Something wrong with Karla?" Maja's aunt asked.

Anna told her she was ill and had a severe headache.

"It's the flu," Maja's aunt said. "It's going around."

"Yeah, I guess that's what it is. Anyway, thanks, the doctor is here. I need to hang up."

In the meantime, Jonas had accompanied Karla to her bedroom and the doctor was unpacking his medical bag. "I'll wait in the living room," Jonas said to Anna.

She nodded. "Honey?" Anna held her hand on Karla's forehead. It felt very warm. She helped her undress and pulled back the covers on the bed.

"Anna, I'm sorry about the note."

Anna shook her head. "Yes, well, we'll talk about that later. First, let's find out what's wrong with you."

The doctor checked Karla out, asked her about her symptoms, pointed a light into her eyes, and measured her temperature. "Headache?"

"Yes, it's a little bit better right now, but it comes and goes and it's really bad sometimes."

"Neck ache?" The doctor peered at her.

Karla turned her head left and right, then shook her head. "No."

"Good." The doctor smiled and turned to Anna. "This doesn't look like meningitis. It looks a lot like the flu. I'm going to give her a shot for the headache and the high fever and some medicine." The doctor took a syringe out of his suitcase. Anna left the room to join Jonas.

"It looks like the flu," she said. "I was so scared." Anna only noticed now that her whole body was tense. She sat down and started to tremble.

Jonas sat next to her and put his arm around her. "I'm so sorry. I shouldn't even have mentioned meningitis, but I heard of a few cases. Sorry."

"It's not your fault. I'm glad you reacted so fast. It could've been, you know." Tears welled up in Anna's eyes. A sob escaped. Jonas hugged her; his body felt warm and comforting. Anna leaned her head against his shoulder. They sat quietly for a while.

The door opened and the doctor stepped out. "Okay, she's asleep. Again, I don't think you need to worry about anything more serious than the flu. If anything unusual happens, or if the headache gets worse again, don't hesitate to call me. Here is my emergency number." He handed Anna his card.

"Thanks for coming so fast," Anna said. "I'm sorry I panicked."

"No problem." The doctor smiled and waved as he walked to his car.

Anna sat back down. "I'm exhausted." She tried to get up again. "I better check on Karla."

Jonas held her arm. "Relax. Let me check on her." He got up and quietly opened the door to Karla's bedroom. Anna, who couldn't sit still, joined him. Karla was lying on her side, deep asleep. Her face had lost its ashen pallor and looked more alive again. A tangle of hair hung in her face. Anna gently brushed it away from her forehead, which felt cooler.

"Little devil," Jonas whispered. They watched her sleep for a while, then tiptoed out of the room.

Anna walked to the window and looked outside. The sun had just set and the yellow-leaved birches in front of the house shimmered in the last of the daylight. She turned around. "Thanks."

Jonas grinned. "For what? For scaring you to death?"

"No, for being here. I think without you I would have lost it." Jonas joined her at the window. "You know, Karla has never been seriously ill. I just realized how hard it must be for a single mother—or father—when something like this happens." She took a deep breath.

"I know what you mean." They watched as the last of the sun disappeared behind the trees. "Well, one thing is for sure, she got out of being scolded too much about her little scheming game," Jonas said. "She got sick at the right time."

"Oh, she's going to get it once she is better again," Anna grumbled.

"She's aware she did something wrong. Besides, I was pretty harsh with her. And I don't think it was her idea. I think her little friend had more to do with it."

"Maja?"

"Yes, I think so."

"Doesn't surprise me. I'm still going to talk to her. We can't blame it on Maja. Karla is old enough to know better," Anna said.

Jonas cleared his throat. "Well, to be honest, I actually meant what Karla wrote on the announcement, except for the spelling error, of course," he said with a quick grin. "I did miss you and when I saw you come in, I was very happy. That above all made my day."

Anna nodded. "Yeah, I guess she pretty much summarized my feelings, too. I wanted you to come to the reading."

"Hmm. So aside from being a dirty little schemer, she seems to know us better than we do."

"It's still no excuse," Anna said, then turned to Jonas. "I'm sorry I have been so hard on you. I had no right."

"That's okay. I probably deserved it. Well . . ." Jonas checked his watch. "I guess I'm on my way. You sure you're going to be okay? You can always call me if something unexpected happens."

Anna swallowed. "Actually, I'd love for you to stay . . . if you don't have plans or anything. I'll fix us something to eat. I'm starting to get hungry. I don't have anything fancy, but . . ."

Jonas glanced at her. "That would be perfect."

Anna examined her refrigerator. There was some leftover lasagna she had planned to warm up for Karla and herself. It would have to do. She fixed a salad and asked Jonas to open a bottle of wine. "To spice up the simple meal somewhat," Anna said.

She went to check on Karla, who had woken up and was thirsty. Her headache was gone and the fever was down quite a bit. After drinking some juice, she fell back asleep again.

"I think we can relax," Anna said as she put the food on the table. Jonas poured them each a glass of wine. "She's on the mend."

"Great," Jonas said, then tried a bite of the lasagna. "This as well," he added, pointing at his plate.

After the meal, they sat in the living room, drinking wine, talking, and watching the darkness settle over the woods and the trees in the yard with their colored leaves.

"I love fall," Anna said. "The colors, the fog in the morning, it's mysterious. But it also makes me a little sad or rather melancholic. Soon, the end of the year will be here again."

"Yeah, I know what you mean," Jonas said. "You don't see the changes of the seasons as much in the city, but out here in the countryside, you really become aware of the passage of time."

"Yes," Anna said. "I'm going to build a fire. It's getting a little cool. This is the time when it's too warm yet for the heating but just right for the fireplace and the woodstove."

"Let me get some more firewood," Jonas said and got up.

"The stack is right next to the house," Anna told him and went to check on Karla again. "She sleeps like a baby," Anna said as she came back out. To her surprise, Jonas had turned off the light in the living room. The front door was ajar and he was standing outside on the patio.

"Psst," he said and motioned Anna to come outside.

In the light of the almost-full moon, a group of deer—two adults and two youngsters—were grazing on the field next to the forest. When Anna stepped outside, the tallest one, a buck with antlers, lifted his head and stood absolutely still. Jonas and Anna didn't move and waited. The male lowered his head again and continued to graze.

"They must not have picked up our scent," Jonas whispered into Anna's ear. She felt his breath on her face and smelled the subtle musk of his cologne.

"The wind is coming from their direction," Anna whispered back.

Jonas put his arm around her. The warmth of his body enveloped her like a soft blanket. She leaned lightly against him. They watched the grazing deer for a while. A moment later, the headlights of a car driving around the curve in the road nearby lit up a short stretch of the field. The shy animals froze, then sprinted off and within seconds disappeared in the forest. A cool breeze picked up. Anna shivered and crossed her arms in front of her chest.

Jonas pulled her closer, rubbing her arm. "Cold?"

"It's getting chilly," she said. She turned toward him. Flashes of shadows and light hovered over his face. His eyes, nose, and mouth shone lightly against the dark. Anna closed her eyes and felt his beard against her cheeks and his lips on her forehead. She took his face between her hands. Their lips touched, lightly first, then fully. They kissed for a long time. The warmth and the firmness of his arms felt good. When they stepped apart, Anna's heart was racing.

"Sleep with me tonight," Anna said when they were back in the living room. Her voice trembled a little.

"I'd love to." He embraced her.

In the bedroom, Anna was gripped by nervousness. She tried to remember the last time she had slept with a man. It was all a blur. Jonas kissed her again. He sat on the bed, took her hand, and pulled her down next to him. He pulled off his pullover and loosened the belt of his pants. Anna tried to open the buttons of her blouse. Her fingers trembled, and after the third button, she tried to pull the blouse over her head. It got stuck and she had to pull it back down again. She guffawed and shook her head. "I'm sorry; I'm not used to this anymore."

Jonas smiled. "Just relax." He helped her pull off her top all the way. Anna unhooked her bra; she was glad she was wearing one which closed in the front. Jonas cupped her small but firm breast and kissed her nipples. His hand slid down inside her skirt. The last bit of resistance fell away. Anna closed her eyes and gave herself over to the sensations of pleasure that surged through her body.

They made love off and on until the early morning hours. It took Anna a long time to be able to fully enjoy it, her body slowly reawakening after such a long time of not making love. But Jonas was patient and sweet, making her feel beautiful and young again. In the end, her sex was sore but she felt satiated and happier than she had been in a long time.

They slept late the following morning. When Anna woke up, Jonas was still asleep, his mouth half open, snoring a little. His arm was resting on top of Anna's thigh. Anna heard the kitchen door open. She carefully moved Jonas's hand off her leg and slid to the edge of the bed. She got up, grabbed her robe, and went to the bathroom. She checked herself in the mirror. Her mouth opened with a wide grin. She brushed her teeth, and ran her fingers through her tousled hair, then went outside.

Karla stood in the kitchen, pouring herself a glass of juice. Anna gave her a quick hug. "How are you, honey?"

"Better. My headache is gone, thank God. I'm still a little tired. But I don't think I'm feverish anymore," Karla said. Her facial color was almost back to normal and her forehead felt cool to Anna's touch.

"Well, I want you to take it easy today. Fortunately, it's Sunday, no school anyway."

"Yeah, thank God." Karla took a sip of juice. She pointed outside, to where Jonas's car stood. "So Jonas spent the night?"

"Yeah, he did." Anna felt her face warm up. If Karla saw Jonas coming out of her bedroom, she would know.

"Good," Karla said. "That's nice of him."

"Yes, he wanted to stay, in case you got sick again. Anyway, are you going back to bed again? I think you should." Anna wanted Karla back in her bedroom, so Jonas could get up without her noticing where he had slept. Anna knew she was being ridiculous, but for some reason she felt embarrassed in front of her niece.

"Yeah, I'll lie down for a little longer, I guess. I'm getting hungry though."

"I'll fix us some pancakes for breakfast. You think you can eat those?"

"Sure, I'd love pancakes." Karla picked up her glass of orange juice and got ready to go back to her room.

The door to Anna's bedroom opened, and Jonas stepped outside, dressed in his pants but without his shirt. He brushed his hands through his wildish white hair, which stuck out in different directions. Karla stared at him surprised, then glanced at Anna, who felt heat flooding her face.

"Well, hello, Jonas," Karla said with a big grin on her face.

"Hello, sweetie, feeling better?" Jonas said. He gave Anna a quick glance, but didn't seem embarrassed.

"Well, I'll see you a little later." Karla went back to her room.

Anna rolled her eyes at Jonas and pushed him back into the bedroom.

"What's the matter?" he asked her.

Anna grinned. "Couldn't you have waited a few minutes?"

"Why? And why is your face so red? Ah." Jonas laughed as well, realizing why she was embarrassed. "I'm sorry but I didn't know she was up. Besides, she has to know sooner or later."

"Yeah, I know, but . . ."

Jonas guffawed. "This is funny. You are the aunt and she is the niece. But you behave as if you were the young girl, having been caught doing the unspeakable."

"I can't help it," Anna said with an embarrassed grin. "Anyway, I'm going to take a shower and fix some breakfast."

"Good, I'm going to join you." Jonas took off his pants and stepped into the shower after her.

"Psst," Anna said. "She's going to hear us."

"Anna." Jonas rolled his eyes. "You are an adult."

"Oh, all right."

Anna was stirring the pancake mix when she saw Maja drive up on her bike. She leaned it against the wall and lifted a bouquet of flowers out of the bicycle basket. Anna narrowed her eyes. Seeing Maja again reminded her of the girls' scheming. *I'll talk to them later.*

"I heard Karla was sick," Maja said when Anna opened the door. "May I see her?"

"Yeah, sure, she's still in bed but feeling better."

"Oh, great." Maja seemed relieved.

"Thanks for the flowers," Anna said.

Maja knocked on Karla's bedroom door and disappeared inside. Anna went into the kitchen and put the flowers in a vase. She was just about to open the bedroom door when she heard giggling inside. She listened for a while.

"They slept in the same room?" It was Maja's loud voice. "Great. Love it. See, I told you it would work."

Anna pushed the door open, and caught the two girls giving each other high fives. They stopped as soon as they saw her, their grins fading from their faces. Anna put the vase on the credenza near the window and faced the girls.

"This is just about as good as any time to tell you what I think of your scheming. It's wrong, it's disgusting, and I'm ashamed of you both. If you continue to do this kind of nonsense, I don't want you to hang out with each other anymore." She glared at Maja, whose face turned red. The girl lowered her head and looked down at her feet. "You are friends and you should encourage each other to do the right thing, not to plot and interfere with other people's lives. And, one more thing: what happens between Jonas and myself is none of your business and has nothing at all to do with your dirty little games. Have I made myself clear?"

"Yes ma'am," Maja said.

"Sorry," Karla mumbled.

Anna stared at them for a while. "Okay, that's settled. Karla, get ready for breakfast. Maja, if you're still hungry, you can have some pancakes with us."

"Thanks, I'd love to."

"Breakfast in five minutes." Anna turned around and closed the door a little more forcefully than normal. "Little rats," she murmured.

Jonas sat in the living room, reading a newspaper. He looked up when Anna stepped into the room.

"What are you grinning about?" Anna asked him.

"Tough Auntie Anna," he said and winked at her.

"You should support me and not make fun of me," Anna said, suppressing a smile.

"Oh, I do, I do. Now, what about those pancakes?"

Chapter 48

Jonas was humming as he shaved. He stretched the skin on one side of his face and pulled the razor across his cheek around his beard, inhaling the lemony smell of the shaving cream. He stopped and grinned at the face in the mirror. "You look like the cat that got the cream." He was happy, happier than he had been in a long time.

The doorbell interrupted his musings. He wrinkled his forehead and glanced at his watch. It couldn't be Anna and Karla yet. It was too early. He put the razor on the shelf above the sink and got ready to wash the soap off his face, then hesitated. It was probably Mrs. Schatz, the snoop from next door, bringing him goodies again. Ever since Anna had started coming by on a regular basis again, Mrs. Schatz had been on a baking spree. Her face gleamed with happiness whenever she handed him another plate of her homemade delicacies. "For you and your guest," she would say, and wink at him. She was a good soul, but Jonas was in no mood to deal with her that early in the morning.

He left the shaving cream on half of his face, figuring that he could get rid of her faster that way. When he opened the door, he stepped back startled. "Martina?"

"Hi there, sorry for dropping by without warning. I've just come from the airport and my room at the hotel isn't ready yet. So I thought I'd see if you're around." She pointed at his face and grinned. "I got you out of bed, obviously."

Jonas was flustered. "Well, no, I've been up . . . I'm actually waiting for someone. I thought it was them." *Bad timing, I hope Anna and Karla don't come early today.*

Martina peered at him. "You don't seem glad to see me. Is anything wrong? Aren't you going to ask me in?"

Jonas sighed, stepped aside, and motioned her to come in. "No, I'm glad to see you. It's just . . . kind of inconvenient right now. I . . . How did you get in? It's usually locked downstairs."

"Well, obviously, it was open." She looked at him puzzled. "Listen, I can come back later. I didn't mean to—"

Jonas heard the sound of the door opening downstairs, the cheerful chatter of Karla and the darker, quieter voice of Anna. *The one time I hope they'd be late. Damn it.*

Martina glanced at Jonas, recognition in her eyes. "Ah, I see. I'm sorry, Jonas," she whispered.

When Karla and Anna reached the top, the two women stared at each other. Karla's eyes showed shock and reproach. Jonas cringed.

Martina smiled at them. "Hello," she said. "I just dropped by to give Jonas this." She pulled out an envelope and handed it to him. "There are a few paintings of mine in this gallery. I'm having an exhibition there later. I would love it if you all took a look at them. Just wanted to let you know. I'm on my way. Ciao." She waved her hand and started walking down the stairs. "Great to meet you again," she said to Anna and Karla.

"Come in and don't look at me like that," Jonas muttered.

Anna and Karla followed him into the living room. "Well," Anna said, peering at him. "What do you expect? You're half shaved and a woman just walked out of your apartment."

"She wasn't in my apartment. She just got here. Now sit down and let me explain."

"Who is she?" Karla asked in a belligerent tone. "Is this the same woman who was here before?"

"Yes, it is." Jonas was getting angry. *Damn women.* "Excuse me one moment." He went to the bathroom. Looking at himself in the mirror, he wondered if he should finish shaving first, then decided to leave it. He'd probably cut himself. He washed his face and went back into the living room.

Anna grinned a little. "You look funny with one side shaved."

Good, Jonas thought, *she doesn't seem all bent out of shape.* He cleared his throat. "You want something to drink?"

They both shook their heads. Karla still glared at him.

"All right, here is my confession." Jonas tried to lighten the atmosphere. Two pairs of eyes still stared at him with questioning looks. "Martina has been a friend of mine for a long time. Back when Eva died, she really helped me a lot." Jonas figured he could score some sympathy points by mentioning his wife's death. "We have been friends ever since. At one time, we were dating off and on, but that's in the past. I like Martina a lot but she is not someone I would want to be in a relationship with. She is a great artist, a great friend, but totally unreliable as a mate. She lives in Italy and we see each other every once in a while when she's in town."

"You don't have to explain all this," Anna said.

"Yes, I do." Jonas glowered at her. "I'm not stupid. I see the suspicion in both of your eyes. I don't want you to think the wrong thing."

"So she's not your girlfriend?" Karla asked.

"No. Not anymore."

"It's okay. I trust you," Anna said.

"Me, too," Karla piped.

"Well, wonderful. I'm honored." Jonas couldn't help a touch of sarcasm. "So that's settled. Would you mind if I finished shaving now?"

"I don't know, I kind of like you that way." Anna's eyes showed a humorous glint.

Jonas breathed a sigh of relief.

PART FIVE: JOURNEY HOME

Chapter 49

Anna grabbed her jacket, purse, and umbrella and was getting ready to go to the library when the phone rang. She looked at her watch and wondered if she should let the caller leave a message on the answering machine, then decided to answer. It was still early and her library assistant was usually on time, so she didn't need to rush. She picked up the phone and was surprised to hear Edna's voice. Edna was Richard's sister and Nico's aunt in England.

"I have some sad news," she said. "Richard died."

Anna felt a stabbing pain in her chest. She hadn't even known that he was ill. They had kept in touch off and on over the years and she had even visited Richard once in England. Richard had been very warm and supportive of her.

After hanging up the phone, she sat down and looked out the window. It was the beginning of April, the month of change and instability, and the weather fit the month's reputation perfectly. It had been raining intermittently all night; the snow was almost gone and the last patches were a dirty brown. The wind whipped the branches of the trees where the first buds and tiny green leaves sprouted.

Richard's passing made her realize that the last connection to Nico was gone. His death awakened some of the old grief, but the beauty of the first signs of spring made her feel better again. March had been warm and spring flowers—yellow daffodils and blue and white pansies—erupted everywhere. *Death and new life, so close together,* she thought. She decided to get a card and send it to Edna.

A few days later, she pulled an envelope out of the mailbox with a stamp from England. She expected a card with the notice of Richard's passing and was surprised at the size and thickness of the envelope. In addition to the card, there was a legal document and a letter from Richard informing her that he had left her a sizable amount of money from his estate.

Anna unfolded the letter. *Dear Anna,* it said. *As far as I am concerned, you, too, were Nicolas's wife—now widow—and in the event of my passing, part of the money that would have gone to him will be yours.*

"This is too much," Anna told Jonas. It was Saturday and Jonas was spending the weekend with Karla and Anna. Karla was with her friend Maja, and Anna and Jonas were taking a short walk after dinner. A few sun rays pierced the fading dark clouds and it was pleasantly warm after a few stormy days.

"I can't take his money. I wasn't his legal wife and I'm not his widow. It really belongs to his Mexican wife."

"It was his father's last wish," Jonas said. "And it may have been Nico's wish as well."

"You don't know that." Anna shook her head. "I doubt it. He was legally married to that woman in Mexico and he had children with her. His life insurance policy was in his first wife's name as well. I don't want his money."

"That's your decision, of course," Jonas said. He stopped and peered at her with a serious face. He buried his hands in his lightweight jacket. The wind tousled his hair and gave his cheeks a pinkish glow. "But think about Karla. You could use it for her education. She'll eventually need a more professional art education than I can give her. She may need to take classes abroad to really advance her career. And that can get expensive."

Anna began to waver; Jonas's suggestion did make sense. "I guess you're right. I could use it for Karla." She hesitated. "But I would like to find out how his wife and children in Mexico are doing financially."

"Don't they get some money from the estate as well?" Jonas asked.

"I don't know. I would hope so, but Richard didn't specify. And the woman has three children. I just don't feel right, keeping it all for myself."

"That means you would have to get in touch with the family," Jonas said.

"I know someone who could find out for me." Anna thought of her friend Gloria, the receptionist of the firm Nico used to work for in Guadalajara.

"Perhaps finding out a little more about that part of your husband's life would help you in some ways. Perhaps bring some closure."

"I have enough closure," Anna said in a curt voice. Then she sighed and added more gently, "Perhaps you're right."

"Carmen and her youngest son still live in the same place," Gloria said on the phone. "The two older children have moved out and gotten married. The youngest one is finishing up his studies at the university."

Anna was stunned. "How did you find this out so fast?"

"Pure coincidence. I have a friend who happens to know the family. I explained the situation to her and she went and talked to Carmen."

"Gloria, I didn't mean for you to get in touch with her. I just wanted to know their financial situation."

"They're not rich but my friend found out that they were included in the will. I think they're doing all right. And I didn't tell my friend to contact her. She did it without my knowledge. I guess I should've made it clear not to do that; I'm sorry. But anyway, Carmen told my friend that she knew Nico was involved with a woman in the United States. But she only found out that he had married again after he had died. She was really shocked about that. But she wants to meet you."

"Meet with her? Gloria, are you crazy?"

"Anna, she sounds like a really nice person and I think it would be good for both of you. She's in a similar situation as you. She, too, has only half the story. Don't you think it would help you both to put this part of your lives behind you?"

"Gloria, I don't want to start digging up the past again." Anna sighed. "Let me think about it, okay?"

After hanging up the phone, Anna plopped onto the sofa and groaned. "Just when I finally thought I could move on with my life." Ever since Anna and Jonas had become more involved with each other, Anna had hardly ever thought of Nico. The pain of his betrayal had all but disappeared. Now, it was mostly curiosity that made her consider traveling to Mexico. She wanted to find out once and for all how a person could live a perfect double life for almost ten years.

The following few days, she began to make plans. Karla's spring vacation started in three weeks. She would spend about two weeks in the Ticino with their friend Lena, so it would be perfect timing. Anna could fly to Mexico, spend a few days there, and then fly back via New York to visit with Susan and George, her old friends she hadn't seen in years.

Chapter 50

Karla tossed and turned, unable to fall asleep. She was worried about Anna being so far away. Karla had never been apart from her, except during her vacations with Lena. But that was different; that was just a three-hour drive by car and they talked on the phone every day.

Yesterday, Jonas and Karla had taken Anna to the airport. Karla had cried when Anna walked through passport control. She was afraid she would never see her again, just like her mother. Fortunately, Jonas was with her and that helped a little. Jonas was here now, spending the night. Tomorrow, they would drive to the Ticino to Lena's, where Karla would stay until Anna came back.

Jonas promised he would wake her up in the early morning when Anna called from the hotel in Mexico. If only it was already morning. Then Karla would know that Anna was all right. Karla sat up; she would never be able to fall asleep. She kicked the down comforter aside, got up, slid her feet into her flip-flops, put on her robe, and went into the living room. Jonas was still up, sitting in front of the fireplace, reading. He peered at her over his reading glasses. "Can't sleep, huh?"

Karla shook her head and plopped down on the sofa next to him. She shivered a little. It had been a rainy and unusually cold April. Jonas handed her a blanket. "I'll stoke the fire again. Want something to drink? Warm milk might help."

"Warm milk with chocolate?" Karla said.

"Yes ma'am, coming right up." Jonas got up, and placed a few more logs in the fireplace, then went into the kitchen. He came back with a mug of hot chocolate milk.

Karla warmed her hands on the mug, took a small sip, and burned her tongue. "Ouch." She sat it down on the table, then snuggled up to Jonas, folding her legs underneath her robe. He put his arm around her. It smelled of burning wood and one of the pine logs made a loud popping sound. A meow came from the kitchen. Karla's black-and-white cat had woken up and joined them in the living room. She jumped up on the sofa and crawled onto Karla's lap. Karla stroked her soft fur and Dotty began to purr loudly.

"I wonder where she is now," Karla said.

"Hmm, let's see. She's probably over the Atlantic Ocean right now. She should arrive at around five o'clock in the morning our time. This time difference is a funny thing, isn't it?"

Karla nodded. She leaned forward, trying to grab her mug without displacing the cat. Jonas picked it up and handed it to her. She took a sip, then handed it back to Jonas. "Jonas, are you worried about her?"

Jonas shook his head. "Not really. Well, to be honest, a little bit. Are you worried?"

Karla nodded. Tears collected in the corner of her eyes. A small sob escaped. Jonas hugged her, unsettling Dotty, who jumped down and gave a protesting meow.

"Don't worry. It'll be okay."

"I know." Karla took a deep breath and wiped her eyes. She took a few sips of chocolate milk. The warm liquid felt good and calmed her a little. She started to yawn. Dotty tried to climb back onto her lap again.

"Why don't you try to get a little sleep? You'll be very tired when I wake you up at five."

"I guess I could try," Karla murmured.

"I could tell you a good-night story," Jonas volunteered.

"A fairy tale by Hans Christian Andersen?" Karla grinned. "I know them all by now."

Jonas chuckled. "Here we go again, children growing up. My kids used to love them, and then one day, they laughed at me when I wanted to tell them another one."

"I loved them, too," Karla said. "It's just . . . well . . ."

"Yeah, yeah, I know, you're a young adult now. What about listening to some soothing music? You have all these CDs."

"I guess I could." She lifted Dotty up and placed her next to Jonas on the couch. The cat got up and shook her head, as if to say she didn't like the arrangement. She stretched her body, jumped down from the sofa, and curled up by the fire.

"Don't forget to wake me up," Karla said, yawning. In her room, she put on a CD by Andreas Vollenweider with soothing harp music. This time, she fell asleep fairly fast.

Loud voices calling for help, flashes of fire, and then it was all red. Karla was suffocating. She tried to call, but no sound escaped. She struggled against the fetters. She was trapped. Finally, a scream, then another one. Karla shot up, her heart thumping in her chest.

"It's okay," she heard a voice say. Someone was holding her, tapping her back. "Wake up, Karla."

Karla's rapid breaths slowed down a little. She stared at Jonas, who held her. He was in his pajamas. "You were dreaming," he said. "It's okay now."

Karla exhaled. Another one of her nightmares. She was still trembling. Jonas held her. After a while, she calmed down enough to speak. "What time is it?"

"It's four thirty in the morning."

"And Anna?" Karla was still confused.

"In about half an hour."

"I don't want to go to sleep anymore."

"Well, we might as well get up. I'll get some coffee started." Jonas brushed his white hair out of his face. It stuck out on all sides and made him look like an aged punk rocker, except the different colors were missing. In spite of her shock, Karla had to smile.

In the living room, Jonas lit the fire again and went into the kitchen. After a while, it began to smell of coffee. "Can I have some, too?" Karla asked.

"Hmm. You really shouldn't, but okay for once, with lots of milk." Jonas heated up some milk, poured a shot of coffee into Karla's mug, and added steaming hot milk and sugar to it. He handed her the cup. "Just don't tell Anna."

"She lets me have some once in a while, with lots of milk. I like hot chocolate better, but today is special," Karla said.

"I guess you're right."

They sipped their coffee and looked out the window. Karla watched the play of light and dark as the trees and bushes and the neighbors' houses became visible, as if they were slowly walking out of the dark. She squinted her eyes and examined the sky. There was a band of whitish yellow right above the horizon, then a thick slab of orange leading into crimson. A group of patchy purplish clouds hung above the trees.

The phone rang, startling Karla, who spilled some of her coffee. She put the mug down and stared at Jonas as he answered the phone.

"Hello there," he said into the phone and winked at Karla. "How are you? Good. Listen, someone here wants to talk to you really badly. She's getting ready to rip the phone out of my hands. Here you go." He handed Karla the receiver.

"Anna," Karla screamed into the phone. "How are you?"

"I'm fine. How are you?"

"Fine. I miss you." The relief of hearing Anna's voice brought tears to Karla's eyes again, but she didn't want to make Anna feel bad, so she held them back.

"You sure you're okay?" Anna's voice sounded concerned.

Karla nodded, then realized that Anna couldn't see her. "Yes, I'm fine. I'm just glad to hear your voice. How is Mexico?"

"Busy and noisy." Anna laughed. "I just got here; I'm in my hotel, getting ready to sleep, or at least try to. It was a very long trip and I'm exhausted."

"What time is it there?" Karla asked.

"It's about eleven at night."

"We just got up. It's early in the morning here. We're having coffee . . . and hot milk." Karla grinned at Jonas, who chuckled.

"Well, let me talk to Jonas, sweetie. And be good. I'll call you again tomorrow, okay?"

"Okay, Anna, love you a lot."

"Love you, too."

Karla sighed and handed the phone to Jonas. She listened for a while, then got up and started pacing around the room. She was so happy that Anna was okay. She lifted up Dotty, who was asleep on the rug in front of the fire. She pressed her against her chest so hard that the cat winced, slipped out of her hands, and hissed at her. "Sorry, Dotty, didn't mean to hurt you." Karla patted the cat, who seemed to have already forgotten the somewhat rough treatment. She turned on her back and let Karla stroke her belly.

Chapter 51

Anna was groggy after her long flight to Guadalajara. She felt odd and disjointed, as if hurled back into the past—a past she had tried to put behind her. After talking to Karla and Jonas, she tried to sleep, but although she was exhausted, it took her a long time to settle down. She began to question her decision to make this trip. What was she doing here? What would a meeting with Nico's other wife bring? She could be at home with Jonas and Karla. She had a home, a man, and a child whom she loved and who loved her. Did she have to come all the way to Mexico for it to really sink in? Anna shook her head.

The following day, Gloria, who had picked her up at the airport in the evening, met her at the hotel. Her friend had gotten a little heavier and older but she was still basically the same bubbly person. They embraced enthusiastically.

Gloria still worked for the same engineering firm that Nico had worked for. After filling each other in on the latest news, they went out for breakfast. Since Gloria had to work during the day, they decided to meet for dinner. Anna spent the day doing some sightseeing, but wasn't much in the mood for it. She hadn't slept well the night before, so she went back to the hotel to take a nap.

In the evening, Gloria and Anna went out to dinner. Relaxing with a glass of wine, Anna felt a little better. She loved Guadalajara and the exotic beauty of one of Mexico's oldest cities, and she would be able to enjoy it more if it didn't bring up painful memories of the past.

"I'm still not sure meeting with Carmen is such a good idea," she said, gazing across the street at one of the many beautifully lit cathedrals. "I guess I'm mainly worried that it's going to be awkward."

"Don't you think it would help you understand a little better what happened back then? It may be painful, but it'll also be liberating. I just feel that if something like that happened to me, I would like to know why that man did what he did," Gloria said.

"I don't know. Perhaps."

The following morning, Anna and Gloria walked along the street where Anna had spied on Nico's family that fateful day. Seeing the small house with its neatly groomed front yard brought back a rush of memories. Anna's heartbeat went into overdrive. She took a deep breath, trying to calm her frazzled nerves. Gloria knocked.

Anna recognized the woman who opened the door right away. She had aged, but she was still attractive and slim, with pronounced facial features and penetrating dark eyes. Her long black hair was streaked with gray.

Carmen invited them in and asked them to sit down. Gloria introduced Anna. Carmen observed Anna with a serious face but without malice. She gave Gloria a quick smile and asked if they wanted tea or coffee.

"Coffee would be nice, thanks. What about you, Anna?"

"Coffee is fine," Anna said. "And may I have some water too, please?" Her mouth felt parched.

"I have bottled water," Carmen said.

"Thank you."

"She seems nice enough," Gloria whispered after Carmen left the room.

Anna nodded. She was beginning to sweat and it wasn't even hot.

Carmen came back in with a bottle of water and two cups. As she was getting ready to go back into the kitchen to get the coffee, Gloria got up. "Let me help you." Anna got up as well, but Gloria motioned her to sit down. "Just relax, I'll help."

While waiting for the women to come back, Anna glanced around the living room. The house was modest, with plain furniture, a few pictures, a large TV, and a piano. It looked as if the family was doing okay. Anna wondered if Carmen had married again.

After Gloria and Carmen came back in, carrying the coffee pot and a plate of cookies, they sat down. Carmen poured coffee and they all took a sip. There was an awkward silence for a while.

Then Carmen faced Anna. "I'm sure you have a lot of questions."

Anna was surprised that Carmen spoke English quite fluently. She took a deep breath. "I don't know where to start. Perhaps I should've contacted you earlier, but I didn't have the nerve. I didn't know how much you knew or if you knew anything about me, about the marriage and everything."

"I didn't know he married again." Carmen spoke in a low sonorous voice. "I found out after his death, from the office."

Anna glanced at Gloria, who shook her head. "I didn't say anything. It must have been Eduardo, his boss."

"Yes, Señor Morales told me," Carmen said. "I was really shocked. But it wasn't a total surprise, either. I knew Nicolas was involved with someone in the US, but I didn't realize he went as far as marrying." Carmen brushed her hand across her face.

"You knew he was involved with someone? He told you?" Anna peered at the woman.

Carmen nodded. "He wanted a divorce."

Anna's heart stuttered, and she couldn't help feeling a surge of elation at the news. Did that mean, perhaps, that Nico truly loved her, and did not just use her? "He wanted a divorce?"

"Yes. When Nicolas and I got married, I already had two kids from a former relationship. I had gotten pregnant at a young age.

"When I first met Nicolas, my boyfriend had just left me and I was desperate. Having children out of wedlock was a real blow to my family. They were ashamed of me and I felt abandoned and alone. At the time, I had a teaching job at the same school where Nicolas's father taught English. That's how I met Nicolas. He came by to pick up his father after work. I fell in love and I think he did, too." Carmen's voice trailed off and she gazed at Anna with her dark penetrating eyes. "You sure you want to hear all this?"

"Yes, I do." Anna spoke vehemently. "I want to know everything. I don't know if you understand, but ever since I found out Nico was already married, I've been wondering who that man was I had lived with for all those years. When he died in that plane crash, I was deprived of ever knowing what had happened. I've lived with that uncertainty my whole life since."

"I know what you mean. When I heard that he had married again, I wanted to know who the woman was, but I didn't dare to contact you. And I was angry, too. I was angry at you without knowing who you were."

Gloria, who had been quietly listening so far, cleared her throat. "If you want to talk about this in private, I can leave and pick Anna up later."

"I don't mind you knowing," Carmen said. "It's all in the past now, anyway."

Anna shook her head. "It's okay, Gloria. You were a friend of Nico's. Unless you feel uncomfortable."

"No. I would like to know more, too. I liked Nicolas. We were all so shocked at the office when we found out."

Carmen continued in a low voice. "When Nicolas and I started dating, Nicolas's mother was very ill with cancer and she soon died. It was a terrible tragedy. It was really hard on Nicolas and it almost killed his father. After she died, his father moved back to England. Nicolas was still in college and he was working as a draftsman's assistant with an architectural company.

"After his mother died and his father left, Nicolas was lonely and we became very close. The children and I became a kind of surrogate family for him.

"But Nicolas wasn't ready to settle down. He was a very ambitious young man. He wanted to get ahead in life. He had dreams of living in England or the United States. There were more possibilities there. All I wanted was for us to get married, and I did everything in my power to convince him. I pushed him too much and I came to regret it later on."

Carmen pushed a strand of hair behind her ear. "We eventually did get married. After a few years, however, he became more and more dissatisfied. He felt trapped in a marriage with two kids. In his defense, I have to say that he loved my children and was a good father."

Anna remembered Nico's love of children, but also his hesitation to have any of his own.

"Then Nicolas received a scholarship to study architecture in New York," Carmen continued. "He had applied without telling me. He was afraid I would try to discourage him. If he was accepted, it would mean we would live apart for several years. We couldn't have all lived in the United States. It would've been too expensive.

"I was really upset that he did all this behind my back. But I knew that if I opposed him, I'd lose him for good. He promised it would only be for a few years. Once he had his architecture degree from the US, he would have so many more possibilities in Mexico as well, and we would be able to have a much better life."

Carmen shrugged. "I wanted to believe him, but I was heartbroken when he left. Somehow I felt that this was the beginning of the end of our relationship. At first, things went okay. He called regularly and came to visit whenever he had time to spare. He sent me money. I found out later that his father supported him financially."

"His father didn't seem to know he was married," Anna said.

"Yes, that was another strange part of Nicolas's life." Carmen took a deep breath. "When we got married, I wanted to invite Nicolas's father to the wedding. But Nicolas claimed he had already invited him but his father wouldn't be able to make it. I realized later that this was a lie. He never told his father."

"That's so strange," Anna said. "Why wouldn't Nico want his father to know? He came to *our* wedding," Anna said, and regretted it instantly. This must hurt Carmen.

Carmen, however, didn't seem offended. "I'm not sure. But it seems to me that this was another sign that he wasn't truly committed to the relationship."

"But why all the lies? Why was Nico such a coward? Why didn't he tell me he was married? Why didn't he ask you for a divorce if he wanted out of the marriage? I mean, what he did hurt us both more than a clean break." Anna's voice broke. Resentment and pain flooded her. It was as if the past, a past she had tried to bury for good, was getting ready to swallow her up.

Carmen's face darkened. "Well, his reason for not getting a divorce was more my fault than his. During one of his visits, he told me that he had fallen in love with someone else. He wanted to stay in the US and get a divorce. I was devastated. It was a very emotional time for both of us, as well as for the children." Carmen hesitated. "It was also during this time that I got pregnant again.

"Nicolas was confused. I knew he loved the children and, perhaps, he still loved me, too. At least I tried to convince myself he still loved me. And so I made a last attempt to keep him." Carmen gave Anna a furtive glance, then looked down at her folded hands in her lap.

"I seduced him. We were both raw and vulnerable and one night it happened. We both had too much to drink. I wasn't using birth control and I hoped that if I got pregnant, he'd change his mind."

Anna thought about the birth certificate and realized that it was the time Nico's and Carmen's youngest boy was conceived, the one with the brilliant-blue eyes she had seen in the park on her last visit to Guadalajara.

"A few months later, I realized I was pregnant, but of course it didn't have the result I hoped for. When Nicolas was back on another business trip, I told him. He was furious. He yelled at me and accused me of tricking him. He really lost it; I'd never seen him that angry. He left and slammed the door, and I thought I'd never see him again."

"No wonder he was upset," Anna said with a sneer. "He had been married to someone else for the past four years. He must have been afraid his whole string of deceptions would unravel and he would be exposed."

Carmen nodded. "Yes, I guess so. Anyway, I didn't know what to do. But then two days later, Nicolas came back. He told me he would acknowledge the child and continue to help me support the children. However, he wanted a divorce. As far as he was concerned, our relationship was over." Carmen lifted her hands in a gesture of resignation. "I was sad but also relieved. I knew I had lost him, but at least I wouldn't be destitute. My salary as a teacher was hardly enough to support three children."

Anna felt increasingly sorry for the woman who must have suffered for years. She had always felt that she was the one betrayed, the one who was used by a man she had loved. But at least she and Nico had had a few good years together.

"I found an envelope in Nico's desk with photos of the child and Nico. It showed him holding the baby and smiling. He must have accepted and loved the boy," Anna said.

"Yes." Carmen smiled. "After Nicolas—we named him after his father—was born, Nicolas came back and fell in love with the baby. He seemed really happy and he didn't mention the divorce anymore. I began to hope again. Perhaps we still had a chance. At least Nicolas promised to always support me and visit whenever he was in Mexico. He wanted to have a part in his son's life."

"Unbelievable," Anna said, more to herself than to Carmen. "How did he ever think he could pull this off? I mean, one day, one of us would've found out. Well, I did find out." She glanced at Carmen.

"It happened when I visited Nico during one of his business trips." Anna told Carmen how she had seen her and the children in the park, how she had followed them to their apartment, and how, after returning to New York City, she had found the same address on one of Nico's papers. "It all came out, and then the plane crashed and I never saw Nico again."

Anna stared at her hands, struggling to keep her composure. The pain of that moment erupted anew. When

275

she raised her head, Carmen looked at her with pain-filled eyes. For the first time, she felt a deep kinship with the woman who had been her rival.

"He betrayed us both," she said.

Carmen nodded. They sat in silence for a while.

"He loved you . . . more than he loved me." Carmen turned to Anna. "During his last visit, before the plane crash, he told me that he could no longer live a lie. He had been more distant during that visit than before. Now I think it had something to do with you being with him in Guadalajara. Perhaps having us both around made him realize to whom he really belonged. Believe me; this is hard for me to admit." Carmen peered at Anna.

"And to be honest, I was worn out as well with the whole thing. It wasn't good for any of us. The children only saw their father once in a while. They began to resent him. So finally, I told him I no longer cared. If he wanted to live with that woman in the US, he could do it. He could get a divorce." Carmen waved her hand in front of her face, as if to chase away an insect.

"He seemed relieved. He promised he would continue to support the children. He also said he would have to confess to you that he was married. And he was really worried about that."

Anna sighed. "By then, I already knew."

Carmen gave her a measuring look. "Would you have forgiven him?"

Anna was quiet for a while. "I guess I would've . . . eventually."

At that moment, the door opened and a young man walked in. Anna's heart thudded when she saw him. She inhaled sharply, thinking for a split second she was seeing a ghost. It was Nico, a younger version of him. He nodded at them.

"This is Nicolas, my son," Carmen said.

"God, you look so much like your father." It was all Anna could say. Her heart was beating fast. She gave Carmen a questioning look. "Does he . . . know?"

Carmen nodded. "Yes, he knows. Nicolas, this is Anna, your father's second wife . . . or first wife . . . I don't know anymore."

A quick smile spread across Nicolas's face. "I'm pleased to meet you."

"How could you be?" Anna blurted out. Now, the whole situation seemed ludicrous to her and she uttered a quick laugh. "I'm sorry," she said, "it's all just a little too much for me. I think I'm beginning to crack." She turned to Nicolas. "I appreciate your kindness, but you couldn't really be happy about this."

Nicolas shrugged. "Why should I be mad at you? It's not your fault that my father was an asshole."

"Nicolas, please," Carmen said.

"For God's sake, Mother, why don't you finally admit it?"

"Nicolas," Anna said in an appeasing tone. "Your father made some terrible mistakes, but he had his good side, too. He was . . . weak, I guess. He was torn between two women. He loved them both . . . in his own way. He found himself in a situation and didn't know how to get out of it." Anna couldn't believe herself. Here she was defending the man who had caused her so much pain.

Nicolas's reaction was swift. "I'm sick and tired of you women with your victim mentalities. It's because you put up with crap like this that men get away with murder. I hope the jerk roasts in hell." His dark-blue eyes flashed with anger.

Anna was shocked at his fury. Carmen shook her head but didn't say anything.

Nicolas walked toward the door. Then he turned back and took a deep breath. "Forgive me, I don't mean to be rude. And it's true I'm pleased to meet you. I'm glad you came. Perhaps it will help my mother, too. *Hasta luego.*" Nicolas brushed a hand quickly through his hair, then left.

Anna's heart skipped a beat. It was the same gesture she still remembered from Nico. The three women looked at each other. "I hope he can forgive his father one day," Anna said.

Carmen nodded. "I hope so, too. You know, Nicolas was crazy about his father. He was four years old when he died and he was devastated. He adored him, and when he found out the truth later on, he took it really hard."

Anna sighed. "Yes, I can understand that. All at once, his idol became a human being with some serious flaws."

"It's just hard to understand how Nicolas could live like this for so long," Gloria said. "He was such a straight arrow when it came to his work. He was kind and considerate, and always stood up for his fellow workers."

"It makes me wonder how we can ever truly know another person's thoughts and feelings, even a person we are close to," Anna said.

Carmen lifted her hands in a gesture of helplessness. "I knew he was in love with someone else and I put up with it. I didn't want to let go. I'm in part responsible for the whole mess, too. I helped him live a lie."

"Carmen, that's nonsense. This is not your fault." Anna spoke in a sharp tone. "Nicolas is right. Your son, I mean. We need to stop making excuses for him. He was wrong. He was a good person in many ways. I remember so well . . . but what he did was so wrong."

Gazing through the small airplane window on the flight to New York City, Anna remembered that it was this flight, twenty years before, that Nico didn't survive. She felt uneasy, but the air was calm. People around her looked relaxed, and the flight attendant smiled at her when she served her the food.

Anna spent a few days with Susan and George, visiting old haunts. The two were doing well and had a family with two children. Although it was at times painful to walk through her old neighborhood where she had once been so happy and so miserable, it also felt liberating.

When Susan asked her about her trip to Mexico and if it had brought her anything, Anna said, "Yes. I found out something very important. I know now that Nico did love me and that he wanted to set things right. Unfortunately, he never had the chance to do so. I wish I had found out earlier. It may have made all the difference in my life. I may not have become so distrustful of other men and I may have trusted my own feelings more." She waved her hand. "But it's no use regretting the past. I have to move forward now."

The most memorable and emotional moment of the trip was visiting Nico's memorial. After his death, George, Susan, and Anna had put up a small memorial stone in the yard of the church where they got married and where the memorial service had taken place.

Anna put some flowers down and stood in silence in front of the memorial stone for a while. Tears began to flood her eyes. She swallowed. "Enough," she said. "I once loved you, Nico. I forgive you. Rest in peace."

She picked up her suitcase at the hotel and drove to the airport.

On the long flight back, Anna had time to reflect on the past few months of her life. She was glad she had undertaken this trip. She felt a great sense of relief. She remembered something she had read in some book once: "I have risen from a darkness that threatened to destroy me."

She nodded to herself. *Yes, it's time to move beyond my broken life.* On the descent to the airport in Zurich, Anna marveled how green the landscape had become. The sky was a deep blue and the sun was shining. It still had been cool when she left on her trip, but now spring had fully arrived.

When she entered the arrival hall, Karla rushed up to her, followed by Jonas. "I'm so glad you're back; I was worried about you," Karla said, hugging her fiercely.

It had been the first time that Anna had been that far away from her. She knew it had been difficult for Karla, who was still haunted occasionally by fears of abandonment.

"Welcome back," Jonas said and kissed her. They embraced.

"I'm so glad to be home," Anna said, choking back tears of joy.

Chapter 52

August 15 — My 12th Birthday

Dear Mama:

I haven't written or "talked" to you in quite a while. I have been busy with school and painting and all that stuff. I used to tell you everything before going to sleep, but now I prefer to write to you. I know you probably can't read my letters, but then again, perhaps you can. Anyway, it's fun writing to you.

Yesterday was my twelfth birthday and I am writing in a brand-new journal right now. It's a present from Jonas and it's really cool. It's large and has thick paper, so I can draw and paint in it as well.

Lots of things have happened lately. Anna went to New York and Mexico, without me! But she promised that next time she will take me along. She went to visit her husband's other wife. You know, the husband who died in a plane crash. You probably remember because you were still here then. He must have been a real crook. Can you believe it; he was married to two women? Some guys, I tell you. My friend Maja said that men are that way. They want as many women as they can get. I don't believe her, she always exaggerates. Jonas isn't that way.

Jonas and Anna are still together. They are a couple now. Unfortunately, they aren't married yet. Maja said we have to do something about that. I told her no way. Last time we wrote those dumb cards, Anna and Jonas got very angry.

Fortunately, it ended up being all right, but I wouldn't want to go through that again.

Anna told me I had to trust my destiny more. Sometimes, you just have to take a leap of faith, she said. Perhaps she is right. I guess it's okay, even if we aren't a completely normal family. But you know, there are kids in school who have a normal family—meaning a mother, father, and brothers and sisters. But their parents don't get along or they are getting divorced. So, having a normal family isn't always fun either.

I don't have nightmares that much anymore, just every once in a while. Last time I had one, Anna was away for a weekend on some book thing. Jonas stayed with me. I woke up screaming and Jonas came in and hugged me. He sat next to me until I fell asleep again. That felt really good.

Jonas hasn't moved in all the way yet, but he spends every weekend here and some nights during the week as well. He still keeps his place in Zurich because he doesn't really have enough room here to paint. Besides, he has his art business and his art students in Zurich. And Anna has her bookstore here and her work at the library and I still go to school in our village. So for the time being, we are in both places. It's kind of fun. I like to stay in Zurich, there is much more going on there than here in the village. Sometimes, we go to the movies, or I go shopping with Maja when she comes to town.

Jonas, however, is looking for a place to rent around here for his painting. And I heard Anna once say that they should make it legal (meaning get married). She said they didn't set a good example for me, living together without being married. I had to laugh. Anna is so old-fashioned sometimes. I know that lots of couples live together without being married. But it would be great if they did get married.

Oh, before I forget. Maja just got her period. She is thirteen now. She makes a big deal out of it, of course. You know how dramatic she is. First, I was kind of jealous because I don't have it yet. Anna told me to just be patient. I would get it soon enough and I would have it for a very long time. And, to be honest, it doesn't sound like a lot of fun. Maja has cramps sometimes and feels sick. Oh well, I think I can wait.

School is going okay. My grades are okay—not great, but okay. Except for art, where I always get the highest grade. I still paint and draw and I decided I definitely want to be an artist. Jonas brought home some pamphlets about art courses in Italy and Germany. He said when I am finished with my basic schooling that I could perhaps take some courses there. But first I would have to go to art school here.

And, Mama, I won first prize in an art contest at our school. Not bad, huh?

Oh, I have to tell you about the birthday gifts I got. I received a new dress from my father in Peru. It's really neat. I'm going to wear it when we have our school dance after summer vacation. One of the boys invited me. He's the cutest in the whole class and I'm a little bit in love. The other girls are jealous of me; everyone hoped he would invite them. Jonas said he was a little jealous, too, but of the boy. He had hoped I would invite *him* to the school dance. He was only kidding, of course.

I got some other great presents. Jonas gave me new paints and a gift certificate for the art store and movie tickets for me and Maja. From Anna, I got some books, of course, some money for my savings account, and some new clothes. Cool.

Yesterday, we had a birthday party here. Anna had made a cake and decorated it with lots of colorful icing, so it looked like an American birthday cake. She ordered pizza and sodas. I invited Maja and a few other girls and boys. I invited

Roland, the cute guy, as well. After I opened the presents, we danced outside. The neighbors came over. Anna invited them so they wouldn't complain about the noise. Jonas and Anna had decorated the patio. There were balloons and colorful streamers and in the evening we lit candles and oil lamps. It was really romantic. And Roland kissed me on the mouth when Anna and Jonas weren't watching. (Don't tell them.) It was just a quick kiss and it was okay, not as great as I had expected. I think all these movies exaggerate.

I have to finish this journal entry because I hear that Anna and Jonas are up. Anna is going to fix my traditional birthday breakfast, pancakes or waffles. After breakfast, I'm going to draw you a picture of the party, okay?

Love you, Mama. Anna and Jonas say hello. Be happy in Heaven.

Karla

The End

Acknowledgements

Many people contributed to the creation of this novel. I would like to thank my friends and family in Switzerland and the United States, who believed in me and cheered me on. Thank you to Susan Deming for her friendship and support, to Diane Busch for the beautiful cover design, to Guillermo Becerra for reviewing the information about Guadalajara, Mexico. A special thank you to Scott Nicholson for editing the manuscript and for his invaluable critique and to Neal Hock who not only did an excellent job of proofreading the manuscript but gave me many helpful suggestions.

Christa Polkinhorn, originally from Switzerland, lives and works as writer and translator in Santa Monica, California. She divides her time between the United States and Switzerland and has strong ties to both countries. Her poems have appeared in various poetry magazines. She is the author of three novels and a collection of poems. She can be reached by email at cpolkinhorn@msn.com or you can visit her at her website www.christa-polkinhorn.com or her blog http://christa-polkinhorn.blogspot.com/.

www.ingramcontent.com/pod-product-compliance
Lightning Source LLC
Chambersburg PA
CBHW030630110726
47901CB00002B/391